A Vicarage Family

An autobiographer is one who writes his own history. This – as far as my growing-up years are concerned – I have, to the best of my knowledge, done. For I am the Vicky of this book.

But how does the autobiographer handle a brother and sister? How they looked, how they appeared to me as persons – yes. But were they like that inside?

It is because of my awareness that my portraits of the rest of my family are probably faulty that I have used no real names. The thin shield of anonymity helped me to feel unselfconscious in drawing them, and in approaching the facts of my own life.

The various vicarages in which we lived were our world; outside them I believe we were never completely ourselves. For this reason I have made my cousin, called here John, a permanent member of the vicarage household. In actual fact he stayed with us during many holidays. Apart from allowing myself this deviation from fact, here is the truth as I remember it.

Noel Streatfeild

By the same author

Ballet Shoes
Dancing Shoes
The Gemma Series
White Boots
Ballet Shoes for Anna
Thursday's Child
Far to Go

Judy Gillespie

A Vicarage Family

Noel Streatfeild

Collins

An imprint of HarperCollins*Publishers*

First published in Great Britain by William Collins Sons & Co. Ltd 1963
Sixth impression published by Collins 1999
7 9 10 8 6

Collins is an imprint of HarperCollins*Publishers* Ltd,
77-85 Fulham Palace Road, Hammersmith, London W6 8JB.

The HarperCollins website address is www.fireandwater.com

ISBN 0 00 671229-0

Printed and bound in Great Britain by
Caledonian International Book Manufacturing Ltd
Glasgow, G64

1 The Telegram

The children had known for days that something was going to happen. There were conferences in low voices behind the study door. The servants talked and then broke off abruptly when one of the children passed by. Miss Herbert, the governess, closed her lips more tightly than usual while her eyes, behind her gold pince-nez, said as clearly as if they had spoken: "Wouldn't you like to know what I know."

It was a Saturday morning towards the end of the spring term. The boys were still away: Dick, the youngest of the family who was eight, was in his second term at his preparatory school; John, the cousin who lived with them in the holidays because his parents were in India, was at Winchester where he had been for two years, for John was fourteen.

Bundled in overcoats, for the spring was late that year, the three girls were ordered by Miss Herbert into the garden, or into what at St Peter's Vicarage passed for a garden. It was a strip of lawn not big enough for a tennis court, walled in on the one side by the Parish Hall, along the length of which lay a narrow flower bed. At the far end of the lawn on the top of a bank there was a privet hedge, beyond which, across a path, lay St Peter's Church. This end of the garden belonged to the children for it was divided from the lawn by a wooden trellis, behind which in a row lay their gardens. When as mere babies they had first come to live in the vicarage, the children's voices as they gardened had made passing parishioners think of the twittering of sparrows, but now they were older and had learnt it was ill-manners to raise your voice.

Isobel, crouched over her garden, looked despondently at a daffodil, still only leaves with no sign of a bud in spite of care which had included covering the shoot with sawdust during a hard frost.

"I wish I'd bought snowdrops and crocuses like I did last year. I like to see the beginnings of spring early."

Louise, who had been raking a corner of her bed, looked up. Her voice took a pathetic note.

"If I had all the pocket money you get now you are thirteen I'd have every sort of bulb and every sort of plant. I'd have so many there wouldn't be a space between the plants."

At thirteen Isobel's pocket money had been raised from threepence a week to sixpence. She was a pretty girl with fair hair and clear blue eyes, but she looked, and was, pitifully frail, for Isobel was an asthmatic. Her words had a habit of falling over each other for she could not take as deep breaths as other people and so had to try to say more between breaths.

"I know sixpence does seem an awful lot but I have other things to buy with it."

Victoria, the middle girl who was twelve, had not

been attending to her garden. With her arms folded she had been scowling up at the church spire. She was the plain one of the family. Instead of Isobel's fairness she had hair of a colour which she herself described as mid-mouse.

"I may as well admit to mid-mouse," she would say to her friends, "because anyone can see it's true, and you can't be·vain with Isobel on one side of you and Louise on the other."

This was true, for Victoria was called by those who only knew the girls by sight "the plain one". Actually Victoria and her contemporaries at school could not see why grown-ups raved about Louise's looks, for in that family of fair or near fair hair and blue eyes – for Dick was as fair as Isobel – Louise might have been a changeling. The reason was that she was the only one to take after her mother's family. There was some Huguenot blood there and it had left a heritage of faintly bronzed skin, brown hair and grey eyes. Schoolgirls might believe that true prettiness must have a pink and white complexion, fair hair, preferably curly, and blue eyes, but adults looked and looked again at ten-year-old Louise with her straight brown fringe beneath which was a face of startling perfection. Though Louise might to outsiders look like an angel and even appear one to her parents, her sisters had a totally different angle on her. Victoria took her eyes away from the spire.

"Don't listen to her, Isobel, you know she's going to try and make you buy her a plant." Then, turning to Louise: "And shut up about that sixpence, Louise, you've gone on and on about it ever since Isobel had it, just as if you didn't know that almost all of it goes on extra paints and drawing pencils. So if you want extra seeds or something go looking all sugar and spice at the man in the plant shop. He'll give you something extra. He always does."

Isobel was an artist. She had drawn and painted before she could write the alphabet. With her gift went the artist's temperament; she was a gentle creature but remorseless where her talent was concerned. Now she looked with amusement at Victoria, always the fighter and the rebel.

"You needn't bother, Vicky, you know perfectly well I wouldn't give anything away if I needed a new rose madder or something like that." She looked down at her garden. "I'm not really keen on gardening. If it wasn't supposed to be good for me I'd give it up."

Victoria had brought a rake out with her, now she turned it stem downwards and leant on the prongs.

"I don't see how any of us can be keen on anything with all this whisper-whisper hanging over us."

Louise narrowed her eyes, glad to have a chance to bite back at Victoria.

"If I was Miss Victoria Strangeway I wouldn't wonder why there was all this whispering. I'd know."

There was a second's silence during which colour flooded Victoria's face while her hands tightened on the rake. She was within a pounce of throwing

8

Louise face downwards on her garden and rubbing her face in the earth.

"Don't, Vicky," said Isobel guessing her intention. "You know she'll tell Daddy and Mummy and then you'll be in another row."

"Little tell-tale tit," Victoria muttered.

Louise disliked it when her sisters ganged up against her. She looked pathetically at Isobel.

"I'm only ten and I have to tell or I'd get hurt. I don't tell in the holidays when Dick's here because then we're two."

Isobel disregarded this.

"I don't believe whatever it is that is going on has anything to do with your not being able to go back to school next term, Vicky. I mean there are lots of other schools in the town but Daddy and Mummy aren't looking at them."

"I expect you're being sent to that boarding school for the daughters of poor clergy," said Louise. "I wish and wish Daddy would send you there, it would be much nicer in term time if there was only me and you here, Isobel."

Victoria did not answer that. Not even her sisters must know how desperately she longed to be sent to the boarding school for the daughters of poor clergy.

A boarding school, away from the vicarage, and all the clacking parish tongues which said: "What a pity the dear vicar has such trouble with Victoria." A boarding school where she went alone, without a family, free to be just herself. The boarding school had only been mentioned after that dreadful talk in

9

the study. Victoria loved her father so much that sometimes it almost hurt. It had been shattering when the letter had arrived from Miss Dean and her father had said: "I want to see you in my study after tea, Vicky." The children seldom went into the study for either their father was working or there was someone to see him, so at all times to be called to the study was an occasion. The room seemed dark for there were heavy curtains and two walls were solid with books in dull bindings. The main pieces of furniture were a huge roll-topped desk and a swivel leather-seated chair. There was also an anthracite-burning stove.

In the early years of the century to be cold was expected. In fact the larger the home the colder it was, for those who had only the kitchen to sit in usually had a good fire. But devoted ladies who worked for the church could not bear to see their beloved vicar with his fingers white – for even in those days his circulation was poor – so they collected the money and bought and presented the stove. In the corner of the study was a prie-dieu with above it a crucifix and a reproduction of Dürer's praying hands. It took many hours of prayer at the prie-dieu before the stove was accepted, for in some ways the children's father believed being cold and godliness were intermixed; with what horror had he found a hot water bottle one bitter night in Victoria's bed – Victoria, the healthy one amongst his daughters – so he had removed the bottle as if he were wresting it from the devil. Finally the stove was accepted and kept alight all the winter through and into the spring, for the givers were always popping in and out.

But did the vicar enjoy the warmth? Only he and God knew the answer. Victoria told John, to whom she told everything, that she believed Daddy was glad when his fingers went dead while he was writing a sermon – "I think he feels he is giving more."

Those walls of the study which had no bookshelves were covered in photographs. No man or boy who had ever worked closely with the vicar – either in his first parish as curate, his second a tiny country village where he was vicar, or now at St Peter's, St Leonard's-on-Sea, could let an occasion pass without being photographed and sending a copy to the vicar. Bell-ringers ringing bells; choir boys in surplices; men's societies on outings. There was no end to them and not one was thrown away. The women church workers were only photographed when they were in their graves. There were dozens of photographs of graves, usually at the stage when they were piled with wreaths.

That horrible day over a month ago now when Victoria had been ordered into the study, she had walked in outwardly brave-looking, quietly shut the door and crossed the room to stand by her father's desk chair. He had swung the chair round so that he faced her. His voice was grave and sad.

"I have had a letter from Miss Dean, Vicky. She says she will not have you back at Elmhurst next term."

Victoria was so surprised that for a moment the room seemed to spin round. She steadied herself by putting a hand on her father's arm. She knew she had been found out – she had already had a shattering interview with Miss Dean. All day she had wondered what Miss Dean had written to her father but this was beyond her wildest imaginings.

"Expelled!"

Her father paused for a moment. He had spent a long time at his prie-dieu asking for guidance in handling this talk with Victoria – was he meant to let her accept that word expelled?

"No, not expelled – though it comes to the same thing. Miss Dean says that you will do better at another school. Oh, Vicky, what have you done? Miss Dean said in her letter she would leave you to tell me yourself."

Now, with her father's sad blue eyes fixed on hers, Victoria could see her crime as he would see it in all its blackness. Since her twelfth birthday, phrases new when applied to her had been cropping up. They had cropped up before for Isobel, but for Isobel they had not meant much. For Isobel was good; hard-working when she was well enough to go to school, and bearing patiently her bouts of asthma, quietly painting and drawing as soon as she had the breath to do anything. So what did phrases like "Having a sense of responsibility" and "You are too old to do such a silly thing" mean to her, for about her own things Isobel had a sense of responsibility and she never was silly. But oh, how far was this true of

Victoria. Yet at the time what she had done seemed a good idea, a just repayment for injustice. How could she make her father understand? That horrible, unjust Miss Dean did not matter – but hurting her father did.

"It really goes back to my magazine."

For six wildly happy months Victoria had gloried in being the editor of a magazine. While the magazine had lasted she had been, as her mother remarked to Miss Herbert, "a different child". The truth was that Victoria had found in the magazine an outlet for almost all that repressed her.

It was supposedly a form magazine, each child being allowed to provide contributions, but in actual fact the lion's share of the contributions came from Victoria. She wrote a chapter of a serial for each instalment. In these the heroine led the sort of life and had the type of adventure which she in her humdrum vicarage could never have. She wrote thinly disguised, though quite harmless, snippets of school gossip. She wrote poetry occasionally of outstanding charm and she invented competitions. For these, prizes such as sugar mice or pigs were provided by her parents and the parents of some of the other members of her form. Each child paid a reading fee of one penny which covered the exercise books in which the magazine was written, also for their penny they took the magazine home for two days. There were two rules. The magazine must be returned at the end of the two days or there was a fine of sixpence, and under no circumstances must the magazine be shown to anyone in the school outside the form.

Then one day a child developed influenza just when her two days were up, and, in spite of a high temperature, struggled to get to school to return the magazine. She was only calmed when her mother promised to go to Victoria in her place. As far as a blinding headache and a temperature for 103° allowed, the child did give the right instructions, but the bit about not allowing the magazine to be seen by anyone outside the form was muddled or omitted. As a result, the mother, running in to Miss Dean, gave her the magazine to give to Victoria.

The children's parents afterwards had often discussed what exactly Miss Dean had seen in that harmless children's effort to anger her to such an extent that she had torn the magazine into fragments and then, according to Victoria, stamped on them. The truth was, that though they knew Miss Dean was getting old and crotchety, neither parent had any idea what the Miss Dean Victoria knew was like. She was a product of the last century. A girl of spirit who had insisted – against bitter disapproval from her family, who believed that a young woman's place until she married was beside her mother – that she should be properly educated for a teaching career.

But that was in the last century and now, in this new century, especially since Queen Victoria died, it had become increasingly obvious to Miss Dean that her day was over. She was no longer the pioneer slashing her way through a jungle of prejudices. She was an out-of-date headmistress whom many thought should retire. Her disillusionment showed itself in bouts of violent temper when she could, and frequently did, appear temporarily out of her mind. And it was girls such as Victoria who sparked off her temper, those who did not conform, who thought for themselves, who would not attempt even on the surface to be true Elmhurst types, girls in fact who must have reminded her of herself when she was growing up. Victoria did not understand or attempt to understand Miss Dean, she just loathed her. But how could she make her father see *her* Miss Dean, when the one he met was all sugar and spice who talked piously about morning prayers, and how well the girls were doing in Scripture?

Her father still had his eyes fixed on hers.

"But, Vicky, Miss Dean forbade you to write that magazine last term, so what has it to do with this trouble now?"

Victoria dropped her eyes to the carpet. She must tell it – the truth, in which she believed but in which her father not only did not believe but thought wrong – perhaps even thought of as a sin.

"She had no right to tear up my magazine, it wasn't doing her any harm, and it wasn't true I did it instead of lessons, every word was written at home in play time. It was beastly mean of her so I had to get back on her. I know all you say about turning the other cheek but when a person's as mean as that you can't – you simply can't."

Her father's face was stern.

15

"And what was it you did to 'get back on Miss Dean' as you call it, which was such an offence that you have to leave the school?"

She had to tell it all. There was no way out of it. Victoria lifted her chin defiantly and glared at her father, daring him to side with Miss Dean.

"I founded a society called the Little Grey Bow Society."

"Mummy and I have noticed you wore a grey bow. What did it mean?"

"Well, at first it was me and a few other girls, then everybody in my form wanted to join. Each of us started this term with a hundred marks; we lost a mark every time we were polite to a mistress. An idiotic girl called Maisie got scared and told."

Her father looked in amazement at Victoria. From childhood he had been dedicated to serving God. At his preparatory school and later at Marlborough each day was spent attempting to do rather more, both in work and games, than was expected of him. He had seven brothers and he believed some of them had been beaten once or twice but, as far as he knew, they too had worked hard and played hard and endeavoured in every way to please God and to turn out a credit to their parents. He did not know about his two sisters for they were at home with a governess, but from the air of peace and content- ment which had hung like a rainbow over his home he supposed they too tried and succeeded in giving satisfaction. Never had there been a Victoria stating defiantly that what had been done was a just return for an injustice rendered. It was clear now why Miss Dean wished to get rid of Victoria – the chaos she must have caused in her form with every girl deliberately being rude to the mistresses.

"I don't know quite where to start, Vicky. That I am shocked and horrified you know without my telling you. But first let us tackle the question of 'getting back', as you call it, on Miss Dean. You are a child and as such it is your duty to obey and not to question. I have no idea what Miss Dean had against the magazine but, whatever her reasons, no doubt they were good . . ." He saw Victoria was bursting to argue so he hurried on, "and in any case she is your headmistress so you must accept her ruling. Instead, to dare to form a society whose sole object was to give offence was a shocking thing to do. I find it almost impossible to believe a child of mine could have done such a thing."

Victoria felt anxious; surely Daddy was not going to cry. He could, because he had when he had read them *The Story of a Short Life*. Worse, was he going to pray with her? Twice he had done that: once when she had told a whopping lie and once when she had stolen a greengage off a friend's wall. To distract him temporarily from her sin she introduced a new angle to the talk.

"It's all very well, Daddy, to say I'm a child and so I must obey and not ask questions. But on the Sunday after my last birthday you said I was stopping being a child and so I must have a sense of responsibility and all that. And Mummy said now Isobel and

17

I were growing up we wouldn't sleep in the night nursery any more but have our own room, which was to be called The Girls' Room – and we have it and it is. Why was I supposed to be growing up then and be a child today?"

That was quite a question. Telling Victoria she must start to grow up, and giving her the little honour of a room shared with Isobel had been one of the many schemes tried to make her a better behaved child. It had not been a success. Victoria had remained as nonconforming as ever, a real thorn in the flesh, as her mother frequently said. But this was not the moment to admit failure and reduce Victoria to the easier rôle of irresponsible child. Instead there was the question of punishment.

"No punishment is sufficient for what you have done, Vicky. It is not only that it was wrong of you to think up so dreadful a society, but think of all the other girls in your form who, because of you, became ill-mannered and offensive. For the rest of the term, as soon as you have finished your homework, you will go to your room, where some work will be waiting for you – some of the hassocks in the church want repairing." He put his arm round Victoria and rested his face against her cheek so that she could feel the thickness of his eyebrow. "But, Vicky darling, punishments are no good without repentance. You must pray, Vicky, for help to forgive Miss Dean for what you so wrongfully imagine was an injustice done to you. We all need the help of prayer, Vicky, but you more than most for you have a difficult nature. When you are ready to ask for forgiveness come and tell me and we will talk to God about it together."

Officially what had happened in the study was a secret but apart from the fact of the punishment, which had to be explained, Victoria was not one to keep a good story to herself, so before another day had passed the whole school was whispering, "Victoria Strangeway has been expelled". – "Imagine, Miss Dean has expelled Victoria Strangeway," which delighted Victoria, making her, if not a heroine, at least the centre-piece of a drama. Almost the thrill of being so noticed and talked about compensated for the cold evenings sitting alone in The Girls' Room stitching braid on to hassocks, but not quite, for Victoria was not one to enjoy her own companionship. She especially did not enjoy it when before the fire in the drawing room the others were playing Spillikins or "Who Knows?", and after Miss Herbert had taken Louise up to bed their mother would read a chapter of *David Copperfield* to Isobel.

Now, standing beside her garden leaning on the rake, Victoria realised with rather hurtful surprise that Isobel was right. For two or three days after the interview in the study schools were discussed, and papers were sent for about the school for the daughters of poor clergy. But now – surprising though it was to face the fact that there could be anything more interesting than herself and where she went to school for her parents to talk about – she had to accept that there had not been a school mentioned for at least three weeks. Victoria looked at Isobel.

"Perhaps they've decided I can do lessons with Miss Herbert."

Isobel moved to the other end of her garden to see how her pasque flower was getting on.

"If that was all, there'd be nothing to whisper about, and certainly nothing to go away for. Imagine their going away yesterday and not telling us where!"

Louise had prepared a place for radishes and was marking it off with sticks.

"Whatever else is happening you aren't doing lessons with Miss Herbert. Mummy asked her and she said: 'I would do anything for you and the dear vicar, you know that, but some things are more than flesh and blood can stand.' "

Louise mimicked Miss Herbert's voice well; both Isobel and Victoria giggled. Then Isobel looked up and saw Miss Herbert coming on the lawn.

"Shut up. Here she comes."

In the days before the First World War people of a certain standing, however little money they had, kept servants, and where there were children a nanny or a governess. So, though the children's father was a poor man, for vicars did not earn much money and he had no private means until his father died, there was a cook and a house-parlourmaid and a woman who came in daily for the heavy work, and Miss Herbert.

Miss Herbert was qualified to teach, but she suffered from poor health so had decided on a place where she only supervised. Not that her days were easy by present standards. She had to see the three girls got up and had their breakfast before she walked with them to Elmhurst, which was over a mile away. Back in the house she helped with any clerical jobs the children's father might have until it was time to fetch the children home to schoolroom lunch. For Isobel, when she was well enough and always for Victoria, there was afternoon school and games until four o'clock, during which time Miss Herbert took Louise for a walk. Then came schoolroom tea followed for the elder two by preparation. Meanwhile Miss Herbert changed Louise into a smarter frock and took her to the drawing room. After homework Isobel and Victoria (when she was not being punished) also changed and went down to their mother.

By seven Louise was put to bed and then Miss Herbert supervised while the other two ate their supper of cocoa and biscuits. At 7.30 Victoria went to bed and at 8.00 Isobel. The rest of the evening was Miss Herbert's own, except for any mending the children's mother had asked her to do. Every other week she had a free half day and she was supposed to be free part of each Sunday, but this seldom materialised. Still, as she said to her friends: "A vicarage is a pleasant background," and with care she was able to save much of her salary of £15 a year towards her old age. She was a small, sandy, dyspeptic woman, always neatly dressed in a high-necked blouse and full navy skirt except on Sundays when she wore a frogged coat and skirt with, during the winter, a fur tippet. Now, as she came across the lawn, the sun glinting on her glasses, it was clear from the purposeful look of her that she was the bearer of news. Besides, she was carrying a piece of paper.

"I have had a telegram, dears. Your father and mother will be back this afternoon and they wish you to have tea with them in the drawing room."

The girls stared at Miss Herbert. They never had tea in the drawing room. On their birthdays and on Christmas Day there was family tea in the dining room, but that was different.

"You sure?" asked Victoria.

Miss Herbert gave a little annoyed wriggle.

"My dear child, I can read." She held up the telegram. " 'Back 4.15 tea drawing room whole family. Strangeway.' "

Isobel looked searchingly at Miss Herbert.

"It looks as if at last we are going to be told what is happening, doesn't it?"

Miss Herbert was in a quandary. She did not want to admit anything but still less did she wish to suggest there was anything going on which was a secret from her.

"Now we mustn't be impatient, must we, Isobel? But this I will say – as perhaps this is rather a special occasion – you girls may wear your velvets for tea."

2 The News

"Your velvets" was a grand-sounding phrase for the
frocks concerned and the girls knew it, for all were
conscious they were badly dressed. Isobel's clothes
were the best for she inherited hers from Ursula, a
cousin who was one year older and far larger and
taller than she was. Ursula's father was Uncle Paul,
who came next in age to Father in the Strangeway
family; her mother, Aunt Helen, was American.

On the few occasions when they had met Aunt
Helen, usually at family weddings, the children had
found her alarming for she was a great believer in
organisation. At two weddings at which the girls had
been bridesmaids and Dick a page, this had led to
disaster for Aunt Helen had insisted on such careful
rehearsing before the wedding that the children
became exhausted and confused. The result was that
at one ceremony Dick sat on the bride's train and
was carried up the aisle on it, and at another Victoria
fell flat on her face, scattering the flowers from her
basket on the chancel steps. But though Aunt Helen
might be alarming to meet, her taste in clothes for
her daughter was just the opposite, for everything
bought for Ursula was soft and the colouring in
gentle pastels.

Miss Herbert called Ursula's dresses sweetly

23

pretty; the children thought them terrible. Because their mother was lazy about clothes, taking no interest in them either for herself or her children, whatever came from Ursula was copied cheaply for the other two. Thus the velvets. Isobel's velvet was a pale green with a very full skirt which hung straight from a big plain yoke. Because the material was the best that could be bought, though Isobel liked neither the shape nor the colour, she had to admit it hung gracefully. Victoria and Louise's velvets were made of the cheapest material; Victoria's was brown and Louise's dark blue. Cheap velvet was stiff and unyielding, and though the inexpensive dressmaker who came in by the hour had done her best, nothing could make the material hang properly from a plain yoke. Since even their mother could see that Victoria and Louise's dresses did not become them, in the house they wore over them pinafores of lawn and lace also inherited, though at an earlier date, from Ursula.

"If there is one thing I hate worse than wearing my velvet it's wearing this pinafore," Victoria grumbled as she and Isobel were changing in the girls' room. "Thank goodness it will soon be summer and I should think I'll have outgrown mine by next winter."

Isobel turned her back on Victoria to have her frock fastened.

"I wish it was tea time. I've begun to feel as if I was going to the dentist."

Victoria's face behind Isobel's back became

serious. This was bad; when things hung over Isobel it often meant she would start an attack of asthma.

"You don't feel wheezyish, do you?"

All too well Isobel knew what prompted that question.

"No, but sort of tightish as though I soon might."

There was medicine Isobel could have taken and a type of blotting-paper soaked in crystals that she could have burned, but it never crossed her mind or Victoria's that she might stave off an attack; grown-ups dealt with illness – never children. Besides, in most cases you had to be ill before there was treatment. The saying "prevention is better than cure" was used but in relation to other things, such as moth balls before the moth season or strengthening the elbows of frocks before there was a hole. But Victoria, brought up under the permanent shade of Isobel's asthma, had watched and learnt. Sometimes an attack could be avoided by attracting her attention to other things.

"It's a pity we're too old for this should be a Hallelujah day."

When the children were small the return of their father and mother, even after one night away, became a Hallelujah day. This meant covering the bars of the windows in the day nursery – now the schoolroom – with whatever was to hand which would pass as decorations. Often in those days it was dolls' clothes, bedding from the dolls' perambulators plus any ribbons saved from birthday or Christmas chocolate boxes.

Isobel, her frock fastened, turned round to button Victoria.

"We may be too old but Louise isn't, and we've dressed much too early so it would be something to do."

"I dressed early on purpose," said Victoria. "I think being dressed for something makes it come faster."

"Don't wriggle. This velvet's awful enough to button, even when you're standing still. It would have to be a different Hallelujah, of course, because we have only Jackie's clothes as Louise doesn't like dolls."

Jackie was a golliwog which Louise was supposed to adore. Her sisters knew that she had been devoted to the toy when she was younger, but they had a theory that for the last two years her devotion was largely simulated to please the grown-ups, especially her mother who preferred small children to older ones. Jackie, with his new clothes for Christmas and birthday and the fables collected round him, such as that Louise could not sleep unless he was in her arms, certainly appeared to chain her to childhood.

"We'll make Louise do the actual putting up, then we won't be blamed for being childish," said Victoria. "We could use handkerchiefs and ribbons and our party beads."

So when about an hour later the station fly drove up to the gate of the vicarage, much tapping on the schoolroom window made both the vicar and his wife look up. Mrs Strangeway smiled.

"Oh look, Jim, it's a Hallelujah. They haven't done that for years."

Having paid the cabman the children's father stood in the road to get a better view.

"Bless them. But Isobel and Victoria are getting too old for such nonsense."

The children's mother opened the gate and walked up the path. "Too old!" Jim was always harping on that subject. The girls were too old for short skirts, too old for bare legs in the summer. If only he knew how the thought of growing-up daughters frightened her. Anyway Isobel would never be grown-up in the way Jim meant, for every time she was ill she became a little girl again clinging to Mummy.

Although it was a special occasion as tea was in the drawing room, there was nothing exciting to eat because it was Lent. The three-tiered cakestand held no cake, only white and brown bread and butter. Fasting in Lent, though supposedly left to the free will of all, was actually imposed. It was taken for granted by the children's father that during Lent no one, except on Sundays, would wish to eat sweets, cake or jam. A visitor to the vicarage one Shrove Tuesday when Louise was six had found her sobbing in the garden. Asked what the trouble was she had said: "I can't bear to think there's forty days of farce in front of me." The tea table was laid with the silver kettle over the methylated flame, and the silver teapot, milk jug and sugar basin all with the Strange-way crest on them. There were eggshell thin cups with blue borders and in each saucer a teaspoon

27

again engraved with the family crest. Even with only bread and butter to eat the occasion had style as tea was poured out for everyone. In the schoolroom, tea was slightly-coloured milk. The children's father smiled round at his girls.

"Mummy and I have some exciting news for you. I have been offered a new living. It's the parish church at Eastbourne."

"It's a great compliment to Daddy," their mother put in, "for it's a big and important parish and whoever is vicar there is also rural dean and often finishes up as a bishop."

The girls were so surprised at this news that for a moment even Victoria was silenced. Whatever else they expected it was not this. St Peter's was their home.

"The Bishop wrote to me with the offer two or three weeks ago," their father explained, "but I could not say yes then because the vicarage wants such a lot done to it and I did not see where the money was coming from, but I heard this week that Queen Anne's Bounty will help, and we went over yesterday and spent the night with the present vicar and his wife, and before I left I wrote to the Bishop and accepted. We are going to move after Easter."

After Easter! But Easter was only a few weeks away. That unloosed the girls' tongues. Questions poured out. What was the new vicarage like? What school would they go to? What was Eastbourne like? How many rooms would there be in the new house?

Would Miss Herbert go with them? Would the maids go with them? Was there a proper garden?

Laughing, their father held up his hand.

"One at a time, please. Mummy can tell you more about the vicarage than I can for I spent most of the time in the study with Canon Moore, the retiring vicar, learning what I could about the parish. He's ill, poor man, which is why he is leaving."

Their mother put down her teacup.

"It's a lovely house lying in a big garden. There is a lawn shaded with big trees – one a particularly beautiful cedar. Then, to the right of the lawn, there is a flower garden. It's been let go rather but I saw some nice rose trees. At the back there is a vegetable garden. In front quite a good drive with shrubs on either side. Daddy's study looks out that way so he'll be able to see who's coming to call."

Father's eyes twinkled.

"And under my study window there's a flower bed and whatever Mummy does with the rest of the garden that is going to be properly bedded out."

The girls knew their father's fondness for a formal-looking bed.

"Lobelias in front, geraniums in the middle and marguerites at the back," Isobel suggested.

Her mother looked at her with an experienced eye.

"Are you feeling wheezy?"

"Only tight."

"I wonder if that chair is too low. Victoria, get a cushion off the sofa and put it at Isobel's back."

29

Victoria jumped up and fetched the cushion.

"I don't think it will be an attack; you said you were tight ages ago, didn't you, Isobel, and it's not worse, is it?"

Victoria was undeniably difficult. But that was only a part of the explanation of the effect she had on her mother. She could see she annoyed her, often without apparent reason, but why? She only began to grasp the answer years later.

The trouble stemmed in part from the fact that Victoria was strong and healthy. There had been another sister, Edith, who was a year younger than Dick. From birth Edith had a frail hold on life, and when still a baby she had died. Because she had died while she was still too small to have a part in family life, she had soon been forgotten by her sisters and brother. But not by her mother. Losing that baby whom she had struggled so hard to keep alive left an unhealed wound. She was helped by Isobel's dependence on her, and by the fact that Louise was far from strong, for in part she could give to those two what she could no longer give to Edith. But lively, healthy Victoria must have opened the wound daily. Why should she have all that energy when so little of it, passed to Edith, might have kept her alive?

Edith was never spoken of in front of the children. Victoria could remember the day she died, not because of the death but because she had seen her mother cry. "Go into the spare bedroom and give Mummy a kiss," the children's father had said. Their

30

mother was standing by the window with tears streaming down her face. Shocked, for grown-ups did not cry, Victoria had glued her eyes on a vase of dark red roses from which petals dropped one by one on to the dressing table. For ever she was to connect dropping rose petals with death.

When Granny and Grandfather arrived for the funeral, Dick, who had just learnt how to do it, distinguished himself by sliding down the banisters, shouting to Grandfather as he came: "Did you know our baby was dead?"

There were hideous mauve frocks made for the three girls, which were so unbecoming that they were given away to the mission supported by the school. Isobel and Victoria, passing the cloakroom, heard the head girl and one of the governesses laughing their heads off as they packed the dresses. "Who *could* want these?" the head girl had said. Who? All that mattered to the girls was, that with the dresses out of the house, sadness left too.

Victoria's calm assumption that she knew anything about Isobel's asthma must have driven her mother frantic. Victoria who was always well, who never needed taking care of – how did she dare to forecast whether Isobel would have an attack or not? Could she not imagine the dread that haunted her mother of losing another child?

"I asked you to get Isobel a cushion, not to talk on a subject about which you are fortunate enough to know nothing."

In the children's father's view, his wife – the

woman he had chosen to share his life and bear his children – was without blemish, or nearly so. In his childhood home to criticise either their father or their mother had been unthinkable; they were God-like figures whose least word was law.

But there were occasions – and this was one – when the thought crossed his mind that there was sometimes something not quite kind in the way her mother spoke to Victoria. Of course it was unintentional, it probably just sounded that way, but it was something he must remember in his prayers. Sylvia was the dearest wife a man could have, but he must not forget that she had never known her own mother, that he had married her when she was seventeen, and that she had lost a much-loved child, so small mistakes in the handling of Victoria were understandable.

"I'm sure Vicky was only trying to help," he said gently. "All the same, Vicky, of course Mummy's right. You should not talk about things when you know nothing about them. Now, wasn't the next question about a school?"

Victoria had a lump in her throat. Why must Daddy add that bit about Mummy being right? He always did that and it wasn't fair because she did know about tightness before asthma. Isobel, who sympathised with Victoria, panted into the breach.

"Have you chosen a school?"

Their father nodded.

"I think so. Eastbourne is packed with schools. But most of them are the opposite end of the town

32

from the vicarage, which would mean a walk across the golf links. This would be all right in fine weather but impossible for you, Isobel, if it was wet or blowy."

Their mother broke in.

"But there is one which sounds very nice, it's called Laughton House, you can get almost all the way there by omnibus if necessary. It's a boarding school but we think you can go as daily boarders."

"Do we wear uniforms at Laughton House?"

Isobel could not wait to ask her question.

"Is the art good?"

Louise, hugging Jackie, looked at her mother.

"Will I go as a day boarder too – like the big ones?"

Isobel had to be answered first.

"That is one of our reasons for thinking Laughton House is just the school we are looking for. I understand the art standard is very high. Girls of sufficient promise are taught by a real artist, who comes twice a week."

Isobel's blue eyes shone.

"I do hope I'm allowed to learn with him."

"I think we can take that for granted," said her mother fondly. Then she turned to Louise. 'You'll be a day boarder too, darling, but for little girls like you it will be mostly play in the afternoons."

Victoria was wriggling in her chair she was so anxious for an answer.

"And the uniform? Do we wear a uniform?"

Her mother looked questioningly at her father, who shook his head.

"I shouldn't think so, it's a small select private school. I'm sure Miss French, the headmistress, would not care for it."

Isobel thought the idea of school uniform terrible. She could see Victoria's point of view, which she had heard over and over again, that if only they had to wear uniform at school they would never look worse dressed than anybody else. But her taste was for bright, clear colours, and the thought of spending her days in a navy blue gym tunic or something of the sort was abhorrent. Still, she was sorry Victoria was disappointed. In case Victoria started to argue and demand a school that did wear uniform she changed the subject.

"What about Miss Herbert and the maids?"

Her father answered her.

"Miss Herbert is coming to start with anyway. There will be a lot of work for Mummy when we move and she will need her."

Louise was anxious. What was this? Mummy would want Miss Herbert?

"If Mummy has Miss Herbert who is going to look after me?"

Her father laughed.

"Don't you worry, Louise, you won't be neglected. During the move, which will be during the Easter holidays, you are all going to Granny and Grandfather's."

"All?" asked Victoria. "John too?"

"And Dick?" Louise queried.

Their father smiled wistfully. Though he and Sylvia had been married for over fourteen years, the mere thought of that solid, restful house in the Kent Weald even now made him homesick. He knew himself to be a fortunate man with a beloved wife, splendid children and work to which he was dedicated. But somehow he had never succeeded in reproducing his parents' home life in his own home. In some way the atmosphere was different. It was always a joy to him when the children stayed with his parents. Who knew but that being under the roof they might catch that special something which had made his own and his brothers' and sisters' home life so perfect. He got up.

"Of course you're all going, as if John and Dick would be left out. I must go and do a little more work on tomorrow's sermon. Don't wear Mummy out with too many questions."

Their mother looked at the clock.

"I'm afraid it's time you went to your room, Vicky."

Victoria got up. It was a nasty anticlimax to all the exciting news to sit alone in her bedroom sewing braid loops on to hassocks. But she was used to punishments and accepted them calmly. Besides, Isobel would save up all the rest of the news she got out of Mummy and would tell her when she came up to bed.

Something about Victoria's calm acceptance of her punishment moved her father, while his wife's quickness in remembering it disturbed him. Perhaps this was a moment when leniency would not come amiss. He put an arm round Victoria.

"I think you have been punished enough, Vicky. At Eastbourne you'll be able to make a fresh start. It will mean a new leaf for all of us – but it's come just at the right time for you. Don't forget to thank God when you say your prayers tonight."

3 Sunday

All the children, especially the boys who sang in the choir when they were home, detested Sundays. But it was an underground detestation never spoken of in front of a grown-up because Daddy must never know. He thought his children loved Sundays just as he had loved them when he was a boy, and this was why their Sundays were modelled on Sundays in their grandparents' house.

On Sundays the girls were called at seven thirty by Miss Herbert, who gave each of them their prayerbook open at the collect of the day, which had to be learnt by heart before they got up at eight. On Sundays breakfast and lunch were eaten in the dining room which was, as Isobel and Victoria agreed, the one nice thing about Sundays. For breakfast there were always sausages, and for the children crusts of white bread. This was because the Communion bread was made in the house, but before the loaves were taken over to the church all the crust was cut off and, since "waste not want not" was a family motto, the children ate them and eating them was supposed to be a treat. "Though actually," Isobel had told Victoria, "I'd much rather have toast like the grown-ups."

Special clothes belonged to Sundays. They were

not necessarily better than those worn on weekdays, but they were newer and supposedly smarter. Even those families with large wardrobes, though they had no clothes labelled "Sundays", always wore something good for church.

The poorest families in the country, and there was a great deal of poverty in those days, would have thought they had sunk low indeed if they could not manage special clothes for Sundays. It was unthinkable to send the children to Sunday School unless they wore what was obviously their best. Dad, though he was only going out to buy a drink, was spruced up even if all that could be managed was a clean handkerchief round his neck. And on Sunday evenings Mum would not be seen in church or chapel without a Sunday hat and probably a slightly less shabby dress than her weekday one.

Only too often those cherished Sunday clothes were only in the homes of the poor on Sundays. For most Monday mornings would see Mum hurrying round to the pawnbroker's clutching a bundle.

The girls never looked their best on Sundays for they always seemed unlucky with their Sunday frocks. "It won't show under a coat," their mother would say, so actually Sunday frocks, though conforming in that they were different, were less good than the skirts and jerseys they wore for school. That winter Isobel was wearing a fawn-coloured dress of Ursula's with embroidery round the yoke, which was startlingly unbecoming. Victoria also had a dress of Ursula's; it had been Isobel's last year, it was sage green and the elbows had worn out so new sleeves had been made of a material which did not match.

Louise looked the best because she was still small enough for smocks and her mother smocked beautifully. Unfortunately she never realised it was a waste to put hand-done work into poor material so, though the smocking was still good, the wine-coloured material was rubbed and worn, but it took more than a worn frock to dim Louise's beauty.

Collect and catechism time Sunday after Sunday were wrestling matches between Victoria and her mother. A devil got into Victoria and she had to argue. If she put in a wrong word she swore she had not; if she gave a right answer she managed to say it in a defiant you-thought-I-didn't-know voice. Isobel usually stumbled more or less successfully through her collect but she was apt to dream when it came to the catechism. Louise, who had only to read a thing through once to know it, was the star turn, and week after week Victoria heard: "If Louise can learn it surely you ought to be able to, Vicky." It was a relief to everybody except Louise when at half past ten they were sent up to get dressed for church.

Last autumn Aunt Helen had sent Isobel the most artistic of her creations for Ursula. It was a pale fawn coat in fine cloth with many collars, known as coachman-style. With it came a fawn felt hat swathed in ribbon which was tied under the right ear with a large bow. The coat was a little long for Isobel but the slim line under the many-collared coat suited her admirably, and she looked charmingly pink and white under the fawn beribboned hat. Victoria's copy of this outfit was a disaster. No cheap fawn material could be obtained so instead a pale brown hairy cloth had been bought which Victoria said with truth looked as though it was a blanket. Ursula's hat had been made by a good hat shop; no bending and twisting of brown felt in a cheap shop could achieve the same effect. Victoria looked a comic and knew it. Stumping upstairs to put on these clothes, still seething from her fight with her mother, she muttered to Isobel:

"I wish something awful would happen, like our all getting scarlet fever, so there would be no more collects and catechisms or church for weeks and weeks and weeks."

Isobel, anxious that Victoria should cause no more trouble, merely said:

"Don't forget your clean handkerchief or your penny for the collection."

Louise, looking charming in a pale blue coat that had been first Ursula's and then Isobel's but was still in good condition because it had skipped Victoria, walked sedately into church clutching a picture book of Bible stories which she still, being a child, was allowed to read during the sermon. Behind her, gloved and wearing what the children called church faces, walked Isobel and Victoria. The vicarage pew was on the left of the aisle. In front of them sat the vicar's churchwarden and his family, opposite the people's warden and his family. The vicar's warden's daughter, Joyce Sedman, was supposedly a friend of the children's. She was about Victoria's age, a spoilt only daughter, endured by the Strangeway girls because her father and their father were friends. In exactly the same way their mother managed to seem friendly with Mrs Sedman though actually the two women had little in common. The question of friendship with the people's warden, Mr Sergeant and his family, did not arise. The Sergeants owned a big draper's shop, and therefore were trade; in those days professional families – still less landed gentry to which Father's family belonged – never knew "trade" socially. It was something which needed no discussion, it just did not happen.

This Sunday, after the family had arisen from their knees and were looking up the hymns in their hymn books, something unusual happened. Mr Sedman, who had been creeping about supervising the sidesmen and seeing that strangers had hymn and prayer books, came to the vicarage pew and quietly laid an envelope in front of Isobel. On it was written "The Misses Strangeway". Church rules were rigorous, if not always perfectly observed. Nobody might turn round, not even if somebody behind fainted or, as had once happened in the row behind, a man had sat on his top hat, squashing it flat. There must be no whispering and no nudgings. In fact the family should be a model of how to behave in church. The envelope was a temptation, church had not started, the organist was still playing the voluntary. Isobel stared at the envelope and so did Victoria. Victoria jerked one gloved finger towards Joyce's back.

41

"Birthday," she muttered out of the corner of her mouth.

Louise too was interested. She leant across her mother to see to whom the envelope was addressed. Their mother thought it was stupid of Mr Sedman to give it to the children before church, so she picked up the envelope and shut it in her Bible, but not before she had shown Louise to whom it was addressed. Satisfied, Louise relaxed, but Victoria had not finished with the situation. She waited until the choirboys had filed in behind the cross bearer, and her father and the curate were in their places and the service had begun. Then, leaning so slightly towards Isobel that it was unnoticeable, she sang with the face of a saint her own version of the Venite. She was a past mistress at singing her own version of any part of the service.

" 'O Come let us sing unto the Lord: Let us heartily rejoice in the strength of our salvation . . .' What's the chances we've been asked to her party? But if we have, bets I, Daddy won't let us go. I know he likes Mr Sedman but he's never let us go to parties in Lent."

Victoria had a good ear and she managed to fit the words perfectly to the plainsong of the Venite.

Isobel had no ear for music but even had she been able to reply it would have been impossible for her to do so, for when Victoria decided to sing her own version of a psalm or hymn it invariably made her giggle. She began to giggle now and to cover it pretended to be choking into her handkerchief. Her

42

mother looked anxiously at her. She had seemed all right when they came out; the suspicion did stir in her – was Victoria being naughty? – but if she was there was no sign for there stood Victoria, her prayer book held in two gloved hands, singing beautifully in her clear, choirboy voice. Their mother opened her bag and took out a box of cough lozenges and pushed it towards Isobel, who somehow mastered her giggles while with a shake of the head she denied the need for the lozenges.

"And that was pretty mean," sang Victoria, "for I like them even if you do not."

The children, all through their childhood, heard discussions as to whether people were very high, medium high or low church. As the daughters of a vicar of the Church of England they knew nobody who was not Church of England. Presumably at their school some girls were Roman Catholics and some were chapel, but if this were so they never knew about it. Everyone in their world was very high, medium high or low Church of England.

The girls' father and mother did not agree on the right way for a church service to be held. The subject was never discussed before the children but words were dropped and their sharp eyes and ears missed little. They knew their mother hated what she called "anything high". "High" included the red lamp to show where the reserved sacrament was kept, and "dressing up", by which she meant vestments.

Their father did not wear vestments because he had none, but on grand occasions, such as Easter,

Christmas and the day of the patron saint, Peter, nothing was spared in the way of processions, or to beautify the altar. Once when the Bishop came to stay, the house-parlourmaid, when she came out of the dining room, had said to the cook: "He'd like incense but the Bishop thinks they aren't ready. She's looking as if they'd both gone over to Rome." Isobel, hanging over the stairs, had heard this statement. She had told Victoria and both had gone to Miss Herbert for enlightenment.

"I know about frankincense like the wise men brought to baby Jesus," Isobel said as they walked to school, "but what is incense?"

Miss Herbert was medium high herself though, because of her devotion to the vicar, struggling to like being higher.

"It's stuff that smells when it burns. Roman Catholics put it in little braziers and swing the smoke out over the congregation. Sometimes it is done in our churches too but only in very, very few."

"Would you like it if Daddy used it?" Victoria asked.

Miss Herbert, who had heard nothing of the talk in the dining room, was shocked.

"Oh no, dear, and I'm sure he never would, it's very un-English I think."

"Popish," Isobel suggested.

Miss Herbert thought that was just what incense was, but knowing how "high" the children's father was, he just might not disapprove of the nasty stuff, so she had evaded a direct answer.

"Something like that, but don't let's talk any more about incense on this bright clear morning. Breathe deeply, Isobel, this is just the day to fill your lungs."

During Sunday matins there were "high" moments which the children waited for, knowing their mother disapproved of them; the choir bowing to the altar when they processed in, and before they processed out, and the part at the end of the Creed when their father, the curate and some members of the congregation crossed themselves. And they knew their mother disapproved when during the week their father would slip out in the early mornings to take Holy Communion to the sick. He always went quietly, hoping to meet no one, because in his portable altar case was the reserved sacrament, and to speak would seem to him profane. When he came home, their mother would watch him eat his breakfast in a grudging way, as if she were saying: "Those that run about before breakfast doing what you've been doing don't deserve to be fed." Isobel, when she was at home because of asthma, used to watch her parents on these mornings with amusement, for she did not believe her father noticed how her mother felt or, if he did, that he cared, for in his philosophy a wife believed what her husband believed. The point was above argument.

After morning church a visit was paid to distant cousins. There were two sets of these, old Cousin Violet who was in her nineties and had produced so many children she had long ago lost count of the number, was a cousin on their mother's side. Cousin

Fred and Cousin Pearl belonged to Father's family. He came of Quaker stock, as had their father's grandmother. She was Hannah, a daughter of Elizabeth Fry. There was not a room in the vicarage which had not something in it by which to remember Elizabeth Fry. Busts of her; engravings of her teaching prisoners; a small Bible signed by her; and, in the day nursery, a portrait of her nurse. But Cousin Fred was unique in that he took Elizabeth Fry out of being history and made her real.

Once when he was a tiny boy, he had stayed in a house, he told the children, where each morning he was lifted on to a great four-poster bed to kiss a very old lady. The old lady had worn a stiff white muslin bonnet. Each day she said the same thing. "Hast thou said thy prayers, Fred?" When the child answered "Yes" he was given a reward. The old lady opened a tin and out of it took a piece of barley sugar hanging on a string. Every time Cousin Fred told the story he finished it the same way. "And that old lady was your great-great-grandmother, Elizabeth Fry."

The visits to the cousins were usually turn about except in the strawberry season when each Sunday Cousin Fred let the children loose under his strawberry nets. Cousin Violet, who dressed exactly as had Queen Victoria in a bonnet, with a cape covered in bugles and beads, though devoted to the children's father, was low church. To counteract any Popish tang attached to words, she deliberately mispronounced them, for instance, God was always Gawd.

She had a remarkable memory and delighted the children with stories of her girlhood. Their favourite was of the death of a relative at which she had been present, when, gripping her daughter's hand, the dying mother had whispered as her last words: "Never wear pink. And never know the name of a card."

"Why shouldn't she have worn pink?" one of the children would always ask in order to hear Cousin Violet say:

"No nice girl wore pink when I was young."

In every way Cousin Violet belonged to the past. When the previous Christmas, for the first time, all the children were taken to a pantomime by Cousin Fred and Cousin Pearl, Cousin Violet had said:

"I should never care to go inside a theatre. How terrible if you died there."

This Sunday it was Cousin Fred and Cousin Pearl's turn. As was usual when it was fine they were walking round their garden when the family arrived but this Sunday they were not alone, two very old people were with them. Cousin Fred introduced the children one by one to the old lady, who nodded and smiled. Then, raising her voice, she in turn introduced them to the old man. She started with Isobel, leading her forward, one hand on her shoulder.

"Isobel, thee dost not know thy cousin John Henry."

Walking home to lunch the children were full of questions.

47

"Why do they talk like that?" Isobel asked her mother.

"Because they are Quakers; Quakers don't talk like that now as a rule but those two are very old and haven't changed."

Victoria giggled.

"I felt I ought to curtsey or something."

"It was a good thing you didn't," said her mother. "They don't approve of anything of that sort. An ancestor of yours through Elizabeth Fry lived in Oxford, and for a time Charles II was there too. As a joke, to tease the Quakers, King Charles would sweep off his hat. One day your Quaker ancestor stopped the King just as he was lifting his hat from his head. 'Charles,' he said, 'I did not doff my hat to thee, so thee needs not doff thy hat to me.'"

"Did anything happen to him?" the girls wanted to know.

Their mother shook her head.

"I don't think so. I think probably the King admired him for standing up for his convictions."

As soon as they were back in the vicarage the girls wanted to open their envelope from Joyce Sedman, but their mother said no.

"You've only just got time to wash and tidy for lunch, the gong will go in a few minutes. We'll open it after lunch."

"How mean!" said Victoria as they were washing their hands. "I shouldn't have thought any mother could be as mean as that."

"Any more of that talk, Vicky," said Miss Herbert, who had come up to collect the girls, "and you'll have no pudding."

There was a second when going without pudding almost won, then Isobel tugged at Victoria's arm.

"Come on down," she whispered. "It's not worth it. Going without pudding won't open the envelope any quicker."

In those days, however much a family like the Strangeways might believe in the catechism – "Remember that thou keep holy the Sabbath day. Six days shalt thou labour, and do all that thou hast to do; but the seventh day is the Sabbath of the Lord thy God. In it thou shalt do no manner of work, thou and thy son and thy daughter, thy man-servant and thy maid-servant, thy cattle and the stranger that is within thy gates . . ." – it did not prevent the cook cooking a hot Sunday lunch and the house parlourmaid serving it. The reason, which belonged to the period was that, though it was never actually admitted to, church-going was a class affair. Matins was for the gentry, evensong for the working classes.

In a big household where there were perhaps twenty or more indoor servants, a large part of the staff in uniform attended matins and then congregated outside the church to take off their hats or curtsey to the family for whom they worked when they left the church. But such households did not exist in the vicar's parish, so keeping holy the Sabbath day started for the servants in the vicarage after they had served afternoon tea and laid cold supper in the dining room.

Lunch on Sundays was always the same: a roast joint, usually beef, in which case it was served with Yorkshire pudding, followed by apple tart and custard. Afterwards, because it was Sunday, the one sweet of the Lenten week was eaten, chosen by each in turn according to age, from one of the many boxes given to the family last Christmas. Chocolates, except on special occasions, were only eaten once a day, so sometimes the Christmas boxes lasted until midsummer. During Lent six chocolates were put away each week to be given to a blind child in the parish on Easter Day.

After lunch the envelope was opened. Inside was an invitation card, which said that Joyce was giving a party from four o'clock to eight o'clock and she hoped Isobel, Victoria and Louise would be able to come. There would be competitions and a conjurer. It was this last which drew excited murmurs from the girls.

There were many parties, especially round Christmas, but they were usually only games and dancing; a conjurer was a rare treat at a time when for children such as the Strangeways there was no entertainment save an occasional magic lantern, except those they made themselves. Other children had things called phonographs on which a black tube spun round and tunes came out, such as *A Whistler and his Dog*, but not the Strangeways, such things not only cost too much but were looked at in dismay by their father, who had no love for any invention he had not known as a child in his own home. True, he accepted gas and was to accept electricity, but all his life he sighed for lamps.

"Don't get too excited about the conjurer," their mother warned. "The party is on the Saturday before Holy Week so I doubt if Daddy will let you go."

"It's going to be awkward for him saying 'no' as Mr Sedman's a churchwarden," Victoria suggested.

Her mother wanted to snap but refrained.

"I've yet to hear your father say 'yes' to something he did not approve of."

Louise looked anxious.

"I do hope he lets us go. It's been a very long Lent this year."

On Sunday afternoon the children were taken by Miss Herbert to the children's service, so asking their father had to wait until after tea. They did not mind the children's service which was, though they did not know it, a model of what a service for children should be. There were plenty of popular hymns. A reading from the Bible. A short talk on a theme suitable for children, another hymn and then, what all the children waited for – a story. How the vicar managed to find a new, absorbing story Sunday after Sunday amazed the adults, but the truth was he was a splendid story-teller and could produce a first-class story without much material. When years later Victoria wrote books for children and was asked whether her talent was inherited she always said "yes", thinking back to those Sunday afternoons.

Sunday tea for the girls was in the schoolroom

supervised by Miss Herbert. Because it was Sunday the fast was lifted and there was both jam and a home-made cake. Usually on the Sundays in Lent the girls lingered over tea, enjoying the food they would not taste again for a week, but today they were anxious to get downstairs to learn whether or not they would be allowed to go to Joyce's party.

In the drawing room the children's mother had broken the news of the invitation to their father. He looked at her with a worried face.

"How awkward, and how peculiar of Sedman to give a party in Lent. In the ordinary way I would have told the children to refuse, but as we are leaving it seems unkind."

The children's mother helped herself to a sandwich.

"I expect he would be hurt. He's going to miss you."

"And I him, dear man; yes, I think perhaps the girls must go, but because I say yes this time they must not think it could happen again."

The girls had not thought it could happen once! Before they came down Isobel had implored Victoria not to argue if the invitation had to be refused.

"It won't do any good and will only end in a row."

"If Daddy says no I shall cry," said Louise. "I do so want to see the conjurer."

Isobel looked at Victoria.

"That might be an idea, Daddy hates her to cry."

Victoria stumped off to wash her hands, which

had to be done before they went to the drawing room.

"I'd much rather have a good argument, but if dear little Louise wants to cry, let her."

So it came as an anticlimax when, as the girls came into the drawing room, Isobel holding the invitation, their father said:

"I have decided that as we are leaving the parish it would be unkind if you refused the party, so you may accept."

The girls fell on him.

"Oh, thank you, Daddy," said Isobel as she kissed him.

Louise hung around his neck.

"Did you know there was going to be a conjurer?"

Victoria rubbed her cheek against his.

"I can't pretend I like Joyce much but I'm glad we can go to her party, it's her birthday so there's sure to be a terrific cake."

That made her father think.

"But listen, darlings, although you may go it does not mean that you forget it is Lent. Just stick to bread and butter for tea and, of course, no dressing up."

Horrified, the girls moved away from him. Eating only bread and butter at a party was bad, but no dressing up was much worse.

"But it's a *party*, Daddy." Isobel held out the invitation. "Look, a proper invitation card, everybody will wear party frocks."

"You couldn't mean we're to wear our school skirts

53

and jerseys," said Victoria. "If we do I'd rather not go."

Louise's eyes were full of tears.

"I haven't worn my muslin with the pink sash since Christmas."

Their father looked at their mother for help.

"Couldn't they wear what they've got on? They look very nice to me."

The three girls gave a protesting howl.

"Daddy!"

"Nice!" said Louise. "This smock is so old it's falling to pieces."

Victoria stuck her chin in the air.

"If I have to go to a party in a frock where the sleeves are a different colour to the dress I'm not going."

"Mummy, make Daddy see we can't go in our Sundays," Isobel pleaded. "Nobody, absolutely nobody, could say I look nice in this!"

Her mother looked and thought that perhaps Isobel was right.

"They could wear their velvets," she suggested.

Victoria almost stamped her foot.

"But they're nearly as awful – at least mine and Louise's are."

Their father felt sad. In his home there had never been scenes like this about clothes. Were his children thinking too much of worldly things? He quoted quietly: " 'Consider the lilies of the field . . .' "

That maddened Victoria.

"Oh Daddy! What's that got to do with us?

Nobody could say that Solomon in all his glory was not arrayed better than us in our Sundays *or* our velvets."

Their father did not mean to be unkind but he was a truly unworldly man and could not believe, provided they were suitably dressed, that it mattered what his daughters wore. And also he was convinced that they should have better things to think about than frocks. He got up.

"I must go to my study. Now Mummy and I don't want to hear any more about what you will wear at the party. You will accept the invitation, Isobel, and you will go in the frocks you have on now."

Sunday evenings always finished the same way. Until Louise went to bed their mother played hymns and they stood round the piano singing. When the boys were home, each of whom had a good ear for music, they would often sing *Glory To Thee My God This Night* in canon. But when they were away the girls sang in unison, Victoria's voice soaring like a bird, Isobel and Louise following her, often out of tune. After Louise had gone to bed their mother read to the other two. Not the book they read in the week but what was called a Sunday book. Just now it was *Meg, a Chattel*, about a Negro slave girl in America who was sold away from her family. While their mother read, to keep them from fidgeting, Isobel drew and Victoria cleaned a brass tray. Usually the girls liked the reading end of Sunday, but today they were glad when Miss Herbert called them to have their supper.

55

"I can't – I simply can't wear this at a party," Victoria whispered to Isobel as they climbed the stairs. "I'll have to get out of going."

"Don't fuss," Isobel whispered back. Of course you can't wear it. It would be all our shame with those sleeves, imagine what people would say! I'll think of a way." Then, as they neared the school-room, she added: "Don't talk about it in front of Miss Herbert."

4 The Party

"Everything seems to be happening at once," Isobel said to Miss Herbert, "and it's so strange because usually nothing much ever happens to us."

They were in the schoolroom. Isobel had been in bed for two days with asthma and had now reached the up-in-the-house stage. She was painting, Miss Herbert was packing some of the children's books into a wooden box. She nodded.

"Yes indeed. Altogether too much excitement, I'm afraid, and now the party on top of everything else. I am surprised your father is allowing you to go."

"He only is because we're leaving and it would seem rude not to."

"Then after the party the boys will be home and then there's Easter and then the goodbye party. Has it been decided what you're going to do at that?"

"Vicky's going to do that waxwork thing with John like they did on Boxing Day. I think Mummy's thinking of something for Louise and Dick. If Daddy says I must do something then I'll introduce the others, but I hope I don't have to."

"I shouldn't count on that, dear. I'm sure the parish will expect to see you all. What are you painting, dear?"

"Clothes."

Miss Herbert came to the table to look. Isobel had filled a page in her sketch book with designs for party frocks. All were in the most vivid colours.

'Oh, fancy dress?" said Miss Herbert.

"No, ordinary dresses. When I can choose my own clothes these are the colours I am going to wear."

"You'll be very conspicuous if you do, and you wouldn't like that, would you?"

In amusement Isobel watched Miss Herbert's prim back walk to the bookcase. But the word "conspicuous" lingered with her and gave her an idea.

"Did you know we were to wear our Sundays at Joyce's party?"

"No, dear." Then Miss Herbert thought of the Sundays. Her criterion of good dressing was neat dressing and the Sundays fell far short of that. "Why?"

"Because it's Lent, Daddy says we can't wear party frocks."

Miss Herbert paused with *The Cuckoo Clock* by Mrs Molesworth in one hand.

"We can't expect your father to have noticed but Vicky's dress really should not be seen outside the vicarage, those unmatching sleeves are most untidy."

"It'll make her conspicuous, won't it?"

Miss Herbert sniffed.

"And that is something which Vicky is likely to be anyway."

58

Isobel seemed intent on her painting.

"Daddy said we weren't to discuss what we wore any more, so we haven't. But could you remind Mummy about the sleeves? Perhaps she'd let us wear our velvets."

Miss Herbert's mind ranged over "the Sundays".

"And Louise's smock is only fit for the house now. I was going to suggest sending it to the jumble this summer. Yes, dear, I'll have a word with your mother."

The word was successful, so it was into their velvets that Isobel and Victoria buttoned each other on the Saturday afternoon of the party.

"Let's look in the long looking-glass in the spare room," Victoria suggested. "When you are being offered up as a burnt offering it's best to know how burnt offering-ish you look."

The spare bedroom was a lugubrious place. No member of the family had ever slept in the large mahogany bed so only visiting preachers knew of the horrid bumps in the mattress. The walls were papered with a brownish wallpaper, the dressing table, wardrobe and chairs, as well as the long looking glass, were all in the same heavy mahogany as the bed; in fact all the furniture had been inherited by the children's father from a great aunt. The carpet was old and faded and in places worn. On the walls were prints of engravings of Christ with the apostles – all fly-walked. The curtains were dark green. The only live thing in the room was the clock, a heavy gilt affair under a glass dome with a furry purple snake round the base to keep out the dust; this ticked and chimed cheerfully for, in common with the other clocks in the house, it was wound and kept in order by the clock winder, who called every Monday.

The girls were used to the room so, not noticing its gloom, they went straight to the looking-glass and standing in front of it saw themselves pictured in the mahogany frame; Isobel, her fair hair held back in a green velvet Alice in Wonderland snood, her eyes huge in her thin face above the pale green of her frock; Victoria, lanky but with far more flesh on her than Isobel, her hair parted and held in place by a brown snood, scowling at the outline of herself in the clumsy brown velvet frock.

"I think this is what Miss Herbert calls an unkind glass," Isobel suggested.

Victoria scowled more than ever.

"If it is it's odd it's much unkinder to me than it is to you. It's no good pretending, Isobel, I look terrible, though I do see I'd have looked worse in my 'Sunday'."

Isobel looked at their feet, on which were their stout walking shoes.

"We'll look more partyish when we put on our dancing slippers perhaps."

Victoria shook her head.

"We won't, nothing can make us look right for that sort of party. Two girls in my form are having new frocks for it. Joan's is green silk with frills, and Diana's is lace over satin – imagine!"

It was too much. Without another look at the glass the girls left the spare room and went to their own room to put on their outdoor things. Even best coats were not allowed so both shrugged their way into their navy overcoats and dragged on their tam o'shanters. Then Victoria picked up the bag with the shoes in it.

"I feel like a Christian martyr being thrown to the lions."

"You'll feel more like it when you see the tea and birthday cake," said Isobel, "and us just eating bread and butter."

Victoria put their birthday present for Joyce – a book done up in brown paper and string – in the bag with the shoes. Birthday present books were chosen by their father.

"I'll shove this under all the other presents. She's sure to get lovely things, so I can't see her wanting a book of religious poetry."

Joyce did not go the same school as the vicarage girls but to a smaller, more expensive one, and so more than half the thirty-odd guests at the party were strangers to the children. In the large elegant spare room, where coats were to be left and shoes changed, all their worst fears were realised. The presents for Joyce were trimmed with bows, and many looked like chocolates. From under coats and wraps the most lovely frocks appeared, enough to give any girl dressed in dark, ill-fitting velvet an inferiority complex. To add to the girls' suffering they felt nudges and looks as they joined the party

61

downstairs, and though they could not know for sure what caused them they heard giggles.

"Let's hope it's a specially good conjurer," Louise whispered. "Then we shan't mind the shame so much."

Kind-hearted Mrs Sedman said to a friend who was helping her:

"Look at the vicarage children! I know they're poor but I can't think they need look as dreadful as they do."

"It's a shame," the friend agreed, "for the smallest one is a real beauty."

Mrs Sedman nodded in agreement.

"I shall make a special fuss of them. Keep an eye on them for me and see that they have a good tea."

The tea table was loaded with all the food that in those days was called "party". There was every kind of small iced cake and little cream buns and innumerable plates of fancy biscuits. There were jellies of all shades, some crowned with cream, crystallised violets and cherries, and others with fruit inside them. There were half orange skins filled with orange jelly and made to look like baskets by the addition of handles of angelica.

To crown everything, there was a huge pink and white cake with roses all over it and *A Happy Birthday, Joyce* written in pink sugar on the top. There was not a suggestion of anything savoury – everything was pretty and sugary and the sweeter the better. This sweeter the better idea had even affected the bread and butter for, as an additional party touch, Mrs Sedman had sprinkled it with tiny brightly-coloured sweets called Hundreds-and-Thousands.

Isobel was sitting with some girls in her form at school. Victoria, escaping from her school friends, sidled over to her.

"Do you see what I see? Look at the bread and butter!"

Isobel looked.

"Daddy said only bread and butter."

"I know," Victoria agreed, "but is it our fault if it's covered with Hundreds-and-Thousands?"

"Where's Louise? We better see what she's going to do. She'll tell if we eat it and she doesn't."

"We can't not eat anything, I'm starving."

"How about biscuits?"

Victoria's friends were calling her.

"All sugar. Louise is sitting by Mrs Sedman, let's do what she does."

"Well, Louise dear," Mrs Sedman was saying, "what would you like to start with?"

Louise had not had Victoria's chance to study the table.

"Bread and butter, please."

Mrs Sedman laughed.

"What a well-brought up little girl." She walked down the table and picked up a plate of bread and butter. "Here you are, dear."

Louise gave a gasp, then hungrily she took a slice, folded it and began to eat.

At once higher up the table voices cried:

"Bread and butter for Isobel. Pass that bread and butter please for Victoria."

Steadily the girls ate their way through all the bread and butter on the table. Luckily there was plenty. Then the moment came for Joyce to cut the cake. Isobel and Victoria had made arrangements with their friends for this moment, pushing their slices of cake on to their plates, but Louise had been placed amongst strangers.

"Funny child," Mrs Sedman had thought, "eating nothing but bread and butter. I suppose it's the sweets she likes," but to be sure the child made a good tea she placed an extra large slice of birthday cake on her plate.

"Eat that up, chicken."

The temptation was too great, almost before she knew it a sugar rose was in Louise's mouth then, as she chewed, she felt eyes on her and there was Victoria staring at her. Louise was appalled. What had she done? As usual when in trouble she took refuge in tears. At once Mrs Sedman was at her side.

"What is it, dear? Did you bite your tongue?"

Louise could not speak at first, then she whispered in an agonised voice:

"I've accidentally done something."

Mrs Sedman wasted no time, she seized Louise's hand, pulled her out of her chair and out of the room.

"You can use the downstairs lavatory," she said.

Louise, still crying, shook her head.

"I don't want to, thank you."

"Then what have you done, dear?"

Louise let out a howl.

"I think I've sinned against the Holy Ghost."

After tea they played charades. These were acted in the hall, the guessing side viewing the actors from the stairs. Isobel and Victoria were picked for the same side and it was while they were the guessers that Victoria, driven mad by the rustling of the silks and laces around them, started her own private game.

"What a pity," she said loudly to Isobel, "we didn't know it was this sort of party. We could have worn our blue silks, couldn't we?" She gave Isobel a nudge.

Too well Isobel knew how easy it was to make Victoria behave worse if you tried to stop her so, instead of saying "What blue silks?", she tried to help her.

"Or our emerald green taffetas," she faltered.

"Our accordion pleateds are nice."

"So are our yellows with belts made of rubies."

Victoria saw that Isobel was seeing the game as if she was painting the clothes. Belts of rubies was going too far. She tried to bring her back to earth.

"I think some of our plainer frocks would be better, our lace frocks are nice."

But Isobel had forgotten how the game had started.

"Or pure gold with bands of blue round the bottom."

Luckily at that moment the other side started their charade so the game had to stop. But not before many who had listened were exchanging glances. Poor Vicky! Who did she think she was fooling? As if they didn't all know that Isobel and Victoria's party frocks were pink voile with large collars of lace, or dotted muslin run through with velvet ribbon.

The conjurer seemed to the girls, who had no standards to judge him by, wonderful beyond belief. Some of the more sophisticated of the audience said they saw how some of the tricks were done, but not Isobel, Victoria and Louise, who were so absorbed that it was quite a shock when the entertainment was over and they were back in the everyday world where there were such problems as having eaten Hundreds-and-Thousands and, in Louise's case, a sugar rose, in Lent.

After the conjurer there were more games, then suddenly it was eight o'clock and everybody was given a cup of soup and a biscuit to fortify them before they went out into the rather chilly night air. Then governesses or parents arrived, shoes were changed, overcoats pulled on, the proper thank-yous said while, at the same time, all three girls looked up and smiled. Looking up and smiling when you spoke to somebody had been almost the first lesson each Strangeway child was taught. "I should think we'll all be looking up and smiling as long as we live," Isobel, aged eight, had said after a particularly large mothers' meeting party, at which she had been ordered to speak to everybody. As it turned out her prophecy came true, none of the Strangeways ever forgot that early strict training.

While most of the rest of the guests were climbing into either their own carriages with perhaps a jobbed horse, or into a hired fly, the Strangeways walked home with Miss Herbert. Isobel and Victoria moved ahead out of earshot.

"Do you think," said Isobel, "we should tell Daddy about the Hundreds-and-Thousands?"

Victoria swung the shoe bag.

"I should think so. He won't scold, even he can see we couldn't sit there eating nothing."

"What about Louise's sugar rose?"

Victoria's voice was gruff.

"That's got nothing to do with us, let her tell Daddy if she wants to.'

"But if she asks us what we think she ought to do, what are we going to say?"

Victoria was unwilling to decide things for other people for she resented it when other people tried to decide things for her.

"I shouldn't think she would ask, but if she does and she's feeling bad inside about the rose, if I was her I'd own up. You feel much better afterwards even if there's a punishment."

Back at the vicarage no owning up appeared possible that night for all three girls, after giving their mother a quick kiss, were bustled off to bed. Their father was out at a meeting.

"We'll tell Daddy about the Hundreds-and-Thousands tomorrow," said Isobel drowsily.

"That's right," Victoria agreed. "I wonder how all those handkerchiefs and flowers got into that top hat."

When the next morning Miss Herbert called Isobel and Victoria and gave them their prayer books so that they could learn the collect, she said:

"Be very quiet when you go to the bathroom. I am letting Louise sleep on as she had a disturbed night."

"Was she sick?" Victoria asked.

"No, dear, something seems to have been on her mind. She got up when your father came in. I found her in the passage crying. She insisted on going down to speak to him."

Isobel and Victoria exchanged looks.

"What did she say?" Isobel queried.

"I didn't hear it all as she went into the study, but I did hear her say: 'Father, I have sinned against heaven, and in thy sight, and am no more worthy to be called thy daughter.' She looked so sweet standing there in her little blue dressing gown with Jackie in her arms. Now, Vicky, do try and get your collect learnt properly this morning. You know how it upsets your dear mother when you don't know it."

When the door was shut again Victoria winked at Isobel.

"You must say Louise does things in style. Our confession will seem very flat after that."

Isobel muttered.

" 'Almighty and everlasting God, who, of thy tender love towards mankind . . .' Don't talk or I'll never know it."

Isobel and Victoria told their father about the Hundreds-and-Thousands after breakfast. He heard the whole story in silence. Then he said:

"It was difficult for you. One of those hard decisions to make. I suppose the splendid thing to have done would have been to eat nothing and, when you were asked why, to have explained. I expect Mrs Sedman would have had some plain bread and butter cut for you. But I do see you didn't want to cause trouble or embarrassment, but it was an opportunity lost to testify to your faith."

Victoria imagined the scene. Herself saying: "I can't eat anything on the table because it is Lent and during Lent, as part of my fast, I eat only plain bread and butter." It was like something from one of those awful goody-goody stories Daddy had read when he was a boy.

"It was bad enough as it was. Everybody was looking at us, and we did explain about Lent to our friends when the birthday cake came, we got them to eat our pieces, and it was a gorgeous cake with raspberry cream icing in layers all through it."

Her father smiled.

"That was splendid for, as I suppose you know, poor Louise failed. I have told her to read the first nine verses of St Matthew, chapter four, which describes the devil tempting Christ when he was fasting in the wilderness. I think you girls might read

69

it too. You'll have time between luncheon and the children's service."

In their bedroom tidying to go down for catechism Victoria said to Isobel:

"The same punishment for Hundreds-and-Thousands as for a sugar rose! There's justice for you!"

Isobel thought about that.

"It's not a punishment. Daddy truly thinks it's nice for us to read the Bible. Think how much worse if we'd had to give up our Sunday jam and cake. And it's only nine verses."

"Even nine verses is a lot in our sort of Sunday, but I'll bear it like a Christian martyr because it's Palm Sunday and I like the choir carrying palm leaves and us getting palm crosses."

Isobel did not answer for she was brushing up her collect before they went downstairs.

" 'Almighty and everlasting God . . .'."

The boys came home. Dick, looking ridiculously small in a too-large school overcoat bought to last, his blue eyes shining with happiness, fell out of the train on the Tuesday in Holy Week. John, looking almost elegant in comparison, came home on the Thursday.

Although Dick, on first seeing his family – except Isobel who had asthma – lined up on the platform, hugged them all in turn as if he could never leave go, no sooner had his luggage been consigned to an outside porter to push to the vicarage than he became tongue-tied. So during the walk home talk was one-sided, everybody chattering to Dick while he replied merely with yes or no. It had been the same when he had come home for Christmas after his first term away; he seemed not to be able to shake school off as John did, as if it was a tap which could be turned on and off. But as soon as he was in the house, having kissed Isobel, he dashed up to the schoolroom with Louise and shut the door and then it was as if he had never been away. First there was home news to be caught up with. Of course Dick knew about the move and that they were going to stay with the grandparents through letters, but there were many things he had been worrying about.

71

"What's happened to Alexander?"

Dick's tortoise was called Alexander, and he was devoted to him. Louise was expecting that question.

"He hasn't woken up yet. He's still in that box under all those leaves. Daddy doesn't think he'll be properly awake when we move so he can travel in his box."

"There's a boy at school who has four tortoises but he's never tried moving them. Do you suppose they mind?"

Louise considered the point.

"If a cat is moved you rub butter on its paws. That makes it know it has a new home."

"Do you think I ought to put butter on Alexander's feet?"

Louise thought of Alexander slowly creeping about the lawn from daisy to daisy.

"I shouldn't think you need. I think he'll like it better where we're going. Mummy says it's a big garden and there's a field as well, there's usually lots of buttercups in fields."

"But he could get lost."

"Ask Daddy, he'll know, he said he was sure he'd be all right."

Dick was a keen gardener, by far the best in the family. He could now look after his garden only in the holidays, his mother seeing to it while he was away, but it was still very much his property.

"What about my plants? I won't leave them behind."

"Mummy's doing that. She says any treasures will be packed in sacking with plenty of damp earth."

"It's not the right time to move things, they'll hate it. I hope my yellow carnation doesn't die. Are we going to have gardens in the new place?"

"If we want them, there's tons of room, but I don't think Isobel and Vicky do, they're getting awfully old." Louise lowered her voice. "Did you know Vicky was expelled from Elmhurst – well, almost – anyway expelled is what the girls at school call it?"

"You said in your letter she had to leave. What did she do?"

"She says it was because of a society she started, but one of the girls in my form said her mother said she was tote-ly unmanageable."

Dick, a well-behaved, hard-working child, could not imagine the meaning of the phrase. He looked round the room. Though called, from the beginning of last autumn term after he had left for his boarding school, the schoolroom, it still looked like the nursery it had always been. There was a floor-covering of what was then called cork carpet, shiny and easily cleaned. There was a high nursery guard round the fire. There was a toy cupboard still full of toys. There was the bookshelf which had held all their books from *Little Black Sambo* and the Peter Rabbit books to the new ones they had been given last Christmas, but it was now empty. There was a place too where the wallpaper had faded.

"Where's the dolls' house?"

"Daddy gave it to the orphanage."

Dick was appalled.

"Gave it away! Why?"

Louise knew instinctively that Dick, when he was homesick at school, pictured his home, seeing everything in the exact place where it always lived. The dolls' house had been allowed to go with scarcely a sigh from the three girls, but Dick cared that it was gone. He had never played with it except when small and he had been called on to be a tradesman delivering food. But he knew every room and it was part of home. The yellow drawing room with mother, dressed in blue velvet, permanently lying on the sofa. Father's china legs were loose so that he could only sit or kneel. To get round this difficulty Isobel had made him a clerical collar and placed him in a corner where for ever he could kneel and pray.

"Odd, in the drawing room," Victoria had said.

"There's no room for him to kneel in the dining room," Isobel had pointed out, "and he can't very well pray in the kitchen."

It was true, the blue dining room was over-full, there was a long table with chairs for eight and a sideboard. Even a mouse would have found it hard to sit down. The staff were all wooden peg dolls with shining pink cheeks. The cook wore a mob cap with a print dress and apron but the parlourmaid wore black with a cap with streamers glued on to her wooden head. There was also a between maid but she too had weak legs so she was kept in a lolling position washing-up.

Upstairs there was Nanny, another peg doll, who was in charge of a nursery with cardboard cots with three china babies sleeping in them. In the next room was a tiny wax doll dressed entirely in lace whom the children had christened Queenie. The parents' bedroom was pale pink with blue bows. The dolls' house, when shut, was painted to look as if it were red brick; the windows were glass with lace curtains painted on them held in place with pink bows. The dolls' house had always been in the nursery since a parishioner had presented it to the family when Isobel was four, so they gave it the vague fondness given to an old friend, but it meant far more than that to Dick. He had a lump in his throat when he thought of those peg doll servants. Queenie and her mother and father finding themselves being played with by strange children. He swung round to look at the rocking-horse.

"I hope they aren't going to give Nebuchadnezzar away. He's coming, isn't he?"

Nebuchadnezzar was a handsome striped rocking-horse. When the children had been small Nebuchadnezzar had been lent for a church garden fête, where he could be ridden on for a penny a ride. The vicarage children had queued with their few pennies for rides, which they had so obviously enjoyed that after the fête was over the owner of Nebuchadnezzar had sold him to the vicar for one pound. He had been ridden and loved by all the children until they grew beyond rocking-horses, but he was also a repository for secrets, for his tail could be pulled out and objects pushed into his inside. Now, when rocked, he rattled. He contained drawings of Isobel's which fell below her standards, things pilfered from Miss Herbert or their nanny as punishments for fancied misdemeanours by Victoria. Treasures belonging to all the family taken by Louise, who was a magpie. There were countless objects of Dick's which he valued but which were counted rubbish so he had been told to throw them away; instead they had been entrusted to Nebuchadnezzar. What John had put through the tail hole was not known but that he too used Nebuchadnezzar as a post box was certain.

Louise knew how Dick was feeling but she was a practical child.

"He can't come either. There's going to be no schoolroom in the new house. There's a little room next to the dining room but that's going to be mostly for Isobel to paint in. Miss Herbert is having her bedroom made to sit in. We're going to be day boarders so we won't be home for meals. In the holidays we're having meals in the dining room, except supper, I think we'll have that in bed."

Dick went over to Nebuchadnezzar and rocked him gently.

"What's happening to him?"

"I think somebody is buying him but first Daddy is having a little hole cut in his tummy to take the things out."

That made Dick laugh.

"I should think there'll be baskets full of stuff. I

76

hope he does it before we go to Granny and Grandfather."

"He's going to so we can decide who everything belongs to."

This would clearly be an occasion – so many old-friend possessions coming back.

"It'll be like the hymn 'Father, sister, child and mother – meet once more'." Giggling, Dick climbed on to one of the seats which were at each end of the rocker. "Come on, Louise, let's ride."

John's homecoming was quite different. He was becoming a sophisticated traveller, for, each term since he had gone to Winchester as a twelve-year-old, on "Men's day leave" he had come to London to lunch and to go to a theatre with an aunt. Though he travelled with the school to London he found his way to his aunt alone. John was almost one of the family but divided from them because at the end of each three years his parents came home from India on long leave, and he then made his home with them.

Another reason why he was not quite family was that he was very much better off than his cousins for, as an only son, everything bought for him was of the best quality and he had plenty of pocket money. Being of the family, though independent of it, helped to build confidence, so it was an outwardly calm self-contained John who stepped off the train to greet the children and their mother. For him the station fly was hired to take his luggage to the vicarage. He could have ridden in it but instead he asked his aunt, Louise and Dick to get in, he would walk home with Victoria. Isobel was still housebound with asthma.

"What a shame about Isobel," John said. "Won't she be able to come primrosing tomorrow?"

One of the special joys of the holidays was that John was now classed as an escort, which meant if one of the girls was out with him no grown-up was needed. Victoria found it hard to walk sedately for she wanted to skip, hop and run, it was so glorious that John was home and that she was walking beside him.

"She's nearly better so if it's fine and warm tomorrow she can come."

Oddly enough, seeing how strictly Lent was kept, Good Fridays were for the children happy, much-looked-forward-to days. There was about the house a hush and an air of sadness so that no one could for a second forget this was the day that Christ died on the cross, but there was very little church-going for the children. They were taken to a short service, which included the Commination, but after that Good Fridays were treat days.

Because the choirboys had to sing at the three-hour service, after the short service they were brought out on the vicarage lawn to eat hot cross buns and drink lemonade. No matter how many hot cross buns the choirboys ate, there were always platesful left over on which, after the choirboys had gone back to the vestry, the children fell like locusts, washing the buns down with what was left of the lemonade. They then hurried indoors, collected picnic lunches, baskets and wool and set off to the railway station, where they caught a train to a village where there was a famous primrose wood.

The weather must have changed, for in those days Good Fridays seemed always to be fine. An adult, of course, accompanied the children even though John was there, for the purpose of the expedition was to pick primroses to decorate the church for Easter, so no lounging about was allowed, primrose picking under supervision had to be carried out without pause.

Looking back on those golden Good Fridays it is likely that there was some competition among the adults to take the children primrosing. Most years it was their mother who took them, making an excuse which stood by her on every kind of occasion: "I've got one of my tickly coughs and I don't want to disturb the three-hour service." Occasionally it was Miss Herbert who was in charge – but once, for some unexplained reason, the cook.

Home again, with baskets full to bursting with primroses, it was as if it was the beginning of Easter. The crucifixion was over, the sadness was lifting, for one day away was what the children had been taught was the greatest day of the church's year. They never agreed that Easter was the greatest, for to them Christmas was clearly that, but their father's shining happiness as Easter approached gave Easter Day a quality it was never to lose.

As they climbed the hill from the station John

looked round at the Victorian houses and prim front gardens.

"I shall miss this place. Does anyone know what Eastbourne's like?"

"It's much older than this. There has been a village there since before the Romans came, Daddy said."

"So you're going to a new school. The move has come just at the right time for you; it would have been awkward for Uncle Jim finding another school for you here."

Victoria had few secrets from John.

"There's a boarding school for the daughters of poor clergy Daddy was thinking about. You mustn't tell because Daddy thinks I would hate it, but inside I was hoping and hoping that was where I'd be sent."

John looked at her, an amused twinkle in his eye.

"Why on earth? It sounds ghastly. Low living and high thinking."

"I wanted to get away. You don't know how awful it is being the vicar's daughter if you are a person like me, everybody being sorry for Daddy and wondering how he came to have a child like me. In a boarding school I'd be free – just me."

John thought about that.

"I know what you mean; but it wouldn't be like that, you know – I like it all right at school but I can't tell you how many days I wish I could get back to the vicarage in the evenings. However much you hate Elmhurst you are free of it after school and all day on Saturday and Sunday. If you're a boarder you can never get away. This term I wished it particularly because Dad's worried about me."

"Why on earth? You are doing so well, aren't you?"

"Yes, at work, but he doesn't think I'm becoming a man fast enough."

"Why?"

"Because I was fool enough to write that I was no earthly good at rugger. Dad was good at all games so it's shocked him. He has written in each letter since, reminding me I'm nearly a man and that it's time I decided what I was going to do with my life. And that if, as he hopes, I'm going to India I must learn that men in the Indian Civil are not only expected to work hard but to play hard. The awful thing is, as you know, I am not a bit interested in the Indian Civil, but I haven't had the nerve yet to write and tell him so."

"Have you thought any more what you do want to do?"

A faint flush came to John's cheeks.

"This is only for you, of course. But you know I was that girl in Shaw's *You Never Can Tell*. Well, I liked doing that, every bit of it including rehearsals. You know, Vicky, everyone would faint if they knew – but I'd like to be an actor."

Victoria's breath was taken away. An actor! If Cousin Violet would not go inside a theatre in case she died there what happened to people who worked there?

"Of course I never knew an actor, and we've

81

hardly been to the theatre so it sounds to me a peculiar thing to be. Why do you want to be one?"

John took his time answering.

"I can't paint like Isobel does and I can't write, like you may do one day."

"Me!"

"Of course, idiot – it was immature but quite a lot in those magazines you edited was good. If you stick to it you might write books some day."

"Might I?" Victoria was immensely flattered. "But that's a sort of respectable thing to be and an actor isn't."

"Not if you write like Elinor Glyn it isn't. Anyway actors *can* be very respectable. Look at Beerbohm Tree or the Vanburgh sisters, they are the children of a vicar."

Victoria did not know the names of any actor or actress, for she never read the papers and, of course, actors' names were not mentioned in the house. But she was not going to admit her ignorance to John.

"There'll be an awful row, won't there, when you do write and tell?"

"There certainly will. But it's *my* life, Vicky, so if an actor's what I still want to be when I leave Oxford I shall be one. From what my father has told me and I remember there's a lot that is horrible in India: dirt and smells and dead people being burnt. I'd hate all that. I suppose that's what Dad means when he says I'm not manly – I'm not, anything disgusting makes me ill. When a boy was sick in chapel, I fainted."

Victoria could not shake off the feeling that an actor was not a nice person to be.

"Oh well, there's heaps of time, you're only just fourteen, you may think of something else to be when you go to Oxford."

"It won't be Dad's fault if I don't. He had meant me to have special boxing coaching these holidays. He was going to write to Uncle Jim about it, but he knows now we are going to Granny and Grandfather's so I expect he'll let the matter drop."

That reminded Vicky that she had a bit of news.

"Before we go there's a goodbye party given by the parish. We've all got to do something. Daddy says it's expected. You and I are doing our waxworks again like we did at Christmas."

In those days, when gin was a few shillings a bottle, there was much drunkenness. As a result it was quite usual on the day after a holiday for the wives of working-class men to have black eyes. To try and keep the men out of the public houses, many parishes throughout the country on public holidays and some Saturdays put on a form of entertainment called A Penny Reading. For this the entrance fee was a penny and something read out loud was part of the entertainment. The rest of the programme was made up of separate turns. A would-be comic, songs from a soprano, perhaps a duologue or two and any other talent that could be found.

For the last three years Victoria and John had been a high spot of the Boxing Day entertainment. At the Penny Reading last Boxing Day John, dressed as a showman, had exhibited Victoria as a waxwork doll who, when wound up, could take off various well-known parish workers. Victoria loved an audience, it satisfied the exhibitionist side of her nature; she also loved performing with John, they had rehearsed endlessly and gave as a result an excellent performance.

John was delighted.

"Oh good, I've often thought about us doing that and worked out some more we might have done – it always seemed a waste to do it only once." They were getting near the vicarage. "You do swear you won't tell anyone, even Isobel, what I've told you?"

Victoria flashed round at him.

"Idiot! When have I ever told your things?"

"Never. Only this is so terribly important. Dad mustn't know one thing until I'm leaving Oxford."

The vicar had not been able to get away to meet John at the station but he was in the hall when John and Victoria reached home. He spoke with extra warmth to make John forget he was not part of the family.

"My dear old man! How good to have you home. Vicky has told you all the news, I suppose?"

"Yes, Uncle Jim."

The vicar hesitated.

"I've had a letter from your father, he had wanted you to have some boxing coaching these holidays. I think he feels you are doing so well with your work you may not be giving sufficient time to sport."

John nodded.

"That's it. He was a bit of an all-rounder, wasn't he?"

The vicar looked sympathetically at his nephew.

"They all were. I was the only dunce at games in the family, the only thing I was any good at was running. We had a family cricket eleven, you know, made up of us and various cousins, we used to play other Kent teams. Your father was the prize organizer, I was the family disgrace. I seldom made any runs and I was sent to field well out where no catch was likely to come my way. Still, we don't want to repeat my poor performance. Perhaps part of next holidays I can arrange some boxing."

John was fond of his uncle.

"I can only hope you can't arrange it."

The vicar laughed.

"Shameless boy!" Then he laid a hand on John's shoulder. "I hope you have a splendid holiday, but I'm sure you will with Granny and Grandfather for it's the perfect place to spend it. I only wish I could join you."

John, walking up the stairs to find Isobel, thought in an affectionate, puzzled way of what his uncle had said.

"I wonder what it was about their home that they found so wonderful. It doesn't matter whether it's Dad or Uncle Jim or one of the other uncles, their eyes positively swim when they think of the dear old home. If only they didn't want us to feel the same way about *our* homes."

6 Goodbye

The goodbye party, though for their father and in a lesser degree for their mother it was an emotional occasion, was for the children fun. Even Dick was in high spirits, for Alexander's travelling arrangements were now satisfactorily arranged, and his mother was seeing to the removal of his plants. Moreover there was a half promise made by his father of another family dog.

Three years before, against his better judgment, the children's father had allowed them to have a fox terrier puppy; he was christened Adrian. The reason why their father had up to then set his face against a family dog was the danger of his getting run over. There was a path from the front gate to the back gate which was used unlawfully by errand boys as a right of way. The vicar had never had the heart to take action, for the path saved a good ten minutes for those on their way to the streets that lay behind the vicarage back gate. But errand boys scurrying guiltily through had no time to be careful about closing gates, thus the fear of having a dog. Adrian had been enormously loved by all the family, especially Dick, but, doglike, he had chosen for himself to whom to give his heart – the children's father.

Because of this he tried to go wherever the vicar went, suitable or unsuitable.

According to the children's mother he could always be seen looking reverent, walking behind the vicar when he was carrying his portable altar to someone who was ill. He also went daily to early service, waiting – still more reverent – in the porch for the vicar to come out. These things had made the children's mother call Adrian, rather bitterly, "That high church dog!" Two and a half years after he had become a member of the family a policeman had come to the door carrying his collar – Adrian had been killed by a bus.

"And that," the children's father had said, "settles that. No more dogs, it isn't safe."

But the new vicarage with its big garden and a field was different.

"I'll look out for another fox terrier puppy the moment we are settled," he had promised Dick.

"I hope he's low church this time," their mother said to the children.

Perhaps, if the children had been forced to watch their home ceasing to be their home, they would not have been so cheerful when the time came to go. But because they were leaving the day after the goodbye party to stay with their grandparents, they were not to see their home become an empty shell, with only marks made yearly on the dining room door to show how much each child had grown, and a few other such landmarks to indicate that the Strangeway family had lived there.

The goodbye party was preceded by the operation on Nebuchadnezzar. A small square was cut out of his stomach large enough for a hand and arm to go through.

"But," the children's father said before he started the operation, "no matter what comes out of him there are to be no recriminations. I'm afraid you have all been guilty at some time or another of putting things that did not belong to you into Nebuchadnezzar, but this is a case of bygones being bygones, it's too late now to say who are the culprits."

What had come out of Nebuchadnezzar was truly astonishing: unimportant jewellery; a watch that wouldn't go; clothes which had been made for Jackie; Miss Herbert's purple stone from Derbyshire over which she darned; some fishing flies dating from a period when an uncle had tried to teach John to tie them; dozens of needles and pins; several needlebooks and a pincushion; fourteen pens and pencils; some of Isobel's paintings; eleven handkerchiefs – most of which belonged to Miss Herbert; two pocket knives; a palm cross; a broken Christmas tree ornament; an assortment of smashed china which had clearly been hidden in Nebuchadnezzar to avoid confessing to an accident, and, amongst other miscellaneous oddments, forty-eight buttons. As most of the objects appeared they were claimed by somebody.

"My dear old darning stone!"

"Look at my flies! Who on earth hid those?"

Isobel snatched up her paintings.

"I put those in him because I was so ashamed of them, but really they aren't bad seeing I was only a baby."

Victoria fell on the watch.

"This is mine. It never went, and I got sick of taking it to the jeweller's – which you said I must, Daddy, because it was given me by a parishioner – so I gave it to Nebuchadnezzar."

The children's mother fingered the Christmas tree ornament.

"This was that angel I was so fond of. I wonder which bad child broke that – I always wondered where it had got to."

"Fancy all these handkerchiefs! I was sad when they disappeared because my sister had brought them home from Madeira. Vicky, I'm afraid hiding these looks like your doing."

The children's father lifted a finger.

"We did agree there would be no recriminations, Miss Herbert." He picked up a handful of buttons. "It's extraordinary how many of these seem to have a clerical look."

The children's mother held up a tiny blue velvet coat.

"Look, Jackie's best coat."

Louise took it from her.

"I knew it was there, thank you. I put it in myself."

"But why, darling?" her father asked.

"Well, you know how you are about things made

by parishioners, but I didn't like Jackie in that coat so I posted it in Nebuchadnezzar."

Dick was enchanted to find the penknives.

"I had those two Christmases ago and I've been looking for them ever since."

"Someone was very mean to hide those," said Louise. She looked in a meaning way at Victoria. "I wonder who it could have been? I seem to remember on that Christmas, Vicky, that you were very angry with Dick because accidentally he made a hole in the tube of that trick thing you had that made plates jump up and down."

Victoria flushed.

"It's extraordinary the way some people forget what was said. Poor Daddy, how often have you got to say 'no recriminations'?"

"Yes indeed," her father agreed.

Their mother looked at what was still on the floor.

"Moving is a time to get rid of rubbish, not to accumulate more, so, unless it's something good like Miss Herbert's stone or Dick's knives, please throw all this mess away." She pounced on something she had not before seen. "My silver thimble!"

Isobel had a look.

"Someone's trodden on it, it's quite flat."

"I can see it is, darling," her mother agreed. "But it was given me as a prize for needlework when I was seven, so I've always treasured it."

John laughed.

"Don't let us forget that moving is a time for getting rid of rubbish."

The goodbye party was organised by the parish workers. It took the form of a sausage roll and buns meal with tea out of an urn to drink, followed by a concert. Although the concert was supposedly given by parishioners, the high spots would be the performances of the children.

Ever since they were very small, the children had sung or acted at the afternoon party given by their parents to church workers during the week of the patronal festival; a turn by the children was a "must" on all important parish occasions. In the early days they had sung together some song certain to amuse; one of the most popular had in the verses a list of childish faults and a refrain which went: "But didn't *you* – didn't *you* – didn't *you* – *didn't* you do the same?" On each "you" the children had stretched out an arm to point at some well-known parish figure.

But as they grew older and passed the stage where the audience said "Aren't they sweet!" no suitable songs could be found for a group of which two could not sing at all. So when John was home they acted something. Not that Isobel, Louise or Dick were much good at acting, but in those days duologues or one-act plays were part of most amateur entertainments, so there were dozens of suitable ones to choose from. For the goodbye party, apart from John and Victoria's Boxing Night sketch, Isobel and Dick were to act a mother and son duologue and Louise was to play the piano, which she could do loudly and accurately but with no musicality whatsoever. The evening was to finish with a presentation to the vicar.

How easily pleased people were in those days! A soprano song, a ballad of the sort enormously popular at that time in which invariably the key changed in the last verse from major to minor to add point to the sentimental, sad ending, which was sure to bring tears to the eyes of half the women in the audience. A man sang comic songs, he was probably appalling but he brought down the house. A baritone roared out a song about the sea with one about oaken hearts as an encore. A group of male singers sang *Sweet and Low*. A local music teacher gave a violin solo.

Then came the children. Their mother, oddly enough, had some sense of showmanship so she put the worst on first and the best last, to wind up the evening well. Isobel and Dick must have been as wooden as peg dolls, for their only idea of acting was to say the words correctly and to get off the stage as soon as possible. And Isobel was hard to hear because of her breathlessness. But the audience were charmed, for they took the will for the deed: this was dear Isobel whom they had known since she was a little thing, and Dick was a great favourite because, when he was not away, they saw him every Sunday singing in the choir.

The girls were wearing their second-best party frocks, the pink nun's-veiling with the large lace collars. Isobel and Victoria had to change for their performance but Louise, of course, did not. As she sat confidently down on the piano stool, first placing Jackie on the top of the piano, there were the purrs of pleasure to which she was used. "I think Louise gets prettier every day." – "What a little dear she looks!"

John and Victoria were greeted with tremendous applause as soon as they appeared for they were the accepted star turn. Victoria might be a tiresome girl and a thorn in the poor vicar's flesh, but she was a real little actress. As for John, he got better-looking every holiday, he would be a heartbreaker some day. It was a shame his father and mother were so far away, but still, no one could have a better deputy father than the dear vicar. Lit up by the occasion, John and Victoria were even better than they had been on Boxing Night, and Victoria looked almost pretty as a waxwork doll dressed as a milkmaid, in a pink frock with a fichu and white apron, which Isobel had worn at a fancy dress party. Their performance was greeted with stamps and cheers.

Then the two churchwardens came on the stage followed by the committee, which was made up of what the children's father had once described as "the cream of his church workers". He had regretted afterwards that he had said this in front of the children because they had adopted the expression. "Who was there?" somebody would ask, to be answered with grins by "Just the cream".

It was Mr Sedman, as the vicar's warden, who made the opening speech. He had, as had all his parishioners, a profound admiration as well as a deep affection for his vicar. So it was with emotion that he said goodbye. They would, he said, be extraordinarily lucky if they met so fine a man again. For, not only was the vicar a most sincere Christian – one who would be proud to lay down his life for his faith – but he was also a born leader and a fine organiser.

His voice, much to the children's embarrassment, cracked as he said: "This saying goodbye is going to hit many of us hard, but don't think, Vicar, you've seen the last of us. Eastbourne is not so far away and there are many of us who will find excuses to come over and, though we can no longer call you Vicar, you will still be our friend and, like friends should, we shall want to see how you're getting on."

This speech was followed by a short one from one of the lady church workers. This embarrassed the children even more for tears streamed down her cheeks as she talked. She spoke of the dreadful gap that the vicar's leaving would mean in many lives. (She did not need to say hers, for one.) It would only be when he was gone that they would realise exactly what he had meant to St Peter's. So godly a man who had served them so selflessly, life would be bleak without him.

Then the people's warden got to his feet.

"It's my privilege, Vicar, to present to you a little token given to you by all who attend your services and many who do not. You'd be surprised how many people whom you would least expect came up with a subscription saying they never went inside your church but they looked on you as a friend, so would like to give a subscription."

A twitch of amusement crossed his face.

"One who has given those of us who serve on the bench a lot of trouble," he went on, "said even if you were a clergyman you were a real gentleman, and he was proud to add his little something to the fund. Would you come up here, Vicar?" He paused to give the children's father time to climb the few steps to the platform. Then, suddenly formal, he said: "It is my proud pleasure to present to you this piece of silver, inscribed with your name and crest, and this envelope in which is a cheque to help with your move to your new vicarage."

In those days it was customary to honour an occasion with a piece of silver. It never seemed to cross anyone's mind that a poor clergyman with a large vicarage and limited means, so without a well-trained staff – for well-trained servants, of course, cost more – did not want extra silver which took time to clean. They believed the larger the presentation piece of silver the more it showed in what esteem the receiver of the gift was held. So what the children's father was holding was a vast silver salver engraved with his crest, under which was: *Presented to the Reverend Strangeway as a mark of affection and esteem from his parishioners*. Then, below that, the name of the parish and the date. In the envelope was a cheque for £100.

All their lives the children were to remember their father that night, as he stood there in his best, but nevertheless worn, clerical suit struggling without breaking down to say what was in his heart. He succeeded, for he spoke as he preached – well and easily. His was not a great brain, but his love for his people rang out in his opening words.

"My very dear people . . ." He went on to explain how much he had learnt since he came to St Peter's, his first big parish. He thanked them all for their kindness to him and to his family. Nobody, he said, knew how heavy sometimes was the burden on a parish priest, but he had been helped and supported by their prayers.

At this point Victoria gave John a kick and said out of the corner of her mouth:

"Can you see Mr Sedman praying for Daddy?"

John, looking amused, shook his head.

The children's father turned to his presents. It was, he said, wonderfully generous of them to have given him such splendid gifts. He was not going to pretend the money would not be useful but money was transitory, whereas the salver would be with him until he died; it would be placed where he could see it daily and whenever he looked at it he would think of them.

A hundred pounds in those days was worth at least five hundred today. So it represented more spending than the children's father thought seemly for a clergyman. He tried tactfully to suggest this.

"My wife and I will put our heads together to decide what is most desperately needed in the new vicarage, and such things will be bought out of your

96

present to us. But don't expect to see us living in a luxuriously fitted home. Ostentation is always unbecoming but particularly so in a vicarage. So your gift will be spent frugally on simple, necessary things."

John looked in an amused way at his aunt. It was his guess she had been shopping mentally since she knew the figure of the cheque. How was she enjoying this talk of frugal spending? But there was nothing on the children's mother's face to tell him. Her eyes were on her husband, while her face wore an "aren't-people-kind" expression suitable to the occasion.

The vicar went on.

"Life in my new parish will for a time be hard. Not that I dread a hard time. I welcome it, for it will be a test of my faith and courage. I cannot, of course, allow brawling in God's house and for this I have, as many of you men know, made preparations."

Victoria nudged John and whispered:

"What's he mean?"

John answered through the side of his mouth.

"I'll tell you afterwards."

"But there will be a hard time for me ahead and to face this, my dear people, I ask for your prayers. Pray that I may be unflinching in fighting for what I believe to be right. The devil is always about to tempt us, and one of his most effective weapons is to suggest that giving in over small points is not a great matter, and that the ensuing popularity will be worth a little compromising."

He paused to emphasise his next words.

"This is never true. So I must be constantly on watch, for all of us would rather be liked than dis-. liked. Probably this is particularly true for me coming to the Parish Church, Eastbourne, from the warmth and affection you have always given me so generously, for I shall be disliked by many and reviled by not a few." His voice broke. "So pray for me, my dear people, as all my life I shall pray for you."

The organist had been instructed that the party would finish with the singing of *For He's a Jolly Good Fellow*. "But you know the vicar," he had said. "What he talks about maybe won't be suitable for *For He's a Jolly Good Fellow*. So I'll have some of the choirboys sitting towards the front and a hymn handy." Clearly *For He's a Jolly Good Fellow* couldn't follow the speech the vicar had made so, as the children's father sat down, the organist struck a chord or two to prepare the audience then, when they were standing, played a favourite hymn:

"Holy Father, in Thy mercy
Hear our anxious prayer.
Keep our loved ones, now far absent
'Neath Thy care."

The audience sang heartily even though there were tears in many eyes. It struck nobody, except John, that the words "now far absent" were not really applicable to a move to Eastbourne, which was less than fifty miles away. For in those days, when motor cars were few and it was considered advanced and rather dashing to own one, Eastbourne was far away for it was outside driving distance and no through train connected the two towns. In any case journeys were not undertaken lightly. In most families they only happened once or twice a year. There were "parish" outings but they were by horse conveyances so a journey to Eastbourne was impossible.

Many of the older parishioners in the hall had been born in the town and had never left it even for a day. For wages were low and, though a pound went five times as far as it does today, it could not be stretched to cover journeys, nor indeed would many of the humbler people have wished to travel. "East, west, home's best," was their motto. So "far absent" was just as suitable a hymn to sing to say goodbye to the vicar before he left for Eastbourne as it would have been if he was going as a missionary to China.

The children were sent home first with Miss Herbert, while their parents stayed for a last handshake. Miss Herbert hurried Louise and Dick up to bed. The servants had gone to the party so Isobel went to the kitchen to boil a kettle on the range for cocoa.

"What was all that about brawling in God's house?" Victoria asked John.

They were in the schoolroom, which had a high very wide window seat. John sat on it swinging his legs.

"You know Uncle Jim's fairly high church?"

"Of course, and Mummy's low."

John gave Nebuchadnezzar a little kick so that he rocked.

"Well, I don't know an awful lot about them, but there are people called Kensitites who are what is known as evangelical. They think people like Uncle Jim are almost Roman Catholics. So one of the things they do is to make a row in the church when someone who goes in for what they call ritual is made the vicar of a low church. Eastbourne is very low."

"So's Mummy."

"Not like the Kensitites. They won't have any sort of show, like bowing to the altar. Anyway, Uncle Jim thinks they will try and cause a rumpus when he is inducted."

All the children knew there was to be an induction service, but a rumpus! Victoria, in her sheltered life, had never been near such a thing.

"Bags I sit on the outside of the pew so I can bash somebody over the head if they shout at Daddy."

"It's no good bagging anything. Uncle Jim is bringing some of the members of his men's society here over. They are coming by train as throwers-out. If there is a rumpus it will be all over almost before it begins."

Victoria heard the chink of cups coming up the stairs.

"There's Isobel, don't tell her about the Kensitites, even thinking about them might make her wheeze."

100

Cocoa over, in the girls' room Isobel said:

"I suppose Daddy is almost a saint, only you can't be a saint while you are alive."

Victoria pulled her frock over her head.

"Of course he is. I wonder if God knows how difficult it is being a saint's family."

7 Arrival

The grandparents' house was in every way different from home. The children thought this odd because they knew their father had thought his home so perfect he wanted their home to be modelled on it.

Grandfather's ancestors had come to England from Normandy a century after the conquest of Britain. The King, or his agents, had presented the Norman settler with a strip of land in Kent. This land proved to have iron under it, so the family prospered. But though they became landowners they had never struggled after position, being content to be country squires. By degrees, what must have been in the beginning the simplest form of home, became a gentleman's country house and, finally, a castle – a rather peculiar castle of many dates, but still, a castle. Each generation succeeded in marrying the daughter of another country squire, who brought with her a reasonable dowry.

At the beginning of the nineteenth century Grandfather's father, the youngest son of the family at the castle, decided to build a house of his own. It must have been a prosperous period, probably he had a rich mother, for evidently there was enough money for each child to have his portion. He chose a stretch of country on which to build which was about twenty miles from the castle.

The house he built was typical of its period, with mock tessellated towers, a library with stained-glass windows, and a kitchen wing so far from the dining room that all food must reach it lukewarm. There was a huge walled kitchen and fruit garden. Fan-tailed pigeons in a loft and peacocks strutting on the lawn. And in a remote part of the grounds, there was a grotto for storing ice. It was in this house that grandfather had been born.

Granny belonged to the aristocracy. There was no title in her immediate family but the head of it, though a faraway relation, was a duke. She had been brought up in a massive house about fifteen miles from Grandfather's home. The family had lived simply for those days, but nevertheless with a house full of servants, a garden full of gardeners and stables full of horses and conveyances.

At that time everybody knew what was called "their place" and, as a rule, stuck to it. The great aristocratic families only knew each other and the royal family. People such as Granny's parents, who were on the fringe of this world, knew each other and, on occasion, when their paths crossed, were accepted by the great families.

The landed gentry knew each other and, in a limited way, the better-off of their tenants, but never "trade". Everybody else in the country – who were below the salt from the landed gentry's point of view

103

– again presumably had their own set of standards as to who belonged where.

It was definitely a snobbish age but once you were brought up on its principles it was hard to break away from them. King Edward VII had always known the fabulously rich captains of industry who, by the beginning of the century, were established as a new class, but that did not mean that the upper classes followed suit.

Granny had said, when asking about the parents of the pupils who went to the school with the girls: "I know today it is quite the custom to ask the doctor into your house, but of course never the dentist. They are trade and should go to the back door." And she had no idea what an appallingly snobbish statement that was.

Grandfather, in spite of coming from a slightly lower level, when a young man had become a visitor in Granny's house, and by degrees was accepted as a suitor for her. He was at that time reading for the ministry and when three years later he was ordained curate he and Granny, whose name was Dymphna, were married.

What it had been like for Granny in the small house a curate could afford the children's mother could never imagine, but soon Grandfather was ordained priest and was offered a handsome rectory in a country parish which was in the gift of one of Granny's grand relations.

"Grandfather," her mother had told Isobel, "was never the sort of clergyman that Daddy is. For

Grandfather was always more what was called a squire-son than a parson. But he was a good, devout man and gifted in many ways – especially at painting – but I don't think he ever thought it was his duty to work day and night as Daddy does."

Actually this summing up of Grandfather was wide of the mark. This Isobel knew because, as a small child, she had often stayed for months together with the grandparents. For Amberley, where her father had his first parish, was too damp for her to live there during the winter. She and her grandfather had understood each other, sharing as they did their love of painting. She remembered, before permanent asthma made an invalid of him, an amusing bohemian man who should never have been a parson. Without doubt he loved his wife, but equally he must frequently have found her trying. For Granny was pious morning, noon and night.

Granny's life was lived by what she called "The Book", by which she meant the Bible. She could and did recite pages of it by heart. Her sons, except the children's father, treated her knowledge of the Bible as a joke and would lead her on to play a game. "Now, Mother, I Chronicles XIII 10?" Granny: "Let me think. 'And the anger of the Lord was kindled against Uzza . . .' " "Quite right, Mother. Now Jeremiah III 12?" Granny – " 'Go and proclaim these words towards the north, and say . . .' "

But though her sons might get amusement out of their mother's piousness, they were not with her all the time – whereas Grandfather presumably was. As an escape, he used his asthma. "I must get to the sun," he would say. And off he would go with his easel to France or Italy – returning a few months later cheerful and bronzed, with a portfolio of water-colours to show where he had been.

Isobel told Victoria that it was not only when he was abroad that he painted. When she was about six years old she could remember being taken by her grandparents to the seaside. There was a run of mackerel while they were there so Grandmother, not wishing to waste what she called God's gift, turned every available pair of hands on to pickling and potting the fish. Grandfather watched what was happening. "Come away with me, Isobel," he said. 'We have something much better to do." Then they sat down together to paint the fish. "This is far more important than all that storing and fussing they are doing in the kitchen."

It was years later that Victoria learnt from Isobel what a difference it might have made to her life if Grandfather had not become an invalid. "You see, Vicky, he would have made Daddy send me to a real art school. But he died just as I grew up so I never went to one. Daddy always said: 'You can't go to that sort of place, darling. In art schools they have life classes!'"

Grandfather was still a parish priest when the children's father was first ordained and his son became his curate. But by the time the children were born Grandfather's own father had died, and, as he was the eldest son, he had inherited the property. After this he gave up active church work, except for taking an occasional service, and had settled down to the life of a country gentleman in the large tessellated home his father had built.

Even there Granny did not have the comfort she had known in her own home, for there was nowhere near enough money to keep the place up. There were a cook, kitchen maid and scullery maid in the kitchen and, for the house, a parlourmaid, an upper housemaid, an under housemaid and a between maid, plus Nanny, who stayed on after the children's father, brothers and sisters grew up, to look after the linen. There were large grounds but only three gardeners, a boy, and an odd job man who lived in one of the lodges. So to Granny, used to a proper staff, it was very much making-do.

The children, when they were very small, had stayed in the big house and had loved it, but by the time Isobel was seven Grandfather had given up the uneven struggle to keep that house going and had built himself what was called The Little House on a corner of his property. He had put the big house up to let.

The Little House, which was the one to which the children were going, had a large drawing room with a conservatory off it. A spacious hall, which could be used as a sitting room, a big dining room and, behind a green baize door, large kitchens and pantries. Upstairs there were six bedrooms and a smoking room. There was also a back stair, which was believed to lead to several servants' bedrooms, but no one as far as the children knew had ever seen them.

Over forty years later during the Second World War the house was converted into flats. Dick kept for himself and his family that part which had belonged to the servants, and interested cousins flocked to see his temporary home. This was because, though they had frequently stayed in the house when they were children, none of them had been behind the green baize door, which was next to the smoking room and led to the servants' bedrooms.

At a time when Grandfather had built The Little House, for a gentleman to live without stables was unthinkable, so naturally there were stables behind the lodge at the gate, and a lodge was something else no gentleman lived without.

Naturally also there was a quite large vegetable garden for Westerham, the small town nearby, was a mile away so, in so far as was possible, vegetables were grown at home to save taking out old Sultan, the horse. Naturally, too, there had to be a flower garden; who would think of living without that? And lawns and a tennis court were to Grandfather the ordinary adjuncts of decent living. Then of course he had kept a field for his own use, for there was Sultan for Granny's victoria and a donkey to pull the lawnmower.

But The Little House was vastly cheaper to run than the big house. There were three servants and Nanny instead of seven. There was only one gardener-coachman-handyman and a boy instead of three and a handyman. There was only one lodge to keep up instead of two, and as the gardener-coachman-handyman called Burridge, who lived there, had a wife and a swarm of children, there was always cheap labour about when it was wanted, also there were plenty to carry out the lodge keeper's normal job of opening the gate whenever a carriage went in or out.

The big house, as the children's mother remembered it, had been full of beautiful things, but when the move took place to The Little House many pieces of furniture disappeared. The children's mother supposed, in rather an aggrieved way, that those things had been sold, which upset her for the children's father was the eldest son, which meant he would inherit almost everything some day. As she learned later, the beautiful things had only been stored, to make room in The Little House for all the gifts that over the years Grandfather and Granny had been given by their children.

Most disastrous presents many of these were, for several of the uncles were in the Indian Civil Service and every leave they brought home trophies: a gong held between two carved elephants; brass tables; teak chairs; temple bells, and any amount of brass ornaments standing against Sheraton tables, under pictures by Constable and Gainsborough or between Sèvres and Meissen china.

But packed away in a cupboard were such treasures as a bedspread which had the family coat-of-arms and crest. This had been embroidered in the castle by the servants in the early eighteenth century; cushions, with beautiful hand embroidery, inherited from the same date; some charming china and miniatures and many delicious knick-knacks. But nothing given by what Granny called "my boys", and the children, "the uncles", was ever put away.

The household was run by Aunt Sophie. Up to the First World War, in well-to-do homes, it was taken for granted that one daughter, usually the youngest, would remain in the home to look after their parents in their declining years. As many parents, with nothing to do, started their declining years before they were fifty, the daughter who stayed at home had not only a hard life while her parents lived, but when they died her reward was all too frequently to be left practically penniless.

Grandfather and Granny had begun declining early. Grandfather, who had suffered from hay fever all his life (as did the children's father and Victoria) had taken a cure. This cure though it got rid of the hay fever, gave him asthma – the other family scourge. He did not have it, as Isobel did, in attacks, but had a permanent wheeze – so wherever he went he sounded as though he was carrying a basket of kittens.

Perhaps by nature Grandfather was lethargic and had to force himself to do a day's work, but certainly, when he was settled in The Little House, he moved about so seldom the children were quite surprised if they did not find him in his usual chair in the hall. He would have bursts of energy when he would go to London to ride on an Underground train, which he said relieved his asthma, or to visit a friend who shared his passion for heraldry, but every year his inclination to move about became less and less.

Granny had started to decline much more dramatically. One holiday when the children had stayed in the house she was walking about as usual, and the next visit she seldom moved off a sofa. When she was outside in the garden somebody, usually Aunt Sophie, pushed her in a bathchair. Beyond her gate she travelled as she had always done – in the victoria.

The children, when they climbed out of the train at Westerham, were not surprised nobody was on the platform to meet them. The porter lifted the shabby trunks out of the van.

"Here you are! I said to Mr Burridge, better than the last time he met you – just after Christmas that was, and snowing terrible."

The trunks were left on the platform for the carrier's cart to bring up to The Little House later in the day, so the children trooped into the station yard. There, as they expected, Burridge was sitting waiting on the driving seat of the victoria.

All her married life Granny had somehow obtained certain comforts and refinements to which she was used, and which she had no intention of giving up. One was a carriage and another was a coachman.

It had always been impossible for Grandfather to afford a full-time coachman, but he knew his

Dymphna and had found a compromise. A fawn coat was tailored to fit the then handyman and a top hat with a windmill-like cockade attached to it. The family crest was painted on the doors of the second-hand victoria. Then three rugs were bought. For Grandmother, one fur and one holland, and for the man who was to drive, a dark blue one.

From then on, whenever Grandmother decided to go out calling, or to take little comforts to someone who was ill, a large bell was rung to warn the handyman. He downed tools at once and clumped off to the stable yard. There he would harness the horse to the victoria, wash his hands under the pump, pull on his uniform coat, put on his top hat and his gloves. Then he would climb on to the box and carefully arrange his rug over his muddy working boots and corduroy breeches. Then, looking every inch a liveried coachman, he would drive to the front door.

Presumably all the houses at which Burridge took his mistress to call knew he could never get off his box outside the front door. For the children noticed that when one or the other of them were taken out calling by their grandmother, someone was always about to hold the horse and open the carriage door. Probably, after the door was shut, the carriage was driven round to the back door and there Burridge, who by then would be Mr Burridge, would be invited in to have something to keep out the cold, or wash out the dust, according to the season. Nobody of course being so rude as to mention the corduroys and the boots.

For a long time the children had suffered silently in case one day Grandmother left a house without warning, to find Burridge was not waiting outside the front door. Presently they learnt this never happened. This made them guess that Granny and her friends knew as well as they did that Burridge (who, as handyman, could not aspire to the butler's pantry or the housekeeper's room) was in the servants' hall having his little something. They realised this because the moment Granny talked of leaving the hostess would ring a bell and when the butler came she would say:

"Order Mrs Strangeway's carriage to be brought round."

In the station yard, delighted to see him, the children greeted Burridge. How was he? How were George, Fred, Tom, Martha, May and Tabitha? How were . . . But there Burridge stopped them.

"Time enough for all that later. You come up on the box beside me, Miss Louise and Master Dick. Only Master John is to sit with his back to the horse, for I've got more to do than clean out your Granny's carriage where one of you has been sick."

The children knew Burridge would say this because once, when he was very small, Dick had been sick on the fur rug, but every other time when one or other of them was affected by sitting back to the horse, they had to say: "Stop please, Burridge," which he always did immediately and they had

113

climbed out and were sick discreetly by the side of the road. Granny thought a child's place was on the back-to-the-horse seat, and if it made them feel sick the lesson in self-control was valuable. So, however often they were sick, there was no suggestion of their not being taken for drives or being allowed to sit on the box or beside Grandmother facing the horse. If they were all staying in the house at the same time, on the drive to and from the station two of them had to sit on the box, but it was the only occasion when it was permitted.

On the drive through Westerham, Burridge always retailed news which might be important to one or other of the children.

"Mrs Minns has her Golden Sovereigns waiting for you." Mrs Minns was Nanny, known to the children as Grand-Nanny, and her Golden Sovereigns was a form of immensely strong beef tea, which she made herself and insisted on all members of the family drinking after a journey. "Your Uncle Matthew is home, so there's to be a funeral Sunday, Master John, which he's counting on you to help him with.'

On most fine Sundays when an uncle was home there was a funeral in the afternoon. There was no difficulty in finding a suitable corpse, for if no bird or animal had come to a natural end, a crow or rabbit was shot.

The funeral cortège followed a well-laid plan. The girls wore black crêpe round their hats and all the children wore crêpe arm bands. At the head of the procession walked the youngest child present, ringing at a doleful speed a handbell. Then came the other children each carrying flowers or a tiny wreath. Beside them, or sometimes bringing up the rear, walked the family dogs, each with a crêpe bow tied to its collar. The hearse was a green cart.

This cart was a feature of the grandparents' home. It was big enough to hold four small children. It was used for tobogganing down the slope of the lawn, and for fetching logs and fir cones from the woods. No picnic could have taken place without it.

On a funeral afternoon, on one of the seats of the green cart the coffin – a cardboard box – was laid. This was covered with a piece of black velvet. Behind the green cart walked an uncle draped in a tablecloth. Granny would beg the uncle who was taking the part of the clergyman not to be irreverent – not that it really crossed her mind that one of her boys could be. Just how irreverent the officiating uncle was depended on whether any of his brothers were there to lead him on. Certainly, when several uncles were present, the mutters coming from the parson caused a lot of subdued laughter. For the extra uncles, dressed in top hats with crêpe streamers, were within hearing as they were the undertaker's men.

At the graveside a hymn was sung. The first verse established the identity of the corpse.

> "Found in the garden
> Dead in his beauty,
> Oh, that a . . ."

115

and here was inserted rabbit, crow, frog or whatever
it was –

> "Should die in the spring.
> Bury him carefully
> In pitiful duty.
> Muffle the dinner bell.
> Solemnly ring."

The service, to words composed by the uncle, was
short or long according to his audience. When there
were undertaker's men present part of it was sometimes in Latin.

No one but family was ever present at a funeral,
but of course all the staff knew they took place.
No doubt Burridge, when he said there would be a
funeral, had already said to Uncle Matthew: "I
caught a rat (or whatever it was) yesterday. I got it
hung up ready for the funeral come Sunday."

Now Burridge turned to more personal matters.

"No harm in being warned, Miss Vicky, but your
grandfather's been carrying on alarming at morning
prayers so I hear, on account of a bit of impertinence
in the kitchen. But now you've come you must
expect him to turn his prayers on to you. There's
ever so tiny a little sapling come up in the garden,
that place you painted last summer, Miss Isobel. I
didn't pull it up, not before you saw it knowing what
strange fancies you artists get. Miss Sophie has put
away ever so nice a bit of velvet to make Jackie a
coat, Miss Louise. How's he keeping?"

116

Louise raised her flower-like face to Burridge.

"He's very well, thank you, Burridge, but he can do with a change of air."

Victoria made seasick noises.

Burridge outside the family treated the children with respect, but when alone with them he was a disciplinarian.

"You don't seem to be improving, Miss Vicky. You let your little sister be. Well, Master Dick, how's that school?"

Dick adored Burridge.

"I'm getting on much better now that I have spectacles. I couldn't see that blackboard properly without them."

Burridge remembered a piece of news.

"We had snow here Shrove Tuesday, so Miss Sophie fetched in a shovelful for the pancakes, and so did Mrs Burridge for our'n. Lovely they were, there's no proper pancake not without a spoonful of snow in it."

At the top of the hill Burridge stopped the carriage outside the gates and slashed at them with his whip. Immediately a child so fair she was almost white-haired shot out of the lodge to open them.

Martha was almost the same age as Louise and, if Dick were not staying in the house, the two were sometimes allowed to play together.

"Hullo, Martha!" Louise shouted.

But Burridge wanted none of that.

"Open the gate, lass, remember Mrs Strangeway is waiting, hurry now."

117

Suddenly they were inside the front door and, one after another, in Aunt Sophie's arms. Then, as they moved into the hall, all those things that were part of staying with Granny and Grandfather were with them: the chimes of the clocks, which were special to the house; the smell of pot-pourri; Pears' soap; mustiness; cedar wood and wood smoke. Things that were so much part of the house that, "It smells like at Grandfather's", or "It sounds like at Grandfather's", was part of the children's language. None of the five noticed that they felt different, but each of them relaxed. Then they looked expectantly at Aunt Sophie, waiting for the proper words to be said.

"Run up to Grand-Nanny, darlings, for your Golden Sovereigns."

8 Grand-Nanny

Grand-Nanny was an institution. Ageless, unchanging, understanding, she was security on two legs. To each of her ten original nurslings even more perhaps than their parents she stood for "home". The seven sons who had married had each in turn brought the girl he was engaged to for Nanny to look over. Always her shrewd eyes took them in before she asked her first question: "Can you needle?" Each of her nurslings, especially those who worked in India, when they came on leave, having greeted their parents, was up the stairs two steps at a time to hug Nanny.

Stories of Grand-Nanny were legion. Some she repeated herself, others were told of her. "When my ten were small one or other of them would be sent to stay with your Granny's family. Everything of the best there would be in those houses, for they did not have to count the pennies same as we had to. But I was not going to have the staff looking down their noses at us. There was a very nice dressing gown we had, and I put it away special for visiting. Every child wore that dressing gown one time or another, so I called it Brotherly Love. 'Don't you forget to pack Brotherly Love', I would say to my nursery maid, 'we don't want to be shamed, do we?'"

Then there was the story of the French boots. The children had no idea what French boots were but they loved hearing about them. "Another thing I kept for a visit to your Granny's relations," Grand-Nanny would say, "was a little pair of French boots. Beautiful they were but they never fitted one of my ten. But who was to know that? Every evening when visiting I put those little boots out to be cleaned, thinking to myself: 'I'll let them see we know what's what'."

One story shocked the children for it made their grandmother sound so selfish.

"It was cruelly hard work bringing up all those children with only a little nursery maid to help. In those days new babies were carried for the first three months. You see, they wore long clothes, every inch clear starched. Your granny had been used before she married to having her own maid and didn't seem able to manage without. So it was one of my tasks to sit up to undo her gown and brush her hair – lovely hair she had. But many a night I would drop to sleep over my ironing board waiting for her. You see, when they went out to dinner it was often past midnight before the carriage got home."

Their mother told the children that when she first met Grand-Nanny she kept a cow. It was tethered to the back door and, according to Grand-Nanny, she went down and fetched a jug of milk as and when she wanted it. "There's nothing for children like milk fresh from the cow, Mrs Jim," she told me. "If you want children to keep well, see the froth from the milking is still on the milk."

Children were Grand-Nanny's life, so when her nurslings had babies Nanny was waiting. When a new baby was expected, or a child needed special cosseting, it was to Grand-Nanny they were sent. She had a genius for handling children. She was strict in a way but more as if she ruled a kingdom than imposed her will. "These are my rules," she seemed to say, "and if you live in my kingdom you have to accept them; but if you don't want to there's plenty of other places to go."

The children's father and his brothers and sisters, and their children, had never disputed Nanny's laws; in fact, as the uncles and aunts grew older, they cherished them, for they made them feel children again. "That's no subject to cause an argument while you've having your tea, it only brings on indigestion," Nanny would say. Or, "Such nonsense this talk of not sleeping well. Count a flock of sheep carefully, as you've always done, and you'll be asleep before you can say Jack Robinson. But mind, you've been over-exciting yourself; that's what started the trouble." To each one of her boys back on leave from India it was his first tea with Nanny that made him feel he was really home.

But bringing up babies and little children was Nanny's work and with them she was extraordinary. Louise, as a tiny thing, had suddenly refused to eat. Everything was tried, the doctor was in despair and certain she would die. Then the children's father had said: "I'll take her to Nanny". Nanny received little Louise, who was skin and bone by that time, calmly, merely remarking: "Children always eat in my nursery". And Louise ate. The stories of what she had done for the children of the family were endless but no one knew how she worked her cures, they were her secrets. "I have my ways," was all she would say.

Grand-Nanny always looked the same. She wore black, with full skirts, and a high neck with a little bit of lace round it. On her head was a white cap. Old ladies – and Nanny must have been nearly sixty at the time of the family's move to Eastbourne, which was considered old – wore caps in those days. Round her waist she tied an apron, which changed according to what she was doing. That morning because she had made the Golden Sovereigns it was made of coarse linen. But at some time in the day she would change that for a black silk one to mark her position in the house – as if it needed any marking.

Though she was Nanny or Grand-Nanny to her family and all her friends, she was Mrs Minns – spoken in capitals – to the rest of the staff and to any visiting servants, such as coachmen, who came to the house. Nanny's "Mrs" was not honorary, as it often was for a cook. She had been married and widowed about a year before the children's father was born. Her husband had been a gamekeeper, and while he lived she had been wonderfully happy. But he died of pneumonia and she had decided to return to her profession of children's nurse.

It was Aunt Sophie who had told the children Nanny's story. "So she came to us," she said, "and we became her children. But every year, when the day comes round that her husband died, you can see she is feeling sad, for she has never forgotten him. Our love for her has comforted her a bit, but nothing is the same as having your own family, is it?"

None of the children was old enough to see the pathos of that statement from Aunt Sophie – condemned almost from birth to dedicating her life to her parents. Years later, when Nanny died, the children were to remember Aunt Sophie telling them Nanny's story. It so happened that at the time the eight boys she had reared were in England.

The Little House was quite a distance from the church but they would not allow their old nanny's body to be taken to it by hearse, instead they – each of whom she had carried in her arms – carried her to her grave on their shoulders.

"She would have liked that," Isobel was to write to Victoria. "You remember when we were children Aunt Sophie said how their love had tried to comfort her."

But all that was a long way ahead, and Grand-Nanny was very much herself the day the children arrived.

"Here you are, dears. I've got your Golden Sovereigns waiting. Now run along and tidy. You girls can use the W up here, you boys run down to the one next to the smoking room. There's a jug of hot water in the basin at the end of the passage."

Brown Pears' soap, which smelt faintly of disinfectant and was opaque instead of solid, like cakes of soap at home, was as much a part of Grandfather and Granny's house as the agapanthus plants which grew in the summer in green tubs on either side of the front door. It helped to produce atmosphere.

"Well," said Grand-Nanny as the children sat round her table drinking their soup, "so you are moving. How do you feel about it?" She looked at Isobel, so it was she who answered.

"It's a much more important parish for Daddy."

Nanny looked up from a table napkin she was darning.

"It was time they found him something important to do. I always knew he was born for great things. Such a funny little boy he was, not like the others at all."

They had heard this before but enjoyed hearing it again.

"Tell how the boy hit him," Victoria urged.

Grand-Nanny smiled.

"At a party it was. Let me see, your father was there and so was yours, Master John, and your Aunt Hetty, and I was carrying your Uncle Freddy – long clothes the baby had, every inch clear starched. So your father would have been about six. After tea there were games and races and such, and your father won some prize another boy wanted. Instead of asking for the prize, which I shouldn't wonder if your father wouldn't have given him, the boy gave your father a punch in the face."

"And Grandfather saw," said Louise, "and asked Daddy why he didn't hit back."

Grand-Nanny nodded, seeing again the mid-Victorian party.

"I can see your father now as clearly as I see you. 'Why should I hit him?' he said. 'I like him.'"

"Was he the teeniest bit a prig?" Victoria asked.

Grand-Nanny shook her head.

"No. Just different. I knew then, though really I had always known it, the life he was cut out for. Mind you, don't think he didn't play games and such, like other boys. Why, at that Cambridge he got one of those blues they talked about for running."

Louise was bored with tales of so long ago.

"Did you know we are going to a new school?"

"A little bird told me so." (Little birds always told Grand-Nanny things.) "Do you think you'll like it from what you hear?"

Louise leaned forward.

"Did your little bird tell you Vicky had to leave Elmhurst anyway?"

Grand-Nanny laid down her darning. She looked at Louise, not crossly, but in surprise that one of her children could behave badly.

"My little birds, Miss Louise, are never tell-tale tits."

Louise flushed.

"I only wondered if you knew."

Grand-Nanny never harped on a subject; one reproof she considered should be enough.

"It was time for a new school for you two older ones. You will be young ladies soon and it's easier to make the change in a different place. I remember I said something of that to your granny when your Aunt Hetty was becoming a little woman, or should have – but she was a sad tomboy, always wanting to do what her brothers did. 'Time to change the governess,' I said. 'Miss Box' – that was her name – 'is all right for little Miss Sophie, but Miss Hetty needs treating like a young lady, and then she'll feel like one'."

Victoria rarely felt on edge or irritable when staying with Grandfather and Granny, and never when she was with Grand-Nanny. She spoke up eagerly, knowing she would not be snubbed:

"Did Aunt Hetty suddenly feel a young lady, or did it take ages? You see, they're beginning to tell me I ought to be growing up – have a sense of responsibility and all that – and nothing seems to happen, I feel just the same as I always have."

"I'm supposed to be almost grown-up," Isobel added, "but I'm not."

Grand-Nanny looked fondly from one girl to the other.

"You have always been halfway there, Miss Isobel; your health being poor, you've spent more time with your mother. But I think the change from being a child to a young lady does come suddenly. You know, though she tried hard and behaved like a little lady and down came her skirts and up went her hair, I don't believe your Aunt Hetty really stopped being a child until the day she met Mr Samuel – now your Uncle Samuel."

"How old was she?" Isobel asked.

"I don't remember, dear, seventeen perhaps. One of your uncles brought him to the house – a Saturday afternoon it was – to play tennis. Afterwards, Miss Hetty came up to her room to dress for dinner and I took one look and I knew. Miss Hetty had grown up."

Louise and Dick were bored. They had finished their soup and had got up to look at Grand-Nanny's screen. It had been the nursery screen and she had inherited it. It fascinated all children, for nothing like it was in use any more. It had a dark background on to which had been pasted pictures and rhymes thought suitable for children, and it had then been varnished.

"Look," said Louise to Dick. "That's Queen Victoria giving a Bible to a savage."

Dick was searching for his favourite picture. He found it.

"This is the first train that ever ran."

John got up and joined them. He too had his favourite. It was a mawkish rhyme, probably thought beautiful in the previous century. He read out loud with exaggerated sentiment.

"There's a touch of paint off the bright new whip,
A chip off the horse's ear,

127

But oh, not that to the boy's blue eye
Brings the quickly-gathering tear:
For the baby has gone where never again
Can she ask for his toys to play . . ."

"That's enough, John," said Grand-Nanny. "It
may seem funny to you, but your grandfather chose
every bit that's on that screen, cut it out and stuck
it on himself, so it's not right for you to make fun
of it. And now, if you've all finished, you can run
down and kiss your granny and grandfather."

Both Grandfather and Granny believed that children were fundamentally good, but help was sometimes needed. Aunt Hetty, when young, easily lost
her temper, so Grandfather had illuminated for her
a speech of Katherine's from *The Taming of the
Shrew*: "A woman moved is like a fountain
troubled . . ." and framed it and hung it over her
bed.

Direct intercession at morning prayers and in his
private prayers, had, he was convinced, worked
wonders for all his children and grandchildren. But
what, quite unconsciously for all their children and
later their grandchildren, both Granny and Grandfather had exuded was faith in them. Because they
believed sincerely that every child in the family was
doing his or her best, there was a feeling of ease
and happiness in the house, and they all tried their
hardest not in any way to offend. Even Victoria
behaved well, arriving to meals clean and tidy and
never arguing about anything.

128

Apart from Grandfather's pleading with God to give special help to the children: "Holy Father, Thou knowest into what difficulties our grandchild Vicky found herself at her last school. We humbly ask for Your very special help for her in her new school. Also for help when at home, that she may accept correction meekly, without argument . . ." Victoria always said she could see the bows which sat like small sailing ships on the maids' praying upturned rumps quiver, when Grandfather said "meekly and without argument".

Granny had her own way of pointing a moral or correcting a fault. Every visit she would at some time send for one or other of the children to come to her room after breakfast.

Aunt Sophie would bring the message. "Granny would like you to run up to give her a morning kiss."

When John was sent for on this visit he was, as he expected, cross-examined on what he intended to be when he grew up. You couldn't lie to Granny, so he had to take refuge in a near-truth – that he did not know. Granny spoke of his father when he was a boy, of his love of sport.

"I never interfered, John, with what my boys chose as a career. But then I was at home in England. It is natural, I think, that your father should wish you to follow in his footsteps, for life in the Indian Civil is not only a good life, but offers many advantages. In any case, since he is such a believer in games I think you could try a little harder. Do you not think so, dear?"

Somehow no one resented what Granny said, so John left her bedroom planning to give more attention to cricket.

Granny, Grandfather and Aunt Sophie never stayed in the vicarage. When they visited, rooms were taken in the town. At such times Granny noted and stored away small things she did not like which she would talk about when the children were next under her roof.

"Isobel dear, you are such a good patient girl when you have that horrid asthma that perhaps you sometimes take it for granted that when tiresome things need to be done you will not be the one who is asked to do them. I find that Vicky's face in repose is becoming a little sullen. That makes your grandfather and I very sad. I think – only when you are well of course – that if sometimes you could do some little task instead of Vicky, it might help her. Will you try, dear Isobel?"

Isobel saw at once what Granny had said was true. She left the bedroom determined to watch for a chance to do just what she was asked.

Louise sat by Granny's bed, nursing Jackie. Perhaps because she took after her mother rather than her father, Granny never spoilt Louise as most others were inclined to do. After enquiring how she was enjoying herself and what she had been doing, she said:

"A boy, Louise dear, has to go out into the world; however sad it is for his mummy, she knows that from the day he is born. That is why we send our little boys away to boarding schools; they have to get used to living without mummies and sisters. Dick is a very clever boy, but I think perhaps he finds going away to school harder than other little boys do. You could help him, Louise. You can be such a useful little daughter at home. Try and find other interests than just waiting for Dick to come back from school."

Louise did not resent what Granny had said, she merely dismissed it. "Nothing ever is going to separate me and Dick," she told herself.

Dick, when his turn came, gazed at Granny owlishly through his glasses. He loved her and Grandfather and Aunt Sophie and Grand-Nanny and the house and everything about staying there. He was always an obedient, obliging child, but he was particularly glad when, while staying in The Little House, something special was asked of him. Because, by doing whatever it was, very fast and well, everybody – including the household and, of course, Burridge – could see how much he loved them.

Granny's heart melted in her. He was so like his father, her first-born. He was not perhaps dedicated in the way Jim had been, even as a little boy, but he had the same basic goodness. She held out her arms.

"Come and kiss your old granny."

Dick ran to her and climbed on to her bed. She smelt as he expected her to smell, what he and

Louise called Granny-ish. A curious smell like a Bible. She hugged him to her.

"Dick, can you keep a secret?"

Dick looked up into the wrinkled face. He knew Granny knew that he and Louise never had secrets from each other.

"Not from Louise I couldn't."

"Especially from Louise. How would a secret be between just your old granny and yourself?"

Dick thought about that. Then he knew the idea was impossible.

"Louise and me tell each other everything. The first thing she will do when I come out of your room is to ask what you said to me."

Granny, though thanking God for so truthful a child, wished – for grown-up Dick he would some day be – that what he had said was not true.

"Every one of us has to grow up to be able to stand by themselves. You never tie two plants together, do you?"

Dick giggled at the thought.

"Of course not."

"Some day, you know, you will go out into the world and Louise will not be with you."

Dick wriggled free from Granny's arms and sat up to face her.

"Oh yes she will. We have thought of that. Wherever I go Louise will come too. We are going to build a little house and live in it together."

Granny thought of Louise and her Jackie. They said little girls who played with dolls were little mothers in the making. Jackie was not strictly a doll but Louise appeared to love him as one day she would love her babies. However, naturally that was not something which could be said before a child.

"So you cannot share a secret with your old granny? That's a pity, ain't it?" Granny deliberately mispronounced certain words as had been the fashion when she was young.

Dick nodded.

"Truly I'm sorry but I know I will tell Louise."

Grandmother gave him another hug.

"Very well. Run along."

When the door was shut she picked up the gold half-sovereign which was to have been her secret present to Dick and put it carefully in a box on her bedside table. It must wait there until Dick could keep a secret.

Granny was particularly anxious not to seem to preach to Victoria, for she suspected her mother was at the bottom of the child's trouble. She never said, or even allowed herself to think, ill of her daughters-in-law. When they had married her sons they became family and the family was sacrosanct. The furthest she would go was to say to Grandfather or to Aunt Sophie:

"Vicky is a child who needs a great deal of love and understanding. I do hope dear Sylvia realises that."

The house puzzled Victoria. Why, she wondered, was she so much nicer here than she was at home? Of course she loved everybody, but then she loved almost everybody at home. Only here nobody said things to make her cross, like Mummy and Miss Herbert did.

"Well, Vicky," said Granny, "your very last day. Have you enjoyed yourself?"

Victoria squeezed Granny's hand.

"It's been perfect except, of course, we all want awfully to see the new house."

"Naturally, it would be very strange if you did not." Granny took Victoria's other hand and pulled her gently nearer to her. "Of course I love all my grandchildren, but I have a very special corner in my heart for you, Vicky."

Vicky was amazed.

"Me! But nobody likes me best!"

"That is what you think but you are wrong, I know somebody else who also keeps a special corner of his heart for you."

Victoria was sure she knew the answer to that.

"God."

Granny smiled.

"God loves us all. No, I was thinking of your father."

"Daddy! But I'm the cross he has to bear. Everybody says so."

"But does he?"

"Not exactly – but from the look on his face I can see he often thinks that."

Granny leant back against her pillows.

"Your father is a very special person. He is, of course, a good husband and father, but beyond that he is father in a very real sense to everybody in his parish. This means that he has to give of his love and his strength to many people, and when you give yourself as he does, you often find yourself exhausted. Your dear mother has so much to do, with Isobel so delicate and Louise far from strong, and a big vicarage to look after, that she has not perhaps the time to watch for those moments when your father is most exhausted. But *you* could, Vicky – you could help him in lots of little ways. You will be stepping soon away from childhood to your womanhood . . ."

Victoria giggled.

"Everybody says that, but I don't feel I'm growing up."

"Part of being a woman is the wish to help and comfort, and who better to help and comfort than your own father?"

Victoria looked in dismay at Granny.

"You don't know how difficult it would be. I'm not supposed to go into the study unless I'm sent for, and if I fussed round Daddy, Mummy would be sure to say: 'Run away, Vicky, Daddy's tired'."

Grandmother nodded.

"It will not be easy. But you and your father have a great deal to give to each other. I am sure, when next I see you, that you will tell me you have found this to be true."

The next morning, during morning prayers, each child was commended by name into God's special keeping during the railway journey. An hour later

135

Burridge, in a borrowed wagonette, drove the children to the railway junction for Eastbourne.

"You get them all into the carriage, Master John," he said, "while I slip off to give the guard this shilling what your grandfather sent."

Louise, as she settled into her seat, said:

"If I was God I'd think it rude of Grandfather to give the guard a shilling for it looks as if Grandfather didn't trust him."

9 The New Vicarage

The vicarage at Eastbourne lay well back, partially hidden amongst trees. It looked from the outside dignified, even imposing, for its garden was the boundary for two streets of small houses. When the children came to know the neighbourhood well they were to learn that the small houses were largely lived in by their owners, many of whom were retired professional people, and all probably better off than their vicar.

On the day of arrival the vicarage looked like the house of the Lord of the Manor surrounded by his tenants. The house had a gracious air, it was two-storied, long and low. But one glance inside and it was clear it was very much a vicarage. There was the bench just inside the front hall on which, if several people called at once to see the vicar, they could sit while waiting. The hall, since so many would tramp up and down it, was covered from end to end with linoleum.

The children's father was working, so he was not able to meet them at the station. But their mother was there, so it was she who, with some pride, led the way into the house, expecting her family to be as pleased with their new home as she was. More-over, for a non-house-proud woman, she had worked hard to make it pleasant. But Victoria as usual blurted out her thoughts.

"Oh why do all vicarages smell alike? I wish I didn't have to live in one."

Victoria was partly right. Many vicarages have a beeswax-ish, hassock-cum-parcels-for-the-jumble-sale odour. But it was an unlucky statement when her mother had been working twelve hours a day attempting, without many resources, to create a homelike atmosphere.

"What a stupid thing to say, Vicky. You are very lucky to live in a vicarage."

John hurried to the rescue.

"Let's see that drawing room you're so proud of, Aunt Sylvia."

The family jostled Victoria to the back of the party, giving her dismayed looks which said clearly: "Why must you be such an idiot?"

Nothing was more calculated to irritate Victoria so, though she said no more at that minute, the others could hear her muttering:

"Well, I do hate vicarages. Why shouldn't I say so if I do? I think vicarages are awful."

Their mother wisely was at that moment deaf.

There were some new curtains and carpets, but mostly viewing the house was the excitement of seeing the old possessions in new settings and, of course, the bedrooms. John had for some time slept in his uncle's dressing room but, because of lack of space, his clothes had remained in the night nursery. Louise and Dick had slept in the night nursery with beds on either side of Miss Herbert's. There had been some effort to drop the word nursery and call it the children's room, but it had not come off.

Now there was nothing approaching nurseries under any name; instead, each of the girls had her own room, the boys shared one, and Miss Herbert – which subtly changed her position – also had a room of her own. The girls' rooms were connected, Isobel reaching hers through Victoria's; it had been chosen for her because it was a warm room and had a fireplace. Louise's room faced Victoria's across a passage.

The boys' room and Miss Herbert's bed-sitting-room were at the top of the back stairs. The children's parents' room was at the end of the house beyond Isobel's room, with windows looking over the garden and to the front gate.

What seemed strange and rather dismaying to the children was that their bedrooms were all that belonged to them. They had been told there would be no schoolroom, but they had not managed to visualise a house where they had no general room of their own.

Dick, always the most fearful of change, was the first to express anxiety. "But where do we keep things? I mean, books and games and things?"

Because she herself had qualms as to how it was going to work out, his mother answered in a brisk, don't-be-so-silly voice.

"In your bedrooms, of course. You and John have

a big bookcase and a cupboard. What more do you want?"

But it was not an answer and they all knew it.

The trouble was the house looked big, but downstairs the space was given to two large rooms. The drawing room had a small back room off it, which could be divided by curtains but which was in no sense private. The dining room had room in it for the dining table with every leaf used. This meant it could comfortably seat sixteen and more if necessary. Next to the dining room there was a small sitting room which was the one earmarked as Isobel's painting room but it was not big enough for them all to use at the same time. The only other room was the study. There was nowhere to lay out a game and leave it for another day. No room in which to be noisy and, on occasion, to fight.

When Dick had asked his question, the children were standing in the passage outside Louise's room, and the silence following their mother's answer was growing awkward. She had not meant to face the problem of space the first day the children arrived, but she saw that she could not brush Dick's question aside.

"I know it's going to be a bit difficult at first, especially in the holidays. You've been used to that big schoolroom. But there is this lovely garden with heaps of room to do anything you like. When it rains, except at meal times, you must use the dining room and, of course, you little ones," she turned to

Louise and Dick, "could play in Louise's bedroom . . . Oh, I'm sure you will manage."

As it happened, the rest of the boys' holiday, which was only four days for Dick and three for John, was fine, so the children spent most of their time in the garden.

The garden proved to be even better than it had looked at first sight. There was a small thicket of trees between the house and the garden wall, which the children christened The Wood, and which became very much their own.

The field, used for grazing by a local farmer, and as a sportsground for the parish, was large and at the bottom looked over the grounds of a preparatory school for boys, which promised splendid chances when the school reopened for games of "I spy".

The flower garden was the sort that had space for growing flowers for picking, something the family had never known at the old vicarage.

The kitchen garden had raspberry canes and currant and gooseberry bushes which, though old and badly in need of pruning, held promise. There was a shed big enough, as John pointed out, to hold a motor car – unlikely though it was there would ever be one – as well as all the family bicycles. These, except for the one belonging to the children's father, which was in constant use, were already in the shed when the children first saw it.

The best thing of all about the garden, apart from The Wood, was its trees – three huge, truly magnificent cedars born to be climbed.

On the day of their arrival, all thoughts of being on the verge of being grown-up and being reasonable citizens were forgotten, and John up one tree and Victoria up another established a telegraph service, with notes travelling from tree to tree on string pulleys.

"I shouldn't wonder," said John excitedly, as he and Victoria reluctantly came down to earth because it was too dark to read each other's notes, "if we couldn't work out something to go in at Isobel's window and out at yours. Think how useful it would be if she was in bed with asthma and you were in the garden and wanted to tell her something."

Isobel was truly happy. She had never known, until the little sitting room had been made largely hers, how badly she needed a room to work in. To herself she called it The Studio, though she knew it would never officially be called that, since it was not to be wholly hers. But the shelves and the cupboard had been left empty for her use, and for the first time she was able to lay out her painting and drawing paraphernalia.

She stood her easel by the window, and put clay models of a hand and an ear on the mantelpiece. She arranged the art books she had been given at Christmas and on her birthdays in the bookshelf. A heavy portrait in oils of Elizabeth Fry's nanny, and a picture so much in need of cleaning it was impossible to state what the original subject had been, but which was known in the family as "The Nativity", had already been hung on the walls.

"I'll see if I can't get these put somewhere else," Isobel told Miss Herbert, who had looked in to see how she was getting on. "I'd rather have good reproductions than bad originals."

Part of Miss Herbert's success with parents was her belief that everything they owned was of value.

"We must see, dear," she said. "I'm sure you will only be allowed to move these pictures if some place worthwhile can be found to hang them."

Isobel looked from Elizabeth Fry's nanny to the mystery picture and smiled inwardly – poor Miss Herbert!

Louise and Dick were not ready for even a partly adult world, and the new house would have been more unkind to them than to the others were it not for two things which changed their future.

The first was announced by their father. "There'll be a puppy next holidays, Dick. A fox terrier. I hope you can fetch him when we come back from the holiday, so you can start to train him."

The other thing was dropped quite casually by their mother.

"Next holidays, Dick, if you are very careful at crossings, I think you and Louise might take walks alone. For, though Miss Herbert will probably still be here, she will have other things to do than to take you for walks.'

Alone in Louise's bedroom the two children gazed at each other, unable to believe what they had heard. Then Dick said:

"We could take the puppy with us."

"And go anywhere," Louise agreed. "I shouldn't wonder if we could take picnics."

"Explore."

"Follow people," Louise suggested, "like detectives."

Then, as the full glory came to them, they went mad, rushing round the room, pushing each other about, turning somersaults. At intervals one or the other would gasp:

"Out alone! No Miss Herbert!"

"A puppy! A fox terrier puppy!"

"Just us. Nobody, nobody else!"

The day Dick returned to school was the girls' first day at Laughton House, so only his father and mother were at the station to see him off. He travelled alone to London to Victoria station and there was met and taken to Waterloo to catch the train to his West Country school.

Dick was well-trained to show a stiff upper lip, and somehow had succeeded on his first two departures in leaving dry-eyed. But he looked so small and pathetic in his too-large overcoat and school cap that Isobel and Victoria, when they had seen him off, had to talk furiously about nothing at all or they would have cried. Louise was hopeless at seeing Dick off, for she had no belief in stiff upper lips, so she sobbed unrestrainedly until the train pulled out. It was therefore a relief both to his father and mother that this time the girls could not come to the station. Besides, their absence gave them something to talk about in the last horrible minutes before the train pulled out.

"What a lot the girls will have to tell you in their next letters," his father said. "I expect Louise will start writing to you tonight."

His mother spoke through a lump in her throat.

"I remembered to put a tin of those biscuits you like in your tuck box."

His father felt in his pocket for the half-crown he had put there.

"This will buy some fruit and sweets to add to your lunch."

His mother gratefully heard sounds which showed that the train was about to move.

"You've got your sandwiches, haven't you, darling?"

Dick could not speak, but he nodded and patted a pocket.

"Goodbye, darling."

"Goodbye, old man."

The train chugged away. Both parents were thankful when it turned round the bend and Dick's small, white, eight-year-old face was out of sight. To neither parent did it seem cruel to send little home-loving Dick away to boarding school while still a mere baby. There was always the British Empire to be thought of, which needed countless administrators, and indeed there was work all over the world for British gentlemen; if you wanted the right stamp of young men it was believed you must educate them right. If a country held a great place in the world, it was that country's duty to train men to uphold that position – and how else did you do that save by your system of education?

So, though his father could ill afford the fees and both parents were miserable to see him go, they were upheld by the knowledge that they were doing what was right for Dick.

Somehow, against the lump in her throat, the children's mother forced out:

"Come along, Jim, it's chilly. We'll have some coffee when we get home." It was her misfortune that she sounded not brave but heartless.

None of the girls could afterwards describe clearly their first day at Laughton House. Everything was so different from Elmhurst. But none of them ever forgot their first view of Miss French.

Miss French was as unlike Miss Dean as was possible. She had come to teaching by an easy route. Her father – an artist of some distinction – had lived in Italy and France and there his children were educated, speaking both languages like natives. He had died when Olivia French was seventeen, leaving very little money, so she had applied for and got a position teaching languages in London. She had lived in London with an elderly cousin who had become fond of the girl, so when years later she died it was found she had left Olivia her not inconsiderable fortune. This meant the fulfilment of three dreams for Olivia. She would own her own school, she could be exquisitely dressed and she could take holidays in comfort in her two loves – Italy and France.

Olivia French wanted a boarding school in a healthy spot, so she bought Laughton House. This came suddenly on the market, as a boarding school for girls. Probably she hoped to have the type of school to which the artistic would send their children – and indeed there were a few such children – for certainly great stress was laid on training in all the arts. Actually, the majority of the pupils were not artistic at all. A few were academically-minded, and somehow got to a university, but they were rarities. What was aimed at was a good French accent and an intelligent interest, if no more, in the arts.

Perhaps it was because the original pupils from Laughton House had recommended future pupils that Miss French seldom had girls of the type for which she longed, but she never gave up hope. Because of this, each new girl – even day girls who were considered below the salt in Laughton House – were objects of intense interest and thought.

Miss French had looked forward to meeting the Strangeway girls. Naturally she was drawn to Isobel, the artist – but Victoria was a challenge. After much thought and prayer the children's father had visited her on his own and had confided to her the whole of Victoria's story, including the history of the magazine.

Miss French had been not only interested in Victoria but had found herself immensely drawn to the children's father. She had run her school without help or advice, but that did not say she never needed either; it was, she thought, a privilege to know such a sincerely good man whom she felt would in time become a close friend.

It was not Miss French's custom to force her personality on her girls; she taught them in class and she saw them at meals, soon quite naturally an opportunity would crop up for a little talk. Meanwhile they could get used to her from a distance.

To the girls, used as they were to a huge girls' school, the new school was full of surprises. At Elmhurst they had started in the kindergarten and then moved into the junior school. From there, first Isobel and then Victoria had graduated into the middle school.

The middle school at Elmhurst was as far as many girls reached, for the senior school was made up of scholars. It was because Isobel and Victoria had in turn reached the bottom rung of the middle school, that there had been talk of "now you are growing up", and "having a sense of responsibility". It was from the middle school that prefects and games' captains were usually selected, for the senior school had little time away from their books.

But at Laughton House there was no kindergarten, and only recently had small girls of from nine to eleven been accepted to form a class called officially "The Little Ones" – and by the school "The Black Beetles". This was the form Louise was in, and very pleasant she found it for the school, being unused to younger children, treated them as babies.

Small faults were overlooked and a wonderful amount of time was allowed for play.

The change was far better for Isobel and Victoria, for they were in the classes which a short while before had been at the bottom of the school. They were now called forms two and three, for The Black Beetles were form one – but otherwise, their position at the bottom of the school was unchanged. They were treated as children from whom nothing in the way of leadership could be expected. When leaders were needed they were picked from the top forms.

It was, too, the first time the girls knew even in part what it was like to be a boarder. There was no more scuttling home for meals. No more dragging home satchels of homework. They left for home at six finished with work for the day.

Because the school was small – there were fewer than sixty girls – there was almost a homelike atmosphere which amazed the Strangeway children, used to mile-long wooden floored passages with classrooms opening off on either side, and to the constant clanging of bells. The classrooms at Laughton House opened off the main hall, which was carpeted and had flowers standing about. The school noticeboard hung here, but otherwise it looked like the hall in a private house.

At twelve, when there was a break before lunch, there was a choice of things to do. Officially everyone went for a walk, marching two and two in a crocodile. In actual fact, less than half the school went; those who had colds or other minor ailments could read or play quietly in a pleasantly-furnished little sitting room, in which in the winter there was a good coal fire. Others, who for various reasons would be late for the walk, could roller skate in a paved yard. Gardeners could always stay in to look after their gardens, for any pupil could have a garden of her own. In fact Miss French, always expecting reasonable behaviour, let it be understood that provided permission was asked the walk was for those who had nothing else that they felt they should be at.

All the school had milk and biscuits at mid-morning; that first morning Victoria drew Isobel into a corner.

"Have you seen Miss French yet?"

Isobel nodded.

"Have you?"

"In the distance. She takes our literature this afternoon. What's she like?"

Isobel searched for suitable words.

"She looks like a lady in a shop window. She is thin and tall and she wears pince-nez like Miss Herbert's, but the most gorgeous clothes. She's wearing grey. It's soft and all folds but it fits like a sofa cover."

"Did she speak to you?"

"Yes, and that makes you feel you ought to curtsey. She took our Scripture. She read a chapter of St Paul, she reads so that it sounds as if you were hearing it for the first time. She said: 'I suppose you know St Paul's letters, Isobel?' I felt an absolute fool for she was so different somehow from anyone we've ever met that I stammered awfully, but I did manage to say 'Yes'. She didn't seem to mind my stammering for she just smiled and opened the Bible."

"Are you going for a walk?"

"No. I'm never to go. Miss Grey – she's our form mistress – told me. She said I could go to the studio and paint if it was wet, or I could sketch in the garden when it was fine, or there's a sitting room."

Victoria had heard that.

"I've got to walk today, but all the girls in my form play knucklebones, and the girl next to me, whose name is Nancy, said the next wet day she'd teach me."

"What is knucklebones?" Isobel asked.

"I don't know exactly," Victoria confessed, "but it's played with five knuckle bones out of an animal. You start by having to catch all five on the back of your hand. But there are hundreds of things you do with them. The game is to see who does all the things fastest."

That first day there seemed no flaw in Laughton House. The girls on reaching home raced in calling out "Mummy, Mummy", as they ran. Their mother was in the drawing room.

"Well, how did you get on?"

It was as if they poured out a sackful of news at her feet. What they had learned. What they had eaten. What the girls were like. Only Miss French had not been described for their mother had met her.

"But you never said how tremendous she is," Victoria complained.

Although Miss French had been charming to the children's parents their mother had felt at a disadvantage. Painfully conscious of her hands which, however often she washed, were gardener's hands. And conscious too, which was unusual for her, of the shabbiness of her clothes. She knew that the children's father was completely blind to such things so she had let him describe Miss French lest there should be a hint of how she had reacted in what she said. Now she was glad she had kept silent, and grateful for Victoria's word "tremendous".

"I thought I'd let you find out for yourselves. She is – tremendous – isn't she?"

"I never knew anyone could look so elegant," said Isobel.

"The girls say she always looks like that."

Their father came in. Victoria noticed that he seemed tired.

"Well, how was it?"

Again the sackful of news was poured out. But when the girls spoke of Miss French, he seemed surprised.

"Tremendous," he said thoughtfully, turning over Victoria's word. "Is she?"

Victoria, much as she loved him, felt on this occasion her father was being dim.

"Of course she is, Daddy. Look at her clothes. Even *you* must have noticed them."

"Clothes!" He sounded surprised. "No, I don't

think I did. What I felt about her came from what she said. She seems to me such a sincerely good woman."

His daughters looked sadly at their father. Victoria turned to her sisters.

"I suppose if all you look for is goodness, it's all you see."

"Couldn't you see how different her clothes were from Mummy's?" Louise asked.

"No." Their father put an arm round their mother. "To me, nobody ever looks as nice as she does."

The girls exchanged glances. Of course Daddy loved Mummy, but not to see the difference between her clothes and Miss French's was going too far. Their mother answered for them.

"*Now* you children can see why I say it doesn't matter what I wear."

10 Miss French

Quite soon the new school began to seem less perfect than it had on the first day. Only a few weeks later the girls had a grumble as they walked home.

"Everything nice seems to happen after we've gone home," Victoria complained.

"Sometimes they dance," said Isobel.

"Not in my form," said Louise. "They just go to bed, but they have pillow fights. I wish I'd got someone to have a pillow fight with."

Isobel had a piece of news.

"Did you know we are doing a Greek play?"

Victoria caught Isobel's arm.

"A play! When? Have they chosen people to act in it yet?"

"Me," said Louise. "Miss French came into our form and she put her hand under my chin and looked at me and said to Miss Black: 'I think this little person will look splendid as the boy in our play, don't you?', and Miss Black said 'Yes' but she always says that, whatever Miss French says."

Victoria was outraged. She was the family actress, it was all wrong that she should be the last to know a play was being acted, and it was certainly all wrong that Louise should be given a part before she was.

"Do you think Miss French will ask which of us can act?"

Isobel knew the answer to that.

"It's a play they've done before. We do it in the garden, all the speaking parts are taken by the top form."

Louise skipped to catch up.

"Except me."

Isobel ignored the interruption.

"But everybody in the school is in it. We have our hair done by a hairdresser and wear Greek dresses."

"It sounds boring," said Victoria. But though she had barely spoken to Miss French, she had at that time almost a crush on her, so anything Miss French planned she was prepared to accept. "Did you know Miss French goes round and kisses every girl good night?"

"Well, Daddy and Mummy kiss us," Isobel pointed out.

Victoria kicked a stone into the gutter. She loved Isobel but why was she always so contented? Couldn't she see what fun the boarders had? That it would be easier to be one than to be sort of half in half out as they were, with home to worry about as well as school?

As if she could read her thoughts Isobel said:

"I do hope Cousin Alexander isn't there. It's awful pretending not to hear him shouting in the study, when he's making the doors shake.'

Louise giggled.

"What would Miss French say if she heard him?"

The other two laughed, for one of Miss French's strictest rules was that no pupil of hers must ever on any occasion raise her voice. One of the greatest crimes that could be committed at Laughton House was to scream while playing a game. Cousin Alexander (sickening for Dick's tortoise to have the same name, Louise had said) would indeed have come off badly had Miss French had anything to do with him.

Cousin Alexander was a churchwarden and a distant cousin, and exceptionally low church. Every smallest change made by the children's father he regarded with suspicion, and when suspicion was borne out by fact he rushed round to the vicarage and stormed into the study. He gained nothing, for the children's father, where what he believed in was concerned, was a rock against which all could hurl themselves in vain. But Cousin Alexander was exhausting, so too often lately there had been a feeling of strain when the girls got home from school.

Cousin Alexander was not there that night, so both their father and their mother came into the hall to greet them. But, although they seemed outwardly full of interest, both Isobel and Victoria noticed they looked tired.

The truth was that a great deal about the new parish was not easy. The last vicar had been ill a lot, so many people had got into the habit of running things their own way and intended to go on doing so.

Eastbourne was a very different parish from St Leonard's-on-Sea. It was well-to-do, and the vicar of the parish church was a leading figure in the town, so everybody of the calling class left cards. But the town was scattered, the residential areas split by a golf course and a stretch of downland. The majority of those who left cards were what the children's father jokingly called "carriage folk", which was an expression used when he was a boy. Some indeed of the more modern townspeople had motor cars.

The children's mother looked dismally at the silver bowl full of calling cards. How ever was she to get around to return all these calls? The buses seemed never to go in the right direction. It was maddening that she had to go out paying calls now, when there was so much that wanted doing in the garden, but she kept her worries to herself. The suspected trouble at the induction service had not happened, but too well she could see that almost every hour of the day there was some nagging worry waiting for the vicar.

"The trouble," he told her, "is that there is too little love; this whole parish wants loving and playing with."

That was the kind of statement which the children's mother found hard to take. But she knew her husband and what he could do.

"You'll win them in the end, darling, you know that."

Her father told Victoria part of his problem. He ran into her at the bottom of the stairs one evening when she was on her way up to bed.

"There is a rather depressing Mothers' Union

157

group here, I mean they never seem to have an outing or any fun. But they do have a tea party next month. Do you think you could arrange a little entertainment, Vicky?"

Victoria looked at him with a we-understand-each-other expression.

"You know how Isobel and Louise are, except of course Louise could play the piano. I suppose Isobel and I could do a duologue. What a pity John isn't here. It would be better to start with something good."

Her father smiled at that.

"They won't have very high standards – next Christmas will be the time for flying high."

Victoria knew he was feeling sad in a way he had never done in the old parish; she laid a hand on his sleeve.

"We'll do something terrific." Then a colossal idea came to her. "We could use masses of the parish children."

She was rewarded for at once father lost his sad look.

"Now that would be something. We'll do it on Boxing Night. Can't you see all the parents streaming in to watch their children?"

"Isobel can design all the clothes and we'll write the play between us."

Her father kissed her.

"Dear Vicky, you are a great comfort to me."

Victoria saw herself again sitting by Grandmother's bed, and heard her say: "You could help him in lots of little ways."

"Truly? Am I truly a comfort to you?"

He made a face at her.

"Sometimes. But you're like the little girl who had the curl right down the middle of her forehead. When she was good she was very, very good, but when she was bad she was horrid."

Isobel was cheering her mother up.

"Isn't there anybody you've met who could draw a map or something to show where all these roads are? You could get through masses of calls, if you found which people live near each other."

Her mother, disgusted, turned over the cards.

"It's such a waste of time when there's so much to do in the garden, and they're such grand people and I haven't the right clothes."

Isobel picked up the bowl to put it back on the hall table.

"If I were you I'd get them finished with. They will only haunt you if you don't."

That night Victoria went to sleep with a singing heart. She was improving, there was no doubt about it, she was stepping away from childhood just as Grandmother had said she should. She was being a comfort to Daddy. He had said so.

Her happiness was short-lived. She was disturbed at three in the morning by Isobel calling breathily from the next room.

"I've got an attack, Vicky. It's bad, I can hardly breathe. Get Mummy."

One knock on her bedroom door and the children's mother had on her dressing gown and slippers.

"Is it Isobel, Vicky?"

"Yes."

Her mother turned back to the bedroom and called out:

"Go to sleep, darling. Isobel has asthma, I'll see to her."

In a sickroom the children's mother could be superb. Quiet, confident, knowing just what to do. In no time the blotting paper soaked in crystals was burning, Isobel had swallowed her medicine, she was propped up so that she could breathe more easily, and she was relaxed because her mother was there.

"I'm afraid," said her mother, pulling back the curtain, "you forgot to shut your window, and it's raining. Damp blowing in is enough to give anyone asthma."

Now that there was no schoolroom the family breakfasted together. The children's mother, who was not strong, was feeling tired after her disturbed night with Isobel. Victoria, perhaps because she had been disturbed in the night, came down with what is known as having a black dog on your shoulder. The weather was frightful, rain lashing against the window. At once Miss Herbert started to fuss.

"As Isobel can't go to school today, and it's too wet for the other two to walk, I think I should be happier if I took the girls. They have never yet been on the motor-bus."

Victoria, feeling black dog-ish, took that as an insult.

"Thank you very much, Louise and I are quite capable of going on the bus by ourselves."

"Vicky," said her father sternly, "that is not a nice way to talk."

"No, indeed," her mother added. "You can't imagine Miss Herbert is suggesting going out in this weather for pleasure."

Victoria did not want to be scolded, she wanted to be loved and to hear her father say that she was a comfort to him, but it was as if she was on a slippery slope and could not stop.

"Fuss, fuss, fuss! One minute you say I ought to have a sense of responsibility and the next I can't even take Louise on a bus."

"Perhaps," said her mother coldly, "we'll feel more like trusting you when we see some sign that you have a sense of responsibility." She turned to Miss Herbert, "Thank you very much, Miss Herbert, and perhaps you would go into Laughton House to see the girls change their stockings."

That stirred even Louise.

"Oh Mummy! We aren't babies. We can change our own stockings."

"Imagine what fools we'll look with Miss Herbert having to watch us." Victoria turned to her father: "Please, Daddy, if we promise to change our stockings, need Miss Herbert come further than the bus stop?"

The children's father seldom interfered in his fam-

161

ily's day-to-day arrangements, thinking that their mother's business, but now something in Victoria's agonised look touched him.

"I think, Sylvia, for Miss Herbert's sake, it will be enough if she sees them on to the bus. I think we can trust the children to get off it safely."

But even having won that concession did not take the black dog off Victoria's shoulder. In those days, if there were rubber boots, the children had never worn them; instead they wore goloshes over their shoes, which were tiresome to pull on, and wretched to get off, when they were wet and muddy. Mackintoshes were bought to last, so they came halfway down the girls' legs, and the sleeves had to be turned back like cuffs. Also, since mackintoshes had no hoods, the girls had to carry umbrellas – objects Victoria detested. So one way and another she was in a bad mood when she entered her classroom for the first lesson.

On Miss French's instructions, if possible nothing was to be said or done to put Victoria's back up.

"I imagine she was difficult at her last school," Miss French had told Miss Brown, Victoria's form mistress, "but I also think she was stupidly handled. So pass the word round that unless it is something serious I want her to be left alone until she loses her 'agin authority' feeling."

So far Miss Brown had found nothing to complain of and neither had the other mistresses. Victoria, enjoying the new school, was alert and behaved well. But that morning, even as she marked the attendance book, Miss Brown could sense that Victoria wanted trouble. "And that, my lady, you shall not have a chance to make," she thought.

Then she turned to the class to discuss what she supposed to be a non-controversial subject.

"As it is wet Miss French wondered if some of you would like to sort out the properties for the Greek play."

That was just the opening Victoria wanted.

"I would have thought before people were chosen to act in the play someone would see if any of the new girls could act."

There was a gasp from the class. The play was Miss French's from start to finish. She produced it every four or five years, chose the cast and, though this would be the third time she had put it on, never once had she even asked her staff for their opinion; she was the high priestess and ruled alone.

Miss French was so strong a personality that her staff was made up of women who preferred to be organised. Each form had a mistress, who taught not only her own form but in her particular subject, the whole school.

A large proportion of the teachers came from outside, usually from London, two or three times a week. Miss French made no secret of the fact that she found the company of the outside teachers more congenial than that of her staff, talking to the language specialists in her beautiful French or Italian or discussing science with the scientists. Though the expression was not used at that date, her teachers –

and still more their young assistants – were apt to have "inferiority complexes". Now, looking rather like the White Rabbit in *Alice in Wonderland*, Miss Brown gazed in nervous wonder at Victoria.

"The actresses are all sixth formers, dear."

Ordinarily that would have been sufficient answer for Victoria, but today her black dog drove her on.

"I call that silly. People who act in plays should be chosen because they can act, and not because of which form they are in."

Miss Brown could see that if not checked Victoria would argue all the morning.

"What you may think is neither here nor there, Victoria. Now, girls, hands up those who would like to help sort the properties."

Every hand except Victoria's was raised.

"Thank you," said Miss Brown. "Many hands will make light work. Now, if you will open your history books, we will get on with our lesson."

Victoria had cut off her nose to spite her face. It was no fun when morning lessons were over having to watch her whole class follow Miss Brown to the basement, leaving her alone in the hall. There was no one to teach her to play knucklebones, no one even to talk to. Then, while she was wondering what to do, Louise came down the stairs with her fellow Black Beetles. She looked in surprise at Victoria who had so far been popular with her class, so was never on her own.

"Where's your form, Vicky?"

Victoria scowled.

"What's that got to do with you? Go and play with the other babies."

Louise sang to the tune of *Nuts in May*:

"Vicky's been sent to Coventry. Vicky's been sent to Coventry."

All the frustrations of the day fused together and came out in blind anger. Once, Victoria in a temper had banged Louise's head on the nursery floor, and Louise had never forgotten it. She saw now the look in Victoria's eyes and ran from it up the stairs, along a passage, down another flight of stairs – anywhere to escape. The rest of Louise's class tried to bar Victoria's way; they failed, but it gave Louise a start. Light of foot, she shot down the small flight of stairs, at the bottom of which was Miss French's study, ran into the day-girls' cloakroom, banged the door and locked it. Victoria, guessing what Louise planned to do, tried to catch her by jumping the last few steps; instead she caught her foot and fell, spraining her ankle. The pain was excruciating.

Victoria let out a howl. Miss French opened her door. Since the beginning of term she had been looking for an occasion to make friends with Victoria. But now she thought of nothing but the noise Victoria was making. In a voice that seemed to have ice in it she said:

"What is the meaning of this noise, Victoria?"

Victoria was swinging to and fro holding her ankle.

"It's my ankle. I think I've sprained it."

Miss French's voice was more icy than ever.

"That may be. But a sprained ankle scarcely seems an excuse for raising your voice."

Victoria never forgot those words. Years later in London, during the Second World War, she was in a house which the third of a stick of bombs was clearly likely to hit. Actually it just missed, but caused a lot of damage. When the dust, rubble and broken glass had settled Victoria heard herself say quietly: "You may nearly have been killed by a bomb, Victoria, but that scarcely seems an excuse for raising your voice."

But that morning had other effects than teaching Victoria not to scream. When, bandaged, she hobbled down to lunch and sat between two of her classmates, she said:

"Well, I've spoken to Miss French at last – and I hate her."

166

11 Settling Down

The first meeting on their own between Miss French and Victoria was, of course, a disaster. Miss French knew this the moment it happened, and, much as she disliked a raised voice, because it was a sign of lack of control, on that one occasion she wished she had not scolded – or at least not so sharply. There is nothing that is so shattered as a fallen idol, and for Victoria Miss French was just that, for to her it seemed cruel to talk to someone with a sprained ankle in the way that she had.

"It was worse than the Pharisees passing by on the other side," she told Isobel later. "It was like kicking the injured."

It was true that, the reproof over, Miss French had knelt down to examine the ankle, and had then said in a voice which Victoria grudgingly admitted she supposed was meant to be kind: "You have indeed sprained it. I will send for Matron, she will strap it for you."

But even if Miss French had looked after the ankle herself, it was too late for her to climb again to the pedestal on which Victoria had placed her. She was off that for good, and Victoria, scowling as she waited for Matron, was back at her favourite mutter: "She's mean. She's mean."

From that time onwards Victoria ceased to try to get on at school. If they were mean to her, she told herself, she would be mean to them. It was not that she was noticeably tiresome – she was not at that time in a position to lead the other girls, and it was a bore making a nuisance of yourself alone – but she made no effort to learn. Class after class she sat through, outwardly conforming, but actually trying to take in as little as possible.

"It's a stupid school," she wrote to John, "so I am not bothering with it. In class I pretend I am somewhere else."

John was a scholar so he loved learning, he gloried every time he felt he was really getting a grip on a subject. But, like many of his sex at that date, he did not think it mattered if girls were educated, and anyway, from what he could hear, all girls' schools were crazy, so he wrote back:

"As you have promised Uncle Jim you will write a play for the parish children, if you have nothing better to do during a class you might work on that. It will have to be one of those 'enter a crowd of elves' affairs if you are to use all the children who will want to take part."

So Victoria dreamed up a play and when she could manage it without being noticed she wrote a page or two of dialogue.

In the vicarage things were improving. Somehow the children's mother had got through her calls, helped on a few afternoons by lifts in other people's carriages. Cousin Alexander, after a last blazing row, had retired as church-warden and the local chemist, a gentle man who had taken an instant liking to his new vicar, took his place. But there were still undercurrents in the parish, a kind of grudging unwillingness to believe that anything the children's father did could be right.

Isobel came up against this outlook; it was the Saturday of the Mothers' Union tea for which Victoria had promised an entertainment. A helper who was cutting up bread and butter said in an unkind voice:

"So we are to have a treat today. I understand it will be something quite new in amateur entertainment."

Isobel flushed and stammered.

"Vicky can act and Louise plays the piano well for somebody of ten, but I'm no earthly good at acting so I'm afraid we won't shine."

"That is hardly the impression your father has given us."

Isobel kept that conversation to herself, for she was subconsciously aware that such pin-pricks were her parents' general lot. But actually that first effort to entertain did help. The Mothers' Union members, unaccustomed to being amused in any way, were delighted and grateful, apart from being interested to meet the new vicar's family. And a cautious but friendly-toned report filtered round the parish.

"Nice young ladies. That Vicky is a card. Little Louise played the piano ever so nice. Their mother

169

was pleasant, talking to everybody. Having a real job getting that garden straight, poor thing."

Taking the children to the Mothers' Union entertainment was the first chance the children's mother had to get to know the poorer parishioners, and the poor parishioners were the ones whom she understood the best. She had learnt this when her husband was given his first parish – a country village. At that time Isobel and Victoria were toddlers, Louise a baby, and Dick was expected. In those days there was so little money every penny had to be counted but, believing it the vicar's wife's duty, she had made some broth for a woman recovering from pneumonia and left it at her cottage. When the woman was on her feet again she came round to the vicarage carrying a basket of vegetables.

"Don't you try to give things to the likes of us," she said, thrusting the basket into the children's mother's arms. "You've got all you can do to fill the bellies of your own."

The children's mother, who was not at that time twenty-one, had been brought up to know herself to be a gentlewoman and, therefore, set apart from the poor. Because of this the woman's remark and the gift of the vegetables was a shock. For in those days the hymn which stated: "The rich man in his castle, The poor man at his gate, God made them, high or lowly, And order'd their estate" was believed by almost everybody. The children's mother might not belong to a castle, but she had believed, however poor they were, that they did not qualify for "The poor man at his gate". But after the gift of the vegetables she was no longer so sure. If not quite at the gate, they were pretty near it.

That they were not only poor but were accepted as such by the parishioners was something which, in the few years they remained in that country parish, the children's mother had come to accept, and this altered her outlook. She was as fond – or even fonder – of the poor neighbours than ever, but now almost as an equal for she never again offered to give them anything, in fact, she became a receiver of gifts, especially of advice.

Probably the parishioners felt motherly about their vicar's young wife, thinking her rather helpless, with a husband, bless him, who must make life difficult when you were hard up, for he would give away the coat off his back.

The whole family would have eaten better if the children's mother had treasured half the advice handed to her, but she was never a good caterer. "With all the mouths you have to feed," a farm worker's wife told her, "you want to do what I do. Every Sunday I give mine a chicken which, with my man and six growing boys, would not go far, surely. But I cook a gurt big suet roll and serves it with a right big jug of gravy. Then I says there's not a bite of chicken for the one of you till that roll's eaten. The chicken goes round fine after they be stuffed with suet roll."

Another woman, finding the children's mother buying a packet of jelly, said:

"You don't want to buy that stuff, you want to make your own, something their teeth have to work on. Do you know, ma'am, my jellies sit so firm and so sweet you can throw one against a wall and it won't break, but will bounce right back at you."

In that parish she also learned that even had she wished to give, only certain forms of giving were permitted; certain lesser gifts might be considered an insult. A not-much-liked vicar of a nearby parish had given, after his Sunday School treat, each child a bun. That evening a half-eaten bun with a note had been delivered to him. The note said: "Buns is common food. Mrs Brown says if she wants them for her children she can get them for herself respectfully Mrs Brown."

By the time the children's father was appointed to a town parish the children's mother, educated by her country friends, had a clear view of herself and her family. They were poor, but poor in their own way. She would visit and make friends with her neighbours, but she would not give them anything, except perhaps a little at Christmas, because she had nothing to give. That parish at St Leonard's-on-Sea was full of desperately poor people, for many were out of work and, in those days, there was no unemployment pay. But also in those days there were many anxious to help.

Remembering the offence given by the bun the children's mother, first establishing it would be acceptable, started what was called a soup kitchen, which was open three days a week all through the winter. The butchers gave bones and meat, the greengrocers vegetables, the grocers such things as barley, and the bakers stale bread. The children's mother collected a group of workers and together they made the soup, boiling it for hours in a copper. Then at twelve every other morning the doors would be opened and women and children would pour in, everyone carrying jugs, basins and mugs. A full jug and enough bread for the whole family's dinner cost a few pence, but always the children's mother was watching, and frequently she would whisper "Extra bread, and only take a penny", or sometimes "No charge".

But Eastbourne seemed to have no poor, at least not poor as the children's mother meant poor – not soup kitchen poor. The truth was, the town was full of boarding schools, all of which needed servants. The schools shopped locally so the tradesmen prospered and they too needed workers. In the summer it was a popular holiday resort, so the hotels were always full and required staff. Many of the schools were let for the summer and the guests not only needed waiting on but again the shops prospered.

The public gardens were magnificently laid out, which took a small army of gardeners. The roads were beautifully kept and washed, which meant employment. In fact nobody who had their health and strength, and was prepared to take what work was going, needed to be unemployed in Eastbourne.

So much was this so that until the Mothers' Union party the children's mother had seen the new parish as a well-kept lawn. It was hard to know where to burrow to look for weeds. It had not been the intention of those who ran the meeting that she should have burrowed; they had intended she should appear as an honoured guest and then depart, but they reckoned without their vicar's wife. In no time she was talking gardening and, unashamed of a hard-luck story, was admitting how much space she had and how few plants to fill it. Soon the offers were pouring in.

"You come up and see me, dear, I've some lovely seedlings you can have."

Or:

"You wait till the autumn, my husband can give you some cuttings."

In other ways the vicarage was shaking down. The cook and the house-parlourmaid, who had worked for them in the last parish, had not come with them to Eastbourne, as they were local women and did not want to move far from their homes. They had started at Eastbourne vicarage with an enormously stout cook called Mona, who seemed a perfect choice, for she was always laughing. The house-parlourmaid, who preferred to be called Hodges, would have been a jewel anywhere else but she was out of place in the vicarage, for she was used to first-class service and was worthy of it, having been highly trained in every branch of her work.

"Oh, why did she come to *us*?" the children's mother would moan. "And why did I take her? She terrifies me."

174

But the children's father rather liked Hodges for she understood valeting a gentleman. All the same, he hated to see his wife upset.

"If you don't like her give her notice."

"But what for? She doesn't do anything wrong. The only thing I could possibly say is, she won't come to morning prayers."

From the beginning Hodges had made a stand on this.

"I do not attend prayers, madam," she had stated the morning after she arrived, and when asked why, she had said: "I don't hold with attending."

"If you don't like her you must get rid of her," the children's father advised. "No good having somebody, however good, who makes you unhappy."

Then something happened which changed the whole situation. Every day at seven o'clock Hodges came to call the children's parents with a tray of tea and thin bread and butter. Having placed the tea tray on a table by the bed, she drew the curtains before going out to fetch in the two copper jugs of hot water for washing and shaving. On this morning, as she drew the curtains, she remarked quietly: "Cook is ill, madam."

"Oh dear!" said the children's mother sleepily. "What's the matter with her?"

Hodges drew back the other curtain.

"I should say she was in advanced labour, madam."

In no time, the doctor was sent for, and the children who, at that date, were not supposed to know anything about babies, were hurried through breakfast and off to school. When they returned that evening Mona was gone.

"What do you suppose Mona did?" Isobel asked Victoria.

It had been understood without being put into words, that their mother did not want Mona talked about.

"Why shouldn't Mona leave?" she had asked in a shutting-out voice when the girls expressed surprise that Miss Herbert was cooking the supper.

Isobel and Victoria had exchanged looks which meant, "Wait until bedtime".

Now, as they undressed, Victoria came to Isobel's door.

"I think it's a deep, dark mystery – because I know something."

"What?"

"Doctor Gay came."

"How do you know?"

Victoria came into Isobel's room and swung on the end of her bed.

"You know Alice Gay's in my form. Well, she told me. She said: 'Daddy tore up to the vicarage before breakfast'."

Isobel was amazed.

"But if Mona was ill, why wouldn't Mummy tell us?"

Victoria gazed at Isobel, her eyes glittered with excitement.

"I think Alice knew something; she didn't tell me, she asked in a funny voice if anything was wrong."

Isobel and Victoria, if they knew nothing for sure, knew there were things they did not know – things to do with wombs, as mentioned in the Bible.

"Oh!" said Isobel. "Something like that. Then we shan't be told, at least not yet."

And though both girls probed for the truth they at last forgot about Mona, so it was not until they were grown up that they heard what Hodges had said that morning.

Mona's departure meant that Annie arrived in the house. Annie came from an orphanage. She was a skinny, tough, black-haired little creature of immense strength, who had been well trained as a plain cook. Never having known a home of her own, her ambition was to acquire one, and the moment she stepped into the vicarage she knew she had found it.

"This will just do me nicely," she said to Hodges.

Hodges looked at Annie with disgust. Mona may have slipped up and had a baby, but she did know what was what. But this chit from an orphanage she could never work with. The very next morning immediately after breakfast she gave her notice.

"I do not think Annie and I will get on, so if she is staying I wish to leave, madam."

The children's mother tried to sound dismayed.

"Oh dear! But I am afraid Annie is staying. I think she will suit splendidly."

"Very good, madam," said Hodges, correct to the end, "I will leave when you are suited."

Nothing like Hodges replaced her; instead, a simple creature willing though not well-trained, but a strong churchwoman, arrived. Her name was Hester. It was understood her husband had died, for she had two children who lived with their grandmother. Over a first cup of tea she said to Annie very much what Annie herself had said.

"I like this place. I think I could settle."

Annie, telling the story later, said:

"I gave my tea a stir and then I said: 'There's only one fly in the ointment, and that's that Miss Herbert; neither drawing-room *nor* kitchen, if you get me'."

It was not long after Annie and Hester had settled in that Annie made the remark which made her "family". The children's mother had gone to the kitchen to order the day's food and discuss plans.

"It will soon be August and we always go away then. This year we are going near Canterbury so that I can see something of my father. We've taken a house. It would be convenient if you and Hester came too."

Annie raised herself to the full height of her five-foot-two.

"Convenient! That's a funny way to talk. I can't see you managing on your own. Of course we're coming."

12 Summer Holiday

St Margaret's Bay remained for always a mountain-top of a holiday; one by which all others could be measured. Afterwards the family all knew what was meant by "Nearly as good as St Margaret's Bay".

Every year in the spring the children's father would look up from a letter and announce as if it was an award he had won: "This year we are going to . . ." and then would follow the name of some minute village in Wales, Devonshire, Essex, Derbyshire or wherever he had rented a cheap house for the month of August. Later, snippets of information would come out in letters to the boys, and by word of mouth to the girls. First, the historical background of the place to be visited and later, bits culled from tourist guides. "The part of Essex where we are staying is called 'Poppy-land'." "In North Wales on Sunday nights choirs sing hymns on the beach." "In Derbyshire they eat cheese with cake."

To the children's father, whose day started at seven, except on Sundays, Saints' days and special occasions, when he was never up later than six; who seldom got to bed before two in the morning; who never sat down between these hours except in church, at a meeting or for hurried meals; who went everywhere on foot so that anyone could waylay him; that distant holiday must have looked an oasis indeed. But his family, though they had enjoyed the holiday when they were small, were now outgrowing it. They never said so in so many words, but there were occasional slips. After the holiday spent in an exceptionally dreary house on a bleak spot on the Essex coast Dick was heard to say:

"Isn't it glorious to be home after that awful Poppy-land!"

And after the Derbyshire holiday Isobel, swallowing some new medicine, remarked:

"It's nearly as nasty as Derbyshire."

All such slips were either laughed off or crushed as heresy by the children's mother, who saw all too clearly the gap widening between the children's father's dream family, built on his boyhood home, and his real family. No doubt family holidays when he was a boy might have been fun, for there was less shortage of money. But no one could blame his children if they got quarrelsome and bored in the let's-get-away-from-it-all houses far from anywhere which were all they could afford. For, contrary to belief, Augusts in those days were just as wet as they usually are today.

During the Derbyshire August it rained every day, and the only dry spot was a waterfall the family had tramped miles to see. The cheap houses were totally unfitted for amusements indoors for a growing family, for they seldom had any books – and never any games. Yet somehow, however depressing the holiday, the children's mother helped to keep the myth going that a jolly holiday was being enjoyed by all, for otherwise it would be only too easy for her husband to say: "I don't think I need a holiday this year."

There were many reasons why St Margaret's Bay was a landmark holiday. First, the weather was kind, it was an exceptionally hot, dry summer. This made bathing, always the high spot of their father's holiday, able to be enjoyed by his children, which in wet summers it never was.

"I can just see my father and Uncle Jim and all the other uncles swimming halfway to France," John had told Victoria as, with blue faces and chattering teeth after a bathe, they ate buns on an icy beach. "I think summer must have been warmer then."

It was the North Wales year. Victoria looked at her father, also blue of face, coming out from behind the rock he had used as a dressing-room.

"I bet you it wasn't, Daddy thinks it more fun when it's cold and rough."

And it was true for at that moment her father, blowing on his fingers which were white where the circulation had stopped, said:

"I think that's the best bathe we've had. Wouldn't it be fun, if it doesn't rain, if we came down again this afternoon, for the tide will be in, and the waves should be much bigger."

"Have a bun, darling," the children's mother said. "I think one bathe is enough, and if it keeps fine I thought we'd go blackberrying."

But at St Margaret's Bay bathing was a real joy,

so no one needed to pretend, and no excuses had to be found why there should not be a second bathe.

Another reason for the success of the holiday was that St Margaret's Bay catered for visitors. In those days it was a quiet little village, highly suitable for the family parties of what were then called gentle people who stayed there. But to encourage young visitors, various amusements were planned for them. A tennis tournament. A dog show. A decorated bicycle competition and a sports day. The children's father, when he first heard of these goings-on, had said to the children's mother hopefully:

"I don't think the children will want to get mixed up in any of that, will they?"

But his wife was ready for that question.

"Of course they will, Jim. You know what fun you say you always had at tennis tournaments."

"But that was just amongst ourselves and a few friends."

The children's mother thought of those eight sons and tried not to give an impatient sigh. But it was an opportunity too good to be missed to sow a seed which needed sowing.

"It's good for the girls to meet boys. You only had two sisters, so of course amongst yourselves and your friends they always had partners. But Isobel will soon be needing partners, and she meets no boys at all."

"Your father," she told the girls years later, "laughed out loud at that. Then he looked at you, Isobel, and, though you were almost fourteen, you were still a child – and a very pretty one. 'I can't see my Isobel growing up to be a wallflower,' he said."

The children's mother was quite right when she said the children would want to enter for anything that was going on. Not that any of them, except Dick who was a sprinter, were much good at sport – but it was the done thing if you stayed at St Margaret's Bay to enter for everything, so even John entered for the tennis tournament, though he drew the line at the sports. But as it happened, Victoria became a sports enthusiast, and this led to one of the few reproofs she earned on that holiday.

Victoria and John were walking round the village when in the window of the chemist's shop they saw a prize for the sports displayed. Victoria clutched at John's arm.

"Oh look! Isn't that the most glamorous prize!"

The prize was a small dressing-case, fitted with what looked at a quick glance like a gold dressing-table set: a brush, a comb, a clothes' brush and two pots with apparently gold lids. John saw at once that the case was of no value; it was probably a novelty displayed at Christmas which had not sold. But he kept his thoughts to himself; poor old Vicky with her cast-off clothes never owned anything nice – it was no wonder she had fallen for the trashy little case.

"You could win that. Look, it says: 'Potato race. Girls under thirteen'."

Victoria clasped her hands.

"If only I could! I should be the proudest person

in the world. I never knew anyone who had a fitted dressing-case. I've always wished and wished my birthday was August, but now I'm glad it's December or I wouldn't be under thirteen."

From then on until the day of the race Victoria practised, using pebbles from the beach instead of potatoes.

Victoria's race came halfway through the afternoon and all the family, together with the local vicar and his wife, were there to watch her. For the sports afternoon she was wearing a last year's brown holland frock, once Isobel's, which was getting too tight and too short. She had bare legs and gym shoes. Naturally, as she raced to and fro with her potatoes, she had to stoop and this showed not only the backs of her knees but her bloomers. So much so that her father's mind was taken off the race, and he was caught unawares when the local vicar's wife said to him:

"She runs like a hare, that child. No wonder she's won."

At that moment Victoria, flushed with triumph, came racing up. Her father had meant to say "Well done, Vicky," but she spoke before he had a chance.

"Got it, John."

As other people were there the children's father made no comment either to Vicky or about her at the time. But later he said to the children's mother:

"Don't you think, darling, Victoria is too big to run about with bare legs?"

The children's mother was determined not to spoil the holiday by a major row with Victoria.

"She's only twelve. Perhaps next year I'll make a change."

On the way home her father spoke to Victoria.

"Vicky, I didn't say anything at the time but sporting people don't run to win prizes, they run for the fun of the thing."

"Not me," said Victoria. "I ran for my dressing-case."

"But the race would have been fun in itself even if you had not won."

Victoria thought about that.

"I doubt it, Daddy. It was hard work. It was only the dressing-case that kept me trying hard."

"I don't know what to make of Vicky sometimes," the children's father told their mother that evening. "I cannot remember that I needed to be told that it was the joy of something attempted that was the prize – not the prize itself – but Vicky refuses to see the point."

The children's mother was determined not to reopen the stocking question, or indeed to discuss Victoria.

"I wouldn't take what she says too seriously. She did want that dressing-case. She's talked of nothing else since she saw it. I'm sure she would take real sports seriously, but you can't call running for potatoes real sport, can you?"

John went with Victoria to claim her prize. The chemist was surprised at her rapturous gratitude.

"It's not much," he said awkwardly. "But I'm glad you're pleased, miss."

Victoria let out a blissful sigh.

"Oh, I am!" She stroked the brassy back of the hairbrush. "I never had anything gold before."

The chemist cleared his throat then, over Victoria's bent head, he caught John's eyes, which said as clearly as eyes could: "Leave it alone. Don't say it. What harm can it do?" So the cleared throat, which had been intended as the beginning of a statement as to the value of the case, changed into:

"Can I wrap it for you, miss?"

Victoria looked surprised.

"Of course not. I want everybody to see me carrying it home."

On the road back to the house John said:

"I bet whatever other prizes you win, Vicky – and I dare say there'll be a lot – nothing will be so good as that case."

Victoria was puzzled.

"What do you mean – lots? I don't suppose I'll ever win another. I don't know anywhere else that has potato races."

"You are a juggins. It's not only for potato races you win prizes. There are all sorts. I mean, we can win medals and things all our lives."

"Not me," said Victoria. "I won't do the sort of thing that wins medals – but I expect you will."

John looked at her with an odd expression on his face. He never thought of girls as having careers, for girls like his cousins didn't; they helped at home until they married – except of course Isobel, who might sell some of her pictures. But while Victoria was answering him he wondered if she was right. He could not imagine what she might do with her life, but somehow neither could he see her helping at home until the right man turned up. He let the subject drop and instead questioned Victoria about the Greek play at her school, about which he had heard nothing except that she had written it was boring. But his impression that Victoria might draw something exciting out of life's bran tub was not to leave him.

From the children's mother's point of view, the especial charm of St Margaret's Bay was that it was sufficiently near Canterbury for her to visit there, and for her father to come to St Margaret's Bay. She had been one of a family of four girls and one boy, but the boy had died while he was still a young man. When she was five years old her mother had died and soon after her father had married again.

His new wife, a highly-connected but to her step-children a rather cold and alarming Scot, though she had never taken to her stepchildren, had done her best by them. As a result, when they were small they were brought up largely by a German governess. From what Isobel and Victoria, when they had stayed at Canterbury, could pick up, the governess had been what is known as a treasure.

"Though I can't think anybody can be quite a treasure who teaches people to be sorry for themselves," Victoria often said. "Of course it must be

187

awful to have no mother, but they seemed to have lots of money and they did go to a boarding school."

Isobel always tried to be just.

"There was that awful Christmas when they drew lots who should go and ask if there were any Christmas presents, and Mummy drew the short piece of paper, and when she got down her stepmother said: "Oh yes, it's Christmas Day, isn't it? Look in that cupboard, there are two work-baskets and two books – divide them between you girls."

"Daddy said that was because Scottish people don't keep Christmas."

Isobel nodded.

"I know. And she was good about other things for when they all married their stepmother did see they had twelve of everything, which we'll never get when we get married."

"You bet we won't," Victoria agreed, "and though Mummy says they were dreadfully plain and neat their clothes were always of the best quality. I wouldn't mind being able to say that just once."

Isobel still struggled to be just.

"But sometimes she did dreadful things. Remember Mummy going to school with Aunt Penelope's last-term everyday hat as her Sunday best?"

"That must have been awful," Victoria agreed. "But none of the things Mummy tells us would make me feel sorry for myself for ever and ever, which Mummy and the aunts are."

"But wouldn't you hate to be brought up by Canterbury Grandmother? I would."

Victoria shuddered and hunted for a suitable, forbidding simile.

"It would be like being brought up by a graven image."

There had been no visits to Canterbury for some time for, though Canterbury Grandmother was not exactly ill, she was, the children were told, not very strong.

"Though she looks as strong as one of those horses which pulls beer," Victoria said when she first heard the news.

In a way the children missed Canterbury, for Grandfather was an enthralling guide to the cathedral, especially to the last minutes of Thomas à Becket's life. All four children in turn had been enthralled when Grandfather said dramatically: "And his body lay here dead, while the fleas ran out of his hair shirt."

Almost equally enthralling was Grandfather's description of a conversation between the devil and the east wind. "Wait for me here, the devil said," Grandfather would state, pointing to a corner of the cathedral. "I'm just going inside for a few minutes. So the east wind waited and waited" – and here Grandfather would pause – "and is still waiting, for the devil never came out."

But except for dramatic visits to the cathedral the children had never known Canterbury Grandfather well, for on a visit he was usually going out with or talking to their mother. So it was that during the St Margaret's Bay August they got to know him in a new way, and a very inspiring companion they found him. John, who had not met him before, was captivated by him.

"I can't think why you've never told me about him," he said to Victoria. "He's a brainy old bird."

Actually, Canterbury Grandfather's gifts were varied. He could recite how the Jumblies went to sea in a sieve delightedly, with lightning illustrations done with coloured pencils – green for their heads and blue for their hands. But he could also talk of history so vividly he could bring the past to life.

He was, too, surprisingly – compared with the children's other grandparents – modern in outlook. He drove slowly, with many breakdowns and much hooting, a second-hand car. He travelled easily, without preparation or fuss, twice during that holiday carting the children's mother off to have lunch in Calais. To go to France at all was considered quite dashing, so to go for the day was in their family life revolutionary.

John increasingly took to Canterbury Grandfather, for his fine brain and detached manner was just what he most admired. He spoke to Isobel and Victoria about him, a conversation both girls were to remember.

"I don't wonder one of his ancestors was one of Oliver Cromwell's generals. If there was a civil war today I can see him taking the opposite side to his neighbours."

Isobel and Victoria were surprised that John was admiring, for they had considered Canterbury

Grandfather's Cromwellian ancestor a skeleton in the family cupboard. For, on the other grandfather's side, one relative was supposed to have been a friend of Charles the First – close enough, so it was said, for him to have been given a piece of the garter the King was wearing when he was beheaded. This alleged piece of garter, now reduced to a few threads stitched on to a piece of silk embroidered with the royal coat-of-arms, lived in a glass case in Granny and Grandfather's drawing room, where it could be viewed with respect by visiting grandchildren. Isobel was just beginning to be conscious that John sometimes thought his cousins stupid, so she chose her words with care.

"No nice person could have been one of Oliver Cromwell's generals, could he, John?"

John tried not to sound impatient.

"Oh, Isobel, of course he could! As a matter of fact I should think it was much harder to find a good reason to fight for Charles."

In the children's world, bound as it was within the walls of the vicarage and their school, everything was clear-cut. God was in his Heaven; the King on his throne; you voted Conservative; the English were the finest people in the world; there was no grey about it – you were right or you were wrong. What John had said gave their world a little rock.

"I don't believe you mean that," said Victoria. "Anyone who wasn't bad would fight for their king."

John could have shaken her.

"I think that's nonsense; apart from the reasons

why Oliver Cromwell felt he must depose the king, I don't believe I would fight for any king just because he was a king. After all, he might be a bad man. Take the late lamented Edward the Seventh: lots of people disapproved of him."

When Edward the Seventh had died at the beginning of their first term at Laughton House, the girls had worn black crêpe bands on their arms, and Miss French had sent a wreath to the funeral from the school and had received a letter of thanks from Queen Alexandra's secretary. Up to that moment the girls had accepted the fact that the whole nation was bowed with grief, so Victoria spoke truculently.

"Oh! What had he done for people to disapprove of?"

John had gone too far. Only too well he knew the gaps in his cousins' knowledge. Although Isobel was now fourteen he was sure she knew nothing of the facts of life. Still, they learned history, surely letting in a little light could do no harm.

"He loved other ladies besides Queen Alexandra."

"Why shouldn't he?" Victoria demanded. "I suppose, in a sort of way, Daddy loves Miss Herbert."

John roared.

"Respect, I think, not love."

Then John grew serious. "You girls want to widen your reading a bit or you will be surprised when you come out into the big, cold world."

That night when they were going to bed Isobel said, "I've been thinking. Mummy's not the sort of

192

mother who talks to her children, but I think she'd be glad if we tried to help ourselves. I'm going to ask her if, now I'm fourteen, I could read her library books."

"I don't see how that's going to help me," Victoria objected. "Besides, if it's going to make me hate kings in the way John does, I don't want to."

"John doesn't hate kings, he didn't mean that. I just think he thinks we are rather ignorant, and I don't mean to be that. So I am going to read grown-up books and, if I get a chance, Daddy's newspaper – and if you've any sense, so will you."

13 Christmas

As a result of that discussion it was, in Victoria's opinion, a more knowledgeable girl who met John when three months later he came home for Christmas. Isobel and Victoria had planned to hold a carefully rehearsed conversation as they walked him home from the station.

"We'll show him," Victoria had said, "he's not the only one who knows anything."

"How shall we start?" Isobel had asked.

Victoria was full of ideas.

"First you'll say, as if it was the sort of thing we always talked about: 'Oh, by the way, Vicky, did you read that speech Mr Asquith made yesterday?' "

"How do we know he said anything yesterday?" Isobel objected. "I haven't been able to get hold of the *Morning Post* for days."

At that time even sober papers such as *The Times* and the *Morning Post* were seldom read by the women of a household such as the Strangeways, for nothing in a national paper was supposed to interest them. So the morning paper left the dining room under their father's arm and presently came to rest in his study, from which it could only be borrowed if it was known he was out and how long he would be away. But not having seen a paper did not bother Victoria.

"Prime Ministers make speeches every day, so he's sure to have said something."

Isobel had giggled.

"John's going to think we've changed a lot if you and I are supposed to talk about Prime Ministers' speeches."

"Well, we have changed a lot. Then I'll say something about Lloyd George."

"Why him?" Isobel had asked. "We don't know much about him."

"Annie does. She calls him 'that liar from Wales'."

"I tell you what would be good to talk about," Isobel had suggested. "Suffragettes. After all, we do know about them."

Actually, except that the name of Mrs Pankhurst was on everyone's lips, the girls had the sketchiest idea of what the suffrage movement was about. They did know that their father was strongly opposed to it, for a parishioner had stopped the children one day on their way back from school and had asked Louise if she would like to wear a white frock and a purple and green sash to present a bouquet to a very important lady. Louise was, of course, charmed and burst into the house calling out her news. Her father, who was in the hall, had said:

"*What* coloured sash did you say?"

"Green and purple," Louise announced proudly. "And a white frock."

Their father spoke quite angrily.

"Listen, girls, those are the colours worn by women who defy the rules by which all good women live. They want to behave like men and vote for members of Parliament – which would mean blue murder – the ruin of the country."

But the political conversation planned for John could not take place when he did arrive for Isobel had asthma, but Victoria intended to manage alone.

"I'll even let him know that we know now how babies come," she promised Isobel.

"I wouldn't," Isobel advised. "For we aren't absolutely sure yet what makes people have them. I'd wait to tell him that until we know for certain."

John as usual put his luggage in the station fly, which still functioned though taxis were taking the place of horses, and walked home with the family, which now had a new addition – a fox terrier puppy called Spot. Presently the children's mother, Louise, Dick and Spot were left behind and John and Victoria were striding ahead, John full of questions about the subject which had been uppermost in Victoria's letters – the Boxing Night play. But Victoria stopped him.

"I'll tell you all about that but now I think we have more important things to discuss."

"What?"

Victoria took a deep breath.

"What do you feel about suffragettes?"

John stopped walking to stare at Victoria.

"What do I *what*?"

Victoria faltered. Hadn't she got the question right?

"Do you approve of suffragettes?"

John had temporarily forgotten the conversation of St Margaret's Bay.

"What is this? Have you been taking a general knowledge exam?"

Victoria lifted her chin into the air.

"Did you think you were the only person who read about things?"

John wanted to laugh, and would have, except that Victoria looked so serious. Certainly it was true he had never thought his cousins read anything, but then girls didn't.

"What is this? Is it a game?"

Victoria was furious. Here were she and Isobel struggling with boring grown-up books and trying to read that horrible *Morning Post* and John had forgotten it was he who had told them to.

"I think you're hateful. Don't you remember anything you say?"

"Say? What about?"

"I suppose you never said people disapproved of Edward VII because he loved other ladies, and that Isobel and I ought to read more so we'd know that sort of thing."

Then John remembered.

"My dearest Vicky, you shouldn't take me so seriously. What have you been reading?"

"When I can get it, Daddy's *Morning Post*, and sometimes the *Church Times* – but not often, for it's

197

terribly boring. Isobel reads Mummy's library books and I read bits of them too."

John felt a new warmth of affection for Victoria. He could see her sneaking into the study for the *Morning Post*, hoping to please him with her knowledge.

"I wouldn't bother with the *Morning Post* if I were you; after all, you won't be thirteen until Christmas Eve. I read papers at school so I'll pass on to you important things you ought to know, but I could suggest books you might tackle, and some poetry."

"Poetry! That's a school thing."

"Don't you believe it, it's the stuff dreams are made of! How about this?" And all the way home he recited *Kubla Khan*.

It was not like the Christmases at St Leonard's-on-Sea when, for days beforehand, the bell never stopped ringing as gifts of all kinds were delivered – but especially useful, helpful presents from the parishioners. In those days the tradespeople with whom you dealt sent presents: a turkey from the butcher; a box of crystallised fruits or chocolates from the grocer; fruit from the greengrocer. Even the local undertaker sent a present of wine. Tradespeople's presents still turned up, but at Eastbourne there were fewer presents from the parishioners, though the children's father received enough and from such unexpected sources to make him feel quite overcome.

"How kind they are, dear people," he said as he

received for his wife another pot plant or, for the children, chocolates or something for himself. "I really expected nothing, my first Christmas here."

Then off the children's father would dash, his arms full of little books on Christmas subjects which he had signed for his friends, for it was a strict rule in the family that for a present received one was sent. Even when they were tiny the children were taught this and would work laboriously at home-made gifts. Granny, who even when the children were small was not much good at getting about, still cherished a book-marker made by Victoria just before her sixth birthday. Its text, in cross stitch, said *Hop on hop ever*. Even now, though they had less time, the girls made many Christmas presents, some of which were put away as emergency gifts to send to the unexpected giver, simple presents such as lavender bags; emery cushions for rusty needles; pen-wipers and needle-books; but, no doubt being home-made, they pleased.

There were some things that were new about the Eastbourne Christmas. Always the family had been used to carol singers who came into the hall to sing and afterwards were given ginger wine and mince pies. They stood in a circle pealing out the old favourites while the family sat on the stairs to listen.

"There is something about bells," Isobel said after the bellringers had gone. "As they rang I sort of felt Christmas come into the house."

Victoria's birthday passed, as usual, with one long scurry to get everything done in time.

"It's a shame," said Annie, who had witnessed the glory of the other birthdays at St Margaret's Bay. "Proper cheated you've been, with only Irish stew for your dinner and your cake to be the Christmas cake tomorrow. But Annie's not lettin' you down."

"I know, angel Annie," said Victoria, looking at the hideous pink vase Annie had given her. "It's a gorgeous present."

"I'm not talkin' about the present. It's something else."

"What?"

"Curiosity killed the cat. You wait and see, and if anyone's sarky about it that's up to them."

Annie's secret came out at lunch time for, the Irish stew cleared away, Hester with a flourish put a dish of meringues bursting with cream in front of the children's mother.

"What's this?" she asked. Then she turned to Miss Herbert. "I asked you to tell Annie we'd have baked apples."

Miss Herbert flushed.

"And so I did. Is it likely I would order rich food like that on Christmas Eve?"

The children's father beamed at Victoria.

"I expect it's Vicky's birthday treat. Even if it is Christmas Eve no doubt you can manage a meringue, can't you, Vicky?"

But the children's mother was still annoyed. Brought up during the rest of the year on plain food her family were all too often, if not ill, cross after Christmas and Victoria, who suffered from what

200

were then called bilious attacks, had been known to be ill for days. Grudgingly she put a meringue on each plate.

"Tell Annie I'll see her after lunch."

The feeling of disapproval made the meringues slip down less easily than usual and it was hard to find conversation to go with them, so it was quite a relief when the dining room door was flung open and Annie, very dignified, looking all of her five-foot-two, stalked in.

"You was wanting me, ma'am?"

The last thing the children's mother wanted was to interview Annie in front of the family.

"Yes. I ordered baked apples."

Up shot Annie's chin.

"So you did. But I like to see justice done. I made meringues for Miss Louise's birthday and chocolate éclairs for Miss Isobel's. What's Miss Vicky done to be palmed off with baked apples?"

The children's mother felt quite intimidated.

"But it's not your place to decide what is eaten. And where did you get the materials?"

"It's everybody's place to see fair's fair. I ordered the meringue cases and the cream same as I did at St Margaret's Bay for Miss Louise's birthday."

There was really nothing more the children's mother could say unless she gave Annie notice, and she had no intention of doing that. Then the children's father took a hand.

"All right, Annie, you meant well. But next year

201

ask before you choose what pudding we have for Miss Vicky's birthday luncheon."

Annie, head up, totally unbowed, strutted to the door. There she turned and winked at Victoria.

"Someone has to stick up for you, don't they, ducks? I reckon it's lucky you've got Annie."

When Annie had gone back to the kitchen and the kitchen door was shut the children's father's face crinkled, then his shoulders began to shake.

"Dear Annie!" he said. "She is a character. Please, Vicky, try hard not to let her down by being sick on Boxing Day."

"How could I be?" said Victoria. "Isn't it the day of the play?"

Another feature of that Christmas was the curate. Curates came and curates went and, except on special occasions, the children seldom saw them to talk to because their father kept his curates' noses to the grindstone. But the curates usually came to Christmas lunch and, unless they had anywhere better to go, stayed on for tea and the Christmas tree – and dull and shy the children found them.

That year the curate – a man called Plimsol, known to the children as Mr Cassock because he seldom seemed to wear anything else – came to lunch. Right away he set a new standard for curates by arriving with five boxes of Fuller's chocolates. A box of chocolates of their own was highly thought of by the children, for most of the boxes received were family boxes and were stored in a cupboard to be passed round before bed, when each child was allowed one. So individual boxes from which the children were allowed, with permission, to help themselves were much valued. But that was not all; when the crackers were pulled Mr Plimsol found a blue sun-bonnet in his and not only put it on but sang: "Oh, what have you got for dinner, Mrs Bond?" in a delightfully silly way.

"Bags I you for my team for charades this evening," said John.

Always for Christmas tea and the tree afterwards the vicarage doors were thrown open to those who were lonely or had nowhere else to go. Annie, on hearing the Christmas arrangements, made a remark which became a family quotation: "As at Sandringham."

Either because of the success of Mr Plimsol in the charades or because some special quality surrounded that Christmas, it stayed in the children's memory.

Their mother always decorated the tree and they were never allowed to see it until the candles were lit. That year the tree stood in the small annexe to the drawing room – a perfect place, because there were curtains which could be drawn back when the tree was to be seen in all its glory. That year there were about fifteen waifs and strays, mostly women, all rather shy and sad while they drank tea and ate Victoria's birthday – now the Christmas – cake.

When the tea was cleared, Annie and Hester joined the party, and soon everyone was circling the tree singing *The First Nowell* and then *Good King Wenceslaus*, with John singing the King's verses and

Victoria the page's. Then came the time to strip the tree. The majority of the parcels were for the family of course, but no one was allowed to feel left out, so there were plenty of little gifts for the guests. Annie and Hester (Miss Herbert went to a brother for Christmas) had presents from every member of the family and, as well as proper presents from the children's parents, each received an afternoon apron. Annie said when she opened her parcel:

"Thank you, madam. It will save you buying me one for when you want me to bring in tea on Hester's day out."

The present-giving over and the wrappings swept up, the charades started and, as had been hoped, Mr Plimsol proved a natural comic. It was lovely to see the lonely, rather sad people who had arrived, mopping the tears of laughter off their cheeks.

Then there was more carol singing and then the guests were in the hall putting on their wraps, and another Christmas Day was over.

Usually Boxing Day was thank-you-letter day, with a little rehearsing for the Boxing evening show, but that Boxing Day there could be no letter writing for everyone was busy with the evening play. Victoria had taken John's advice; though there were no elves, there was scarcely a moment when a chorus of sorts was not entering, so that as many children as possible might be used.

There was a simple story running through the play of a bewitched princess lost in a wood who was rescued by a gallant prince. But to the audience the high spots were when their offspring appeared as toadstools, clouds, flowers or fairies, all of which lived in the wood.

The talent was probably nil and Victoria's ability to arrange dances was non-existent, but it was all very cheerful and fast-moving, and Louise was excellent thumping away on the piano. But there were two high spots: Isobel's dresses and John's lighting. Isobel had let herself go, and many of the clothes she had designed were really charming. Few had any money for luxuries, but there was butter-muslin and there was dye. So her clouds danced in grey frocks with rose pink petticoats and rose pink stockings, and her flowers, however awkwardly they moved, almost looked like the real thing.

To add to Isobel's dresses John, with Dick as assistant, with lamps and coloured papers produced what were generally considered stupendous effects. Certainly the audience were more than pleased. "Proper professional," they said. "Better than the panto at the theatre, shouldn't wonder."

Victoria took a curtain as author, Louise as pianist, the boys for their lighting and Isobel for her designs and they were all cheered. But the best moment was talking it over afterwards over cups of cocoa. The children's father said:

"Bless you all, that play will work wonders, it was just what the parish needed."

14 Broken Resolutions

Victoria was sitting on Isobel's bed. It was New Year's Eve and the girls were waiting to hear the bells ring in 1911. Isobel put the alarm clock she had been given as a Christmas present back on the bedside pedestal – something found in every bedroom in those days.

"Luckily I had this or we'd never have been awake. Next year I shan't be here, for I suppose I'll go with Mummy to the midnight service, as I'll be confirmed by then."

"Passing from the old year to the new upon your knees," Victoria agreed, quoting what yearly her father said in church. "Isn't it awful how old you are getting? I hate to think of you being confirmed, it means you won't be there for stockings on Christmas Day. You'll come in from church as if you were a grown-up."

"Well, I will be fifteen in August. That's almost old enough to be married. Mummy married Daddy when she was seventeen."

Victoria looked at Isobel.

"You don't look any different. Your chest sticks out more, that's all. Mine doesn't."

"Well, you're only just thirteen – I expect it will begin this year. What resolutions are you making?"

206

Victoria sighed.

"The same as usual, but I don't know why I make them, for I break them right away. Tonight I will vow not to argue, always to get up the moment I'm called, not to fight with Louise, and to work so hard at school I'll get a good report. But I'm very despairing about keeping any of them."

Isobel looked again at her clock.

"We haven't long." She took a piece of paper from under her pillow. "I've written mine down. Not to mind when Miss Herbert fusses; not to mind when I'm ill; not to mind not going to a proper art school." She hesitated then folded the paper. "That's all."

Victoria made a pounce.

"It's *not* all. Let me see."

But Isobel had the paper tight in her folded hand.

"You can't see – anyway it's time. Go and open your window so you can hear the bells, and don't quite shut my door so I can hear them too."

Victoria flung open her window. The bells of all the churches in Eastbourne were ringing, and from down the street there were voices shouting greetings. Into the night Victoria called her resolutions in the form of a prayer.

"Please, God, don't let me argue once with anyone, not even Miss Herbert. And help me to get up the very minute I'm called. And don't let me fight with Louise, however awful she is. And make me work harder at school however mean Miss French was about my ankle, because then I'll get a good report. And please help me to start to grow up, even if it means my chest has to stick out, which I don't like, for don't forget I'll be fourteen next Christmas."

Isobel, as midnight passed, whispered the last resolution on her list.

"And I resolve not to let Vicky do everything, like Granny said she did. I must do my share."

Nineteen hundred and eleven was what Victoria called "a beast year", which meant it was the year when John's parents, Uncle Mark and Aunt Catherine, came on leave from India. Even the first time it happened, though she was only four, Victoria had resented their arrival and had shown it by hiding under the dining room table when they called, refusing to budge and shouting, "Go away! Go away!" It was perhaps this unfortunate start which had given Aunt Catherine the impression that her niece Vicky was a boorish child.

The next time they came home Vicky had been seven and, as on the last leave, they had found John rather at a loose end during the summer holiday, they tried the experiment of staying in an hotel near the villa-type house in Devonshire the children's father had rented for August. This was a great success from the men's point of view, for the brothers were devoted, but it was in every other way a failure for the children's mother and her sister-in-law had nothing in common: Aunt Catherine, a smart bridge-playing type, much preferred the hotel to the beach, and she was unable to disguise the fact that, had there been any other suitable relations to whom she could have entrusted John, she would have done so. John had not helped matters by escaping from the children staying in the hotel whenever he could, to join his cousins – particularly Victoria.

Because when John went back to school at the end of the Christmas holidays, both he and Victoria knew they were unlikely to meet again before next Christmas, their parting, though outwardly off-hand, had been discussed between them for days.

"Let me know how you get on with the reading, Vicky. I expect everything on that list I gave you will be either in Uncle Jim's study or your school library, but if they aren't let me know, I always get extra pocket money when the parents are home."

"I hope you get into that shooting team before your father comes, then he won't fuss so much about other games."

John too had made New Year resolutions.

"I'm going to try and look keen on OTC things. That really will please my father."

Victoria had often heard John on the subject of the Officers' Training Corps, whose every enterprise was anathema to him. The drills, the route marches, the field days. The spit and polish and rewinding of muddy puttees.

"Could you?" she asked doubtfully. "I shouldn't think anyone was less like a soldier."

"I've got to try, Vicky. If he thinks I'm sloppy he'll be on again about boxing, which I'll hate worse."

209

He looked amused at his thoughts. "Smart soldierly type, that's me."

The day before he left Victoria had said:

"You will write and tell me everything, even in the holidays, won't you – especially if Uncle Mark says anything about what you'll be when you grow up?"

"You know I'll write. But don't worry. My father can talk his head off. I know the sort of life I couldn't lead. I'd loathe India, with all the filth and burning ghats and everything; I'll pretend to agree, but when the time comes I'll do what I want."

"Aren't you brave!" Victoria had said admiringly. "I wish I could feel like that."

John had caught hold of her hands.

"You will, Vicky, when you are older. Just think – you have only one life, so it's up to you to see that you use it as perfectly as you possibly can. You must understand that."

Victoria was still too much a child to look upon her life as her own; what she did was decided for her by her parents. But John's enthusiasm was catching.

"I can't see it quite as you do because I'm a girl, I suppose – but I do hope you do what you want, and that sometimes I can share in the things you do."

Fortified by her resolutions, Victoria began the school term determined to do really well. It was bad luck that apparently other people had made New Year resolutions; among them was Victoria's form mistress, Miss Brown, and evidently one of her resolutions had been to be more strict, especially with Victoria Strangeway. Unfortunately, both Victoria and Miss Brown were so busy thinking about their own resolutions that neither had time to wonder about other people's.

The first period of the term in each form was taken up in making out time-tables. The main outlines of these time-tables were the same, save for special subjects: music lessons and music practice, extra dancing and elocution, special art classes and so on. All girls in those days learned to play the piano – it was expected of a lady – but Victoria was an exception; instead she learned the violin, which she played abominably.

The reason for the violin went back many years to the day when Victoria, aged seven, having fought at every lesson against being taught to play the piano, arrived at her own solution. She turned both hands upside down, and neither punishment nor bribes could persuade her to play with them in any other position.

"It is no good my teaching Vicky," the young woman who came to the vicarage to give piano lessons confessed. "She's determined not to learn, and I'm afraid that if I go on trying she might damage the piano."

That was one of the occasions when Victoria was sent for by her father to come to his study. He was looking sad.

"This is very, very naughty of you, Vicky. Poor

Miss Carney says she can't teach you the piano any more."

"Good," said Victoria. "I hate learning, Daddy."

"I dare say," her father agreed. "But it is not for you to decide what you learn. But, as Miss Carney will no longer teach you, Mummy and I have decided you will learn the violin."

Victoria had scarcely at that time seen a violin.

"The violin! But I haven't a violin. And who will teach me?"

That was soon settled. A violin was bought and a Miss Gardener found to give lessons. From that time on nightmare sounds filled the vicarage whenever Victoria practised or had a lesson. Her mother would have let the violin lessons drop, but her father refused to give in; because Victoria had been naughty, she must not be excused learning an instrument.

"Stick to it, darling," he said. "One day you will be a great help to me."

"How?" Victoria had asked suspiciously, hoping her father had no wild ideas about her playing at parish concerts.

"If you could play hymns they could be of the utmost help when I am writing a sermon."

That day at her violin practice Victoria started to pick out the tune of the hymn "Art thou weary, art thou languid . . .". At once her mother came into the room.

"I don't believe Miss Gardener told you to play that. Go back to your scales."

Up had shot Victoria's chin.

"If you want to know, Daddy asked me to learn it. It's to help with his sermons."

The children's mother with a muttered, "What nonsense!" had retired, so Victoria went on struggling with the hymn. She could not know it then, but when she grew up and at last stopped learning the violin, the only tune she could play with any accuracy was "Art thou weary, art thou languid . . .".

When the move came to Eastbourne the violin, of course, travelled with Victoria. She was to learn, she was told, with a man – a George Bring – who came to Laughton House twice a week to give lessons. What Victoria did not realise was that it was only musical girls with some talent who learned the violin and that Mr George Bring had a sense of humour, and when pressed, would sometimes give an imitation of Victoria playing the violin.

Another thing Victoria did not know was how much the governesses disliked chaperoning her during her violin lessons. Even more unpopular was it when one or other of them had to play her accompaniments during her daily practice.

It was impossible to arrange time-tables absolutely fairly. There were many music rooms, but they were always in use, so some of the girls had to fit in their practice during recreation periods. Possibly Miss Brown had done her best, and annoying Victoria was not in her thoughts when she arranged the time-tables, but certainly Victoria had been unlucky. On two mornings she was down for violin practice after morning school, and on two afternoons between tea and homework. The second Victoria heard the half-hours allotted to her, away went her resolutions about arguing.

"But it's not fair, Miss Brown. You've given me practice in free time almost every day."

Away too went half of one of Miss Brown's resolutions, for to the intention to be more strict, she had added "but just".

"I will not have any discussion about the time-tables, Vicky. In my opinion day girls should do their practice at home. But since Miss French allows you to do it here, if anyone is to be inconvenienced, you must see it is not fair it should be one of the boarders."

Miss Brown had not said "who are the most important people in the school" but it was clearly what she thought. Victoria seethed.

"Boarders, boarders, boarders!" she said. "If you don't mind me saying so, it seems to me mean to speak of us day-girls in that despising way."

Miss Brown's voice was icy.

"One more word from you, Victoria, and you will leave the room."

Victoria said no more because her friends made faces suggesting "It's only old Brownie" and "Don't let her annoy you". But it was hard work being silent, and for the rest of the morning she was muttering "She's mean. She's mean."

Having broken one resolution or rather, in Victoria's opinion, having it broken for her by Miss

Brown's meanness, another good resolution quickly followed and Victoria was back where she had been last term, learning as little as possible.

In March Isobel was confirmed. She was sent a charming white dress by Aunt Helen which Ursula had worn when she was confirmed. Both grandfathers came for the service and so did Isobel's godparents, Uncle Paul (with, of course, Aunt Helen) and Aunt Hetty and mother's sister Aunt Penelope. Victoria was impressed with the service and thought privately Isobel looked like a saint in her white veil, but she was surprised how calm and ordinary she seemed. Nobody actually talked in a quieter voice or was what the children called more "creamish" than usual, but it seemed to Victoria as if they were.

"My goodness," Victoria thought, "I'm glad it's not me being confirmed. I couldn't bear all that sort of 'this is a wonderful day' way they go on. When I'm old enough I'll ask Daddy if, instead of at home, I can be confirmed with my class at school."

Two things happened after the confirmation which left their mark. The first concerned Jackie. Uncle Paul was an amusing, clever man, but very much under Aunt Helen's thumb – as indeed were her two children, Ursula and Henry. Aunt Helen, though she dressed Ursula artistically, was a no-nonsense mother, seeing a daughter from babyhood as a little woman, rather than as a pretty toy.

Though Aunt Helen did her duty by her sister-in-law Sylvia's family, in her heart she disparaged them. Her brother-in-law Jim was a fine man and, of course, they were poor – vicars always were – but need they live *quite* so miserably? The food in the vicarage, in her opinion, was always uneatable. There were never enough fires. The girls – even Isobel in Ursula's clothes – looked unkempt. And, in her opinion, they were stupidly brought up. She was sure if she had Isobel in her care there would be less asthma, it was probably partly bad feeding. As for Victoria, she really was impossible and she was getting to look so sulky; if there was one kind of child Aunt Helen hated it was a sulky one.

Aunt Helen had no idea that her poor Ursula was slowly having such personality as she possessed crushed out of her until she showed nothing, not even sulkiness. Most of all Aunt Helen was aggravated by Louise. This was partly jealousy, the child was so outstandingly beautiful. Just because she was beautiful, that was no reason to baby her.

"Look at Louise," she said to her husband before the confirmation. "She's eleven years old, yet she goes round like a child of six, clutching that ridiculous golliwog."

Uncle Paul was a true Strangeway. He accepted dear Jim's family just as they were without criticism.

"Is Louise eleven? She doesn't look it. I think she only carries Jackie around from habit."

"I don't believe it," said Aunt Helen. "I think Sylvia likes her to have a toy; it makes her feel she's still a little thing. She doesn't want the responsibility of a grown-up family."

Uncle Paul disliked the conversation.

216

"I am sure you are wrong, dear. I tell you it's only a habit."

"Prove it," said Aunt Helen. "You take Jackie from Louise – toss him in the air or something – and see what happens."

Uncle Paul and Aunt Helen were returning to London after the confirmation, but after the service, which was in the afternoon, before they left to catch their train, they were to have tea. It was a fine afternoon and while they were waiting for tea the family went into the garden. Louise had fetched Jackie from her bedroom.

"You're rather a big girl to carry a doll around, aren't you?" Aunt Helen asked her.

Louise clutched Jackie. She knew she was too big to play with him, and that he no longer meant to her what he used to. But though she had no idea of it, in a way Jackie was Dick to her – her friend, confidant and supporter.

"Jackie's *not* a doll."

Suddenly Aunt Helen snatched Jackie from Louise's arms and tossed him to Uncle Paul. "See if you can throw him over that tree."

Uncle Paul had not heard the conversation but he was a cricketer. Up went his bowling arm and Jackie flew, not over the tree, but into one of the top branches.

Louise was always pale for she was anaemic; as Jackie hurtled into space she gave a muffled scream (Miss French's training was taking effect), turned a bluish white and fell down apparently in a faint.

That evening at bedtime when Jackie, with the help of a ladder, was recovered and the fuss had died down, Victoria said to Isobel:

"Do you think Louise really did faint?"

Isobel thought about that.

"She could have. She's silly enough about Jackie."

Victoria swung on the door between the two rooms.

"I hope today makes her give him up. I don't often agree with Aunt Helen, but this time I did – she's too old to carry him about."

"Poor Louise," said Isobel.

Victoria studied her sister with interest.

"Do you feel that? I mean, you don't usually. Is it because you were confirmed today?"

"Idiot!" Isobel retorted. "Shut the door and go to bed."

The other thing that happened after the confirmation was to affect Victoria. Aunt Penelope stayed on at the vicarage for a day or two and on Saturday afternoon she had invited her goddaughter Isobel out to tea.

Going out to tea in those days meant going to a café and eating innumerable cream buns, and was a much-loved treat. Aunt Penelope was the hardest of their mother's three sisters for she had less self-pity, she was too insensitive. Probably she was genuinely sorry for Louise, who had looked white and miserable since the scene about Jackie, but also she had no love for her niece Victoria.

Whatever Aunt Penelope's reason, at the last

moment she invited Louise to tea too – which meant leaving Victoria alone at home. No one had ever behaved like that before, and all three sisters were shocked. Victoria was wounded in a way she had never been before. To be left behind by one's aunt! It was unthinkable.

Her father and mother were out, and so was Miss Herbert. Victoria took Spot into the garden and, while he sniffed round the lawn, she climbed up a cedar tree. She had thought she wanted to be alone to cry, but no tears came. Aunt Penelope's behaviour had hurt her, but that her parents had not interfered and said: "You can't leave Victoria out," cut her to the quick. But it was not her hurt she thought about, but her future.

"This is something I am never going to forget. I'll always see myself on this day, and remember how it felt when people were cruel and I was thirteen."

15 A School Report

Though Victoria was not getting on at school, Isobel and Louise were doing splendidly. Louise shone at theory of music, electrifying everybody by getting a hundred out of a hundred in an examination. Isobel, though often away ill, kept up easily with her form and was likely to be moved up in the autumn. As Louise was frequently at the top of her form, it was obvious she would move up too; but if that happened what was to be done about Victoria? By no stretch of the imagination was Victoria ready for a move, for she was usually bottom of her form.

The form mistresses concerned had a private meeting to discuss Victoria. "I would not mind," Miss Brown said, "if she were a stupid child; but she's not, it's just that she won't work."

Isobel's form mistress, Miss Grey, was dreading the day when she would be given Victoria.

"I can't understand it. Isobel's a dear girl. I tell you what, Brown, why don't you keep Victoria after Louise has moved up? That might shame her into working harder. She surely wouldn't allow her little sister to pass her."

Miss Brown was doubtful.

"The decision will be Miss French's, of course. She's got an idea Victoria needs special handling."

Louise's form mistress, Miss Black, had more spirit than the other two.

"I'd handle her if she was in my form. You're getting white hairs over that girl, Brown."

Miss Grey was afraid of Miss French's decision. Of course some day she must have Victoria – but not yet, surely not yet.

"I should wait as long as possible before going to Miss French. See how Victoria does in the end of term examinations. If she gets bad marks, however strongly Miss French feels she really cannot permit Victoria to move up. She has got the rest of the school to think about."

So, for the time being, things rested as they were, and were not quite so bad as they looked. For though Victoria appeared to fritter away her days and truly did spend as little time as possible on her school lessons, she was becoming a bookworm. Urged on by John she had read since the beginning of the year all of Jane Austen that was in the school library, *Vanity Fair*, *David Copperfield*, *A Tale of Two Cities*, *Dombey and Son*, *The Mill on the Floss* – and was struggling with *Wuthering Heights*. The perverse streak in her would not allow her to talk to anyone, even to Isobel, about her reading. Instead she would hide away to read where no eyes were on her and, when asked what she had been doing, being deliberately aggravating, she would say, "Just playing". During prep she became a past mistress at appearing deep in arithmetic or geometry, while she devoured page after page of her current book.

Probably the effect of her reading would have shown in at least some of her examination papers had not events piled up which made of Victoria an even more complete rebel. During the spring Granny and Grandfather with, of course, Aunt Sophie, had taken rooms on Eastbourne sea front. On the Saturday afternoon of their visit tickets were bought by Aunt Sophie for the theatre on the pier, and she and the girls went to a matinée. To visit a theatre was an unheard-of treat. Once, to make up to Isobel for a bad time at the dentist, the children's mother had taken her and Victoria to see *Alice in Wonderland*. And one Christmas some friends had invited the whole family to see *Aladdin*. But that was the sum total of the children's theatre-going. So the matinée on the pier with Aunt Sophie would in any case have been an event, but the type of entertainment made it memorable, for the performers were all children. It was called Lila Field's Little Wonders. It was a sort of review, partly ballet, a few songs and a short play.

The girls were spellbound and utterly absorbed. For days afterwards Isobel and Victoria had discussed little else. From where did those extraordinary children come who led such different lives from their own? In every spare minute Isobel drew ballet dresses, which excited her for she had never seen one before. As for Victoria, those child dancers stimulated her imagination as nothing had ever done. Where *did* they come from? Who taught them to dance? Where did they do their lessons? Did they earn money? Did their mothers travel with them, or perhaps someone like Miss Herbert? Victoria wove endless stories round that fabulous dancing troupe – sometimes including herself among them. Those lucky, lucky children, so miraculously free from the boring life led by other girls, especially girls whose home was a vicarage.

At the beginning of the summer there had been a holiday for the Coronation. Almost all the boarders, and a large number of the day girls, were taken to London to watch the procession. It would be lovely to have a fairy godmother who sent you in a coach to a ball – it was outside possibility. Instead, on the day of the Coronation, the girls helped run the sports and games organised for children in the parish, and received Coronation mugs and watched the fireworks. Also, to mark the occasion, their summer hats were of royal blue straw trimmed with cerise ribbon, which for some reason their mother believed to be Queen Mary's favourite colours.

Probably not going to the Coronation rankled slightly in Victoria's mind – in a nothing-nice-ever-happens-to-us way; but there was no sense of grievance: it was something else which gave her that. Suddenly everybody was talking about a man. His name was Diaghilev. Not *Mr* Diaghilev, like an ordinary man – just Diaghilev.

Even in the vicarage it was known that the Russian ballet was in London. Miss French had seen the ballet in Paris the previous year and had determined then and there that as many of her girls as possible must see the company when they visited London. So she booked tickets, and all who could afford it were taken to London for three nights. Again, it was a Cinderella type of thing; it never crossed the girls' minds that they could see the Russians, but Victoria, still enthralled by dancers, determined to learn all about them at second-hand. They were ballet dancers so they would, she supposed, stand on their toes as the children on the pier had done. They would wear the same ballet skirts – perhaps with feathers on them like the little girl who had danced as a dying swan.

But what was *extra* about the Russians? Why did everybody talk about them? Even John's letters were full of them and his longing to see them.

At Laughton House the girls did not sit with their forms at meals, but the whole school was mixed up and moved their seats at table weekly. The week after the school visited the ballet Victoria was sitting at the top of the table near Miss French. Around her were several sixth-formers, all of whom had been in the ballet party. Looking round at them, Victoria could see that they and Miss French looked what she called to herself "shiny eyed" as they talked. Victoria listened eagerly, trying to catch some of the magic from what they said.

"I could have watched the Polovtsian Dancers for ever," one girl stated. "Those jumps!"

"What about *Spectre de la Rose*?" sighed another.

"Wasn't Nijinsky wonderful?" gasped a third.

224

Miss French's precise voice cut through these eulogies.

"For myself the ballet I must see again is *Schéhérazade*. The colour! The exquisitely balanced whole!"

Victoria meant only to listen but there was so much she wanted to know. She leaned across the table to the sixth-former who had raved about Nijinsky.

"What was the ballet about the rose? Was someone dressed as a rose? Did they dance on their toes?"

Probably Miss French was tired after three exhausting days. Certainly to someone who had seen the Russians, Victoria's questions sounded puerile. Did they dance on their toes! Such a question to ask of those who had seen *Schéhérazade*! What did the child imagine they had taken time off from school to see? A music-hall turn?

"If you have nothing more sensible than that to ask, Victoria, I should say nothing at all."

Victoria was indignant, but also deeply hurt. She had so desperately wanted to know what the dancers were like. How could anyone be so mean after three lovely days in London seeing ballets as to refuse to describe them to someone who was too poor to go and see them for herself? Scarlet of face, blinking back tears, she shut her ears to the talk and went on eating her lunch. But a thought was chasing round in her head.

"I don't know how I'll do it, but when I grow up, *somehow* I'll have enough money to do all the

225

things other people do – Coronation, ballet, everything . . . You wait, all of you, and see."

It was accepted that Isobel would want to know all about the ballets, and many souvenirs had been brought back for her to see. As a result she came home dizzy with descriptions of colour.

"It must be the most glorious sight," she said to her sisters as they walked home from school. "All colours splashed together – just as I've always wanted them to be."

Louise's form had been considered too young to join the party, but they had heard the ravings of those who had.

On the way home Louise said: "The man who dances the part of a rose wears nothing but rose petals. Could you draw him, Isobel?"

Victoria said nothing. She did not want talking to her sisters to take her mind off her grievance. She was not going to forgive Miss French. She intended to remain aloof and bitter.

As a result of her public snubbing over the ballet Victoria decided to do what to herself she described as "paying Miss French back". This she would do by writing deliberately disgraceful examination papers.

There were two outcomes of this: so bad a report for Victoria that she was sent for to the study to discuss it, and something Victoria knew nothing about – a talk between Miss French and her father. Summoned to her father's study, Victoria, though cold inside for her report really was a horror, came in with an air of truculence. Her father was not at his desk but by his window, Victoria's report in his hand.

Victoria stood beside him and gazed, without seeing them, at the special bed of geraniums, calceolarias and lobelias. Her father did not speak at once. Instead he re-read the report. At last he said:

" 'Could do better' is the best that anyone has found to say about you, Vicky. Why?"

"That's the sort of thing they always say."

Her father put a hand on Victoria's shoulder and turned her round to face him.

"That's not true, there is nothing like that in Isobel's or Louise's report. There I read 'Greatly improved', 'Works hard' and sometimes 'Excellent'."

Victoria had no real answer so she said grumpily:

"I can't help it if they're better than me, can I?"

Her father went on as if she had not spoken. "Your examination marks are a disgrace. Look at this. English literature two out of a hundred."

Victoria could have done fairly well in this subject, so it had been difficult to answer everything wrong.

"Two! I wonder what I got two for?"

For once, her father could feel the aggravation which Victoria's mother so often felt when dealing with her.

"I don't know what to do with you, Vicky. What gets into you that you are always in trouble over something? You are such a disappointment to me and to Mummy."

This brought a lump into Victoria's throat. It

really did hurt her to hurt her father. She struggled to explain.

"Miss French has never been fair. She was beastly when I sprained my ankle, and just because we haven't got enough money to do what other girls do you would think she'd be nice, not nasty. If people are hateful to me I'm hateful back. Why should I work to please her? And she's not the only one; Miss Brown was mean on purpose about my violin practice, I know she was."

Her father gazed over Victoria's head to his front gate. How was he to help this difficult daughter? In what way had they failed her? She had a troublesome nature, but why was she always so resentful? She seemed to have a permanent chip on her shoulder.

"Every school cannot be at fault, Vicky. What you are saying now about Miss French you said once about Miss Dean. I should not blame Miss French if she too asked me to send you to another school."

"I could go to that boarding school for the daughters of poor clergy," Vicky suggested, trying and succeeding in keeping a note of hope out of her voice.

Her father went to his desk and there, his head bowed in his hands, he let out a sort of groan. Victoria was appalled. She followed him and laid a hand on his arm.

"I'm sorry about the report, Daddy. When I was doing the exams, I didn't think about you – only about Miss French and Miss Brown."

Her father raised his head and there were tears in his eyes.

"Why had you to think about anything except the paper in front of you?"

Victoria tried not to sound impatient, but she had told him.

"I had to pay Miss French out for being mean."

Her father's eyes widened in amazement.

"You deliberately wrote bad papers?"

"Yes."

Her father's breath was literally taken away. Presently he said:

"But what I can't get at is, why? I know you have talked about imagined unfairness from Miss French and your form mistress. But why do you feel these things? Isobel and Louise seem perfectly happy."

Why her? How could Victoria explain that? Her resentment at living in a vicarage where she felt all eyes were on her; her consciousness of always being badly dressed in Isobel's old clothes; her longing just once to have new text books like the others in her form, instead of secondhand ones. ("We don't want to cost your father more than we must.") Her knowledge that to the school – though they were all poor and shabby and only day girls – Isobel was admired as an artist, and Louise for her looks and her cleverness, but she had nothing. She was the plain one, the one without talent.

"They both shine at things – I've got nothing. The only things I can do, like write plays and act, we

229

don't do." A sob long held back burst out of her. "It's an awful feeling, to be despised."

Her father put an arm round her.

"I don't despise you, Vicky, and neither does God. I think truly nobody does; you are imagining it. But one thing is certain – there is never to be another report like this one." He hesitated, trying to find the right words to explain what he meant. "I do see that in many ways things are easier for Isobel and Louise. But that is because they use the talents God has given them. You have talents too, Vicky, but you are burying them as the bad steward did in the parable."

"But I told you, they don't do my things at school."

Her father pulled Victoria down to sit on the arm of his chair.

"There is something we all have called personality, Vicky. You have a strong one – the strongest I believe of all my children. A strong personality properly used is a talent, for it is people who have it who make leaders. So if you cannot make your mark at school as an artist, like Isobel, or have the retentive memory of Louise, you could be an influence when you are older – an influence for good."

Victoria thought how little her father knew about girls' schools.

"We don't have people like that in Laughton House."

"You have a head girl, don't you?"

"Oh her! But I could never be that, only boarders are."

Her father sighed. He hoped Victoria was not doing it deliberately, but she was obstructing everything he said. But he knew he was tired; a few days before his annual holiday he was always conscious he was not at his best. Nevertheless he was thinking clearly enough to know that such a report could not be allowed to pass without punishment.

"I don't like our lovely August holiday spoiled so you will not be punished until we come home . . ."

Victoria looked anxiously at him. What was he thinking about? ("Please, God, don't let Daddy and me pray together.")

"Yes, Daddy?"

"Your punishment will be to get up half an hour earlier each day next term: you can saw logs for the winter."

The girls never knew if what their mother said was deliberate or an accident. When asked, years later, she appeared to have forgotten the conversation. It happened the following Sunday. They had finished singing hymns and Louise was having her supper of cocoa and biscuits. Cocoa made with water, and one biscuit – an inadequate, ill-thought-out meal, as were most meals in the vicarage. Suddenly the children's mother said:

"If we are still here when you leave school, Isobel, we must see if we could build a temporary studio for you in the field."

Isobel looked like a startled faun. It was a big step from being "good at art" to having a studio built. But if a studio was built, would it mean that the chance of her being sent to an art school was further away than ever?

"You mean, to keep my paints and things in?"

"I mean to work in," said her mother dryly. "All you girls will have to earn your own livings, you know."

It was an earth-shaking statement. Always they had understood they were to live at home until they married. That is what Daddy's sister Aunt Hetty had done. Nobody before had mentioned earning anything, though actually Isobel hoped, if she got to an art school, to sell her pictures some day.

Louise pretended to give Jackie a sip of cocoa – not that she played with him when alone in that way, but she knew how it maddened her sisters.

"I shan't earn my own living. I shall marry just as soon as I'm old enough, and have lots and lots of children."

Almost as if she could see into the future her mother replied:

"Quite likely that is what will happen. But you will have to marry very young, if it's to happen before you are trained for a career."

"What sort of career?" Louise asked.

Her mother gave a slight shrug.

"Nothing very exciting. You might teach perhaps, or I believe you can earn a good wage if you can use a typewriter. But it will only be a temporary career – if you have one at all – for I can see you marrying early."

Victoria did not want to ask about her future. Too well she could guess the snubbing reply she would get. Perhaps Isobel sensed this, for she asked: "What about Vicky?"

There was a long pause before the children's mother answered.

"I don't know. But it will be nothing ordinary for you, Vicky. I think you will be the one to surprise us all."

Years later when Victoria's first book was published Isobel sent her a postcard. On it was written: "You will be the one to surprise us all."

Victoria never knew what her father and Miss French had said to each other, only that they had met. It was the last day of term and Victoria was with the rest of her class tidying her desk, when a message came that she was wanted in Miss French's study. All her class knew how bad her report had been, for exhibitionist Victoria had not been able to resist telling them, so they made sympathetic faces. Outwardly brave though respectful, but inwardly trembling, Victoria knocked on the study door. Miss French, looking frighteningly smart in a dark shade of blue, was sitting at her desk.

"Come in, Vicky." She pointed to a chair. "Sit down." She clasped her elegant, long-fingered, ringed hands.

"You and I have got to start again, Vicky," she announced.

Victoria gasped: "What?"

Miss French ignored the interruption.

"Your father is a very fine man, my child, and a very devoted father. When talking to him the other day I realised that both you and I have let him down – you as my pupil, I as your headmistress. It is quite hard for him to find the fees for even a day girl, but he has found them. What have we given him in return?"

An answer was clearly expected.

"Not much."

"Only a girl who is as ignorant as the day she entered my school. At your age, Vicky, it is very easy to be misunderstood, for it is difficult for you to express what you feel. I am afraid this is just what has happened, and perhaps I am partly to blame."

There was another pause. Victoria was sure she should have said "Oh no", but she could not bring herself to say it. Instead she said:

"You *were* rather mean about my ankle when I sprained it, and . . ."

Miss French stopped her with a gesture.

"We are not here to rake among the ashes. We are here to make a fresh start. I want us next term to work together, so that at Christmas you can give your father the present of a good report. He is a fine man; he deserves it, Vicky."

Victoria thought of Miss Brown stealing her free time for violin practice, and all the other pin-pricks which were her daily lot.

"I could try," she said, after thought. "But I

shouldn't think it would happen. It's like New Year resolutions, I make those – but I always break them."

"I was not expecting you to achieve what by present standards would be a miracle – alone."

Victoria was disgusted. Having a father who was a clergyman she had to put up with a lot of talk about God, but, except at morning prayers and Scripture lessons, she did not accept such talk from a headmistress. She sounded resentful.

"I know about God."

Miss French looked for a second as if she were going to laugh.

"I was not at that moment meaning God – I am sure a daughter of your father knows how to pray. I was thinking about myself. Starting next term would you promise me, when you think you have been treated unjustly in any way, to come and discuss the situation with me?"

Victoria could hardly believe her ears. Nobody as far as she knew, except the outside teachers, talked to Miss French.

"How could I? I couldn't just walk in."

Miss French opened a drawer and took out a pad of pink paper. She passed it to Victoria.

"If you need me write me a note. Just say: 'May I see you please?' and sign it."

Victoria turned the pad over; it was pretty paper, but she could not see herself writing such a note.

"Thank you very much."

Miss French gave her a friendly nod.

"Run along, dear. I have no intention of letting your father down, even if you have, so if I feel I should have had a note and do not receive one, I shall send for you. Oh – and, Vicky, please tell no one about this conversation. It is our secret."

16 Another August

The summer holiday was spent in North Wales. The weather was kind, but the house the children's father had rented was isolated and a mile from the sea. The scenery, however, was exquisite, and there was fun in talking to the few locals, who spoke with a lilt and phrased their sentences so curiously, so the holiday turned out better than some. Isobel certainly enjoyed it, for she was out sketching from morning to night, and was often joined by her mother, who could paint quite pleasantly. The children's father, as often happened, spent his first week being ill, for he was so over-tired that the sudden relaxation was too much for his system to take. But after that, his daily bathe over, he too often joined the sketchers, for he was quite clever with a pencil.

Louise and Dick were always happy as long as they were together. But that holiday they showed a new independence. The bathe over, for that, still supposedly a pleasure, was accepted by all the children to be a must unless there was a health excuse, the two would collect a picnic lunch and, taking Spot with them, would disappear until dark. What did they talk about, those two? Nobody knew. But clearly one subject had cropped up – Jackie – for one day during breakfast the children's mother said:

"Where's Jackie, Louise? I haven't seen him for days."

Louise was at that moment eating a plate of stewed bilberries that Hester and Annie had picked. She looked up, her mouth black from the juice.

"He's gone."

Dick too was eating bilberries for stewed fruit for breakfast was a special holiday treat. He said:

"We buried him."

Amazed and clearly a little upset the children's mother asked where.

"Just somewhere," said Louise.

"But nicely," Dick added. "Like a funeral at Granny and Grandfather's. In a box."

"The one my sandals came in," Louise explained. "I put that pink handkerchief I had for Christmas over him."

Isobel and Victoria might disapprove of Jackie but he was part of the family life. They could not believe he had just been pushed under the ground.

"But you know where to find him when you want him back?" Victoria asked.

Louise shook her head.

"No. Anyway, I don't want him back."

"She's twelve now," Dick pointed out. "I always knew twelve would be the right age for Jackie to go away."

They looked at Dick with new eyes. He was changing. He wouldn't be ten until October, yet it sounded as if it was he who had decided that Louise was too old for Jackie. Such a strange decision to come from the member of the family who noticed and minded if between one holiday and another an ornament was moved.

"Of course Dick wasn't there when Mummy was talking about what we'd be when we grew up," Isobel said later to Victoria. "But if he had been, I should think she'd say he would be something where a person needs to be extra reliable."

Victoria too had been thinking about Dick.

"Aren't Daddy and Mummy lucky that the only boy is like Dick? Always good, always works hard, as well as being clever enough to be expected to get a scholarship at Marlborough. How awful for them if he'd been like me."

"Or me," said Isobel. "It's all right for me to be an artist, but it's not the sort of thing Daddy would like his son to be."

Victoria had expected to loathe every minute of the holiday. No John to do things with. Even if it was not mentioned and the punishment was waiting until she got home – in disgrace. As she had written to John:

"My expectation of pleasure is low."

As things turned out it was a better holiday than she anticipated. Of course she missed John abominably. Every moment of the day there seemed to be something she wanted to tell him or show him. But in so far as he could he had made up to her for not being free by sending her books.

"Knowing what a muggins you are about keeping your reading a secret," he wrote, "I am sending a parcel of books for you to Annie. Warn her it's not a gift from a swain, though I will put in the box some of that toffee with nuts in it that she and Hester like . . ."

The books were a mixed lot. Because it was holiday time John had changed Victoria's diet. For the box introduced her to Arnold Bennett, Wells and Conan Doyle. But there were also the poems of Keats, Shelley and Coleridge.

"Try getting off on your own," he wrote, "and read one poem out loud each day. It'll sound fine with a background of waves."

Because John ordered it Victoria obeyed and was surprised to find he was right. She also found she grew so fond of some of the poetry that she learnt it by heart. As a result, during a bathe, she would swim away from the family to recite "Swiftly walk o'er the western wave, Spirit of Night" or "O what can ail thee, knight-at-arms, Alone and palely loitering?" But even while she was reciting, she never lost sight of herself, for she would often break off to giggle. "Miss Brown would drop dead if she knew I said poetry because I like it."

Annie, who of course had to know about the books, had some shrewd comments to make.

"Comic, you are. Let your poor father fidget himself to death because you aren't learnin' anything and all the time you've your nose in a book. Why can't you tell him?"

Victoria had no real reason.

"I just don't want to."

"Hopin' to surprise everybody, are you? Well, it will be a nice change. Shan't know ourselves come Christmas, if you come home sayin' you was top in everything."

Until that moment Victoria had not faced up to the problem of next term, but now Annie had sowed the seed, it took root. Victoria never willingly did things by halves. She had not liked the thought of next term because doing better, interspersed with talks with Miss French, had seemed both tame and embarrassing; but after that talk with Annie she began to plan. She would be a different person next term. She would work harder than any girl had ever worked before. The whole school would talk about her.

It was easy to find quiet spots in which to read undisturbed, but Victoria had not as much time on her hands as she had expected; and of all people, the one with whom she spent some of what she had was her mother. From the time they could walk all the children had been taught by their mother to enjoy her hobby of flower hunting. In the early days small prizes were given for the largest collection found on a walk of different flowers, each of which must be named. Later, they helped search for rare flowers, for their mother had the Bentham and Hooker books, which described and showed drawings of every flower in the British Isles. When she found a new flower she painted the drawing of it. In North Wales, though August was not the best time of year for flower hunting, there were rare flowers

241

she had never found; so she was out some part of each day hunting, and Victoria got into the habit of going with her.

At the beginning of the holiday conversation on the flower hunts was confined almost entirely to flowers. Then gradually other topics crept in, until one surprising day Victoria found herself her mother's confidant. There were plenty of stormy patches ahead when the gap of understanding between them was as wide as ever, but in future after each patch closed Victoria was once more someone in whom her mother could confide and, later on, on whom she could lean. A position she was never to lose.

It started on the day the children's mother found a Pinquicula Vulgaria. Only collectors know the sense of achievement that comes from finding that for which they have searched. Regardless of the fact that the plant was growing on a wet rock, she knelt down by it to get a closer view. Then she called Victoria.

Victoria was at that time only a flower collector because she had been brought up to be one, but she could feel triumph at the success of a search. She looked at the bluish-purple flower and the spreading rosette of oblong light green leaves.

"Oh Mummy! It's *it*, isn't it? The Pinquicula?"

Her mother carefully picked one flower and one leaf.

"Yes. I was afraid it was too late to find one as they flower in the early summer."

They turned for home, both slightly exalted.

"I bet Isobel will wish she had been there when we found it," Victoria gloated.

They walked in silence for a little distance, then her mother said:

"I worry about Isobel, Vicky. She's sixteen next year; even perhaps this Christmas she may get asked to dances and we know no boys to partner her."

In Eastbourne parents rented halls and gave what were then called "flapper dances". But there was nothing new in the Strangeways knowing no boys – they never had. Victoria and John had long accepted the fact that he would have to act as escort when Isobel was old enough to be invited to such parties.

"There's John."

"It's not now I'm worried about, but in two years' time when Isobel is old enough for grown-up dances. John will be away at school except in the holidays, and we know nobody."

"How do other people get to know partners?"

Her mother replied with what Victoria found startling candour.

"They entertain. I mean, if I was the sort of person they are, I'd ask John to bring some school friends to stay. But I'm so bad at that sort of thing. I hate bothering about meals and entertaining. And Daddy isn't fond of having visitors in the house – except the Bishop or relations."

"I wouldn't bother," said Victoria. "Isobel's awfully pretty. I expect partners will turn up."

Her mother was again silent for a little. Then she said:

"I don't worry about you, Vicky. You are the sort that can look after yourself. But Isobel isn't, and I know I'm not going to make Daddy understand that we ought to be thinking about things."

Victoria, having only been to children's parties, was incapable of visualising a proper grown-up dance with dance programmes, though of course she had heard about them.

"I wouldn't bother too much yet. Isobel's only fifteen, it's two years before she's old enough for grown-up parties. Perhaps by then Daddy will have a curate that can dance."

On that day the subject was dropped there, but on another flower hunt it was picked up again, in a different version.

"What do the older girls wear at Laughton House for best? I mean, when their parents take them out."

"Very tight skirts so they can't move, and lace blouses and hats with veils – and proper idiots they look."

"Just like smart grown-ups?"

"That's right," Victoria agreed cheerfully. "I expect clothes like that will soon be coming from Ursula."

"Oh, no. They are going to India. Uncle Paul has been offered a secretaryship to the Viceroy. It couldn't come at a better time, Aunt Helen says, as she will be able to bring Ursula out while they are there."

"Won't Aunt Helen send her clothes back to us from India?"

"I doubt it."

They were so used to Isobel being dressed by Ursula that it was almost impossible to imagine her dressed by any other means. Victoria tried to think of something comforting to say.

"Oh well, Isobel won't care. And anyway I think soon Ursula's clothes wouldn't have fitted her. Isobel still looks awfully little-girlish – even her chest doesn't stick out properly for someone of fifteen."

"I expect I ought to be buying her corsets and proper bust bodices."

Isobel, like her sisters, was still wearing what was called a liberty bodice – a plain garment supported from the shoulders by wide straps with suspenders fore and aft, and buttoned all the way down. Both she and Victoria dreaded the thought of boned corsets, bust bodices and beribboned camisoles and petticoats – so constraining, and doubling the time it took to dress.

"Honestly, I wouldn't fuss yet. Grand-Nanny told us Aunt Hetty never stopped being a child until the day she met Uncle Samuel. I expect Isobel will be like that."

"Aunt Hetty had eight brothers," said her mother, "so it didn't matter if she looked grown-up or not. And I don't care if Isobel does or not. But it's what people say. Those smart women I have to call on are always making remarks like: 'You will soon have to be planning to bring that eldest girl of yours out.'

It sends shivers down my spine, Vicky, for I haven't the faintest idea how to do it – and Daddy will be no help."

Victoria could only repeat what she had already said; and indeed to her, Isobel grown up was too remote to imagine.

"I wouldn't fuss. Two years is simply ages away."

Victoria had another occupation which kept her from her reading. Remote as the house her father had rented was from anywhere, there was another house in the area, and occasionally the family staying in it came down to the beach. To Victoria this family was nearly as enthralling as the troupe of child dancers, for their lives were almost as far removed from her own. The family were driven to the beach in a wagonette by a uniformed coachman. With them came a governess, and a manservant who carried the hampers of food to the beach and made himself useful, but he also, after luncheon, played cricket with the children, for he was quite a star bowler.

Victoria, sitting on a rock pretending to be absorbed in a book, was studying the family, taking in every word they said. The eldest was William, then came Marigold, then Harold, then Daphne and there were two little ones, Agnes and Katherine.

They were a cheerful, friendly family, except for Harold, who could fly into furious tempers at a moment's notice, but not especially interesting to Victoria, who adopted the lot. To each one she gave a character, hobbies, gifts – until sometimes the unknown family seemed nearer to her than her own.

Then one day at the end of the holiday when Victoria was out with her mother flower hunting, she learnt something about them which brought them into even sharper focus, and really did make them as fascinating as the child dancers. They were passing the tiny halt from which in a day or two a small train would take two hours to carry them to the main line where they would catch their train via London home. That day, standing on a side line, was a long coach marked "sleeper".

"That," said the children's mother calmly, "must be for the family at The Plas. I heard they were leaving about the same time as we were."

"Sleepers?" Victoria asked. "What are they?"

Interesting flowers could be found on a railway embankment so her mother probably had only half an ear for Victoria's chatter.

"Beds. Very comfortable, I believe."

"Beds!" Victoria thought of the journey home. It took more than twelve hours and her mother, Louise and Hester were sick off and on all the way. Yet there were beds to be had, if you were rich enough to have them. But her mother was just not giving them a thought. She didn't mind that other people had things she had not. As for Daddy, he would be glad they couldn't have beds – he would think it was wrong to be so comfortable. Every inch of the journey home she would imagine William, Marigold, Harold, Daphne, Agnes and Katherine asleep in beds – while they, stiff and cramped, had to sleep propped against each other all night. She did not grudge The Plas family their comfort, but it gave her something to add to her list of intentions.

"When I'm grown up," she vowed, "I won't do anything, not even go on a train, unless I can go in the best way there is!"

The next day was one of those when The Plas family came to the beach. After lunch Victoria, apparently deep in a book, was startled to see Marigold, after a whispered conversation with William, coming towards her.

"We were wondering," Marigold said, "if you'd like to join our game of cricket."

Victoria was surprised at the revulsion she felt. She had made the family up – it would spoil them if she knew what they really were like.

"No, thank you," she said politely, hoping Marigold had not seen she was reading a story about Sherlock Holmes. "I've got to work."

That was the first time Victoria discovered that what she had imagined, and what was real, could get entangled – but it was far from being the last.

17 Autumn Term

Nobody ever began a term more full of great intentions than Victoria. Much to Miss Brown's disgust the question of how to handle the problem of moving up Louise into Victoria's form was got round by dividing the form in half. Victoria was in the A division, Louise in the B and a pupil teacher was engaged to assist – especially in the B division.

"Such pandering to Victoria," Miss Brown grumbled to Miss Black.

Miss Black was scornful.

"You've only yourself to blame, Brown dear. You let Miss French ride roughshod over you."

Of course, exhibitionist Victoria dramatised her reformation. When she remembered she wore a solemn – she hoped saintlike – expression. And openly, though it was not allowed, studied in her free time. When she was spoken to she replied with exaggerated politeness, which the mistresses found almost more aggravating than her previous rudeness.

"At least I could scold her for being rude," one of the outside mistresses complained to Miss Brown. "Now, I can't say a thing."

"I know," Miss Brown agreed. "So sad for her father to have such a difficult daughter, for he is such a splendid man. How I grieve for him."

But though Victoria dramatised herself, in her heart she was a frightened girl. Surely, if you worked really hard and even did arithmetic and geometry in free time, you should get on awfully fast until you reached the top of the class? It was true she got slightly better marks than she had last term, but she never rose above a B which, though better than the disgrace of a C, was a long way from the A-plus she expected.

At last, after some weeks of Bs, Victoria unwillingly took out the pad of pink paper and wrote: "Can I see you please? Urgent. Victoria Strangeway."

An hour later she was in Miss French's study.

"Well, Vicky, what's the problem?"

Victoria poured out her story.

"So you see I'm doing exactly what Daddy asked me to do, and what you said I should do for him, but, as I explained, it isn't doing any good. I only get Bs."

Miss French looked at Victoria. She would, she recalled, be fourteen at Christmas, and she was changing. It would not surprise her, Miss French decided, if this very ungainly fledgling became a swan some day.

"I am not a bit sorry for you, Vicky. You are experiencing what I supposed you would experience. Where did you first go to school?"

"To Elmhurst, when I was seven."

"Seven – and you are now thirteen, nearly fourteen, and, I suspect, working for the first time. Concentration and the power to work are qualities that have to be learned. None of us have them by nature; we may be naturally studious, but we still have to practise application. You have never begun to work until this term yet you expect, as if you had Aladdin's lamp, just to give it a rub – and hey presto, there you are at the top of the form."

Victoria was disappointed in Miss French. She had not known what she would say, but she had thought "bad luck" would have been part of it.

"If it's not going to do any good, I don't see much point in slaving as I am."

"Nonsense. You don't know it, but every day you are learning how to use that neglected brain of yours, and you are learning to concentrate. What you have to work at now is not to get discouraged. It is hard on you to work as you are doing, for small results; but we all have to pay in the end for wasted chances. That is something everybody has to learn – and the earlier the better."

Locked in a lavatory, Victoria had a little cry after the talk.

"Slave, slave, slave and nothing to show for it. I don't see how Daddy's ever going to know I worked hard if all I get is Bs. And I couldn't bear another term of getting up early to saw those beastly logs. If only I could see John! This term is being the longest I ever knew, and I get no time to read. I shouldn't think anything nice would ever happen again."

But in spite of Victoria's gloomy forecast, of course nice things did happen. One was funny: it

251

was on the quiet day which the children's father held for the clergy in his rural deanery. The children enjoyed anything which upset the ordinary routine, and this certainly did that. The day before, meals were eaten in the little room Isobel used for her painting, for the dining room was being given an extra clean by Hester. For the occasion, the dining room table was stretched to its fullest extent.

In those days, all dining tables were made with an eye to an increasing family. When the table arrived, probably as a wedding present, it was quite small, suitable for two people and two guests. But when the children were born and grew old enough to come down to meals a winder opened up the table and a section was inserted which added to its length. Presently, as the family grew, another section was added, and sometimes for especially big families, another. Then, as time passed, the children married and went away to homes of their own, and first one section and then another was removed until finally the dining room table was back to the small table that had been used before the children were born. Two sections were always needed now in the vicarage, since the children had meals with their parents, but for the quiet day a third had to be added.

On a quiet day nobody spoke until tea time. So for days beforehand Miss Herbert had been busy painting direction arrows on pieces of cardboard, and labels to hang on the doors. One glance at those cards and arrows and the girls saw an opportunity for a splendid joke. They and their mother were going to neighbours for breakfast, leaving Annie free to cook breakfast for the hungry clergy who would stream into the vicarage after Holy Communion. To keep an eye on Hester and Annie, Miss Herbert was remaining, but on the understanding that she stayed in her own room except when she slipped down the back stairs to lend a hand in the kitchen or dining room.

"We're leaving at eight for breakfast," Victoria reminded her sisters. "We'll have to nip round and change everything just before we go, or the Herbert will spot what we've done."

"She won't," said Louise. "She's promised Annie to help her dish up. They're eating bacon and eggs and Annie says they'll be hungry as wolves."

Victoria giggled.

"I wish – oh goodness, how I wish I could see them all going into the wrong rooms! We'll put all the WC arrows to Miss Herbert's room and hang WC on her door."

"Do you think Daddy will be very angry?" Isobel asked.

Victoria, set on a task, could see no future dangers.

"I wouldn't think so. He'll be so full of quiet day he won't notice. You know how he is."

The children's father had written to Miss French asking that they might be allowed home by four o'clock so that they could hand round at tea.

"I feel they should know the clergy in my rural

253

deanery, and the clergy should know them," he had explained.

When the girls got back to the vicarage, the rule of silence which had held all day was over, and it sounded like Babel in the dining room. As the girls slipped up to their room to tidy, Isobel whispered:

"I do hope you were right, Vicky, and Daddy isn't angry we changed the arrows. I feel a bit wormish inside."

"Someone's changed them back," Louise pointed out. "I purposely marked Mummy and Daddy's bedroom 'Dining room' and the card's gone."

Looking unbelievably innocent the three girls came into the dining room. Their mother did not see them for she was pouring out tea but their father saw them come in. He beckoned to them, his lips twitching at the corners.

"Here you are! I'm afraid Miss Herbert's very angry with you. And you may have to make your peace with some of my clergy."

That was all that was said.

"How odd," said Isobel to Victoria that night, "that Daddy did not mind about the arrows."

Victoria thought she knew the answer.

"I suppose that was the sort of thing the uncles and aunts did – what Granny calls 'mischief'. I've always noticed he doesn't mind things he calls that."

Another brief spot in that rather dull autumn term was an entertainment the girls arranged. In those days in most parishes there were branches of The Band of Hope, which brought children up to sign the pledge. This meant they promised not to taste, touch or handle strong drink.

Eastbourne had many branches of The Band of Hope, which each year competed for a shield. On the night when the shield was awarded, the largest hall in the town was hired and each branch put on a so-called entertainment. From what the children's father had seen last year, the parish church's contribution to the entertainment had been of even poorer quality than that of the other parishes, for there was no one competent or willing to produce it. So this year he handed the job over to his daughters.

"There is a rule that no branch may spend more than ten shillings on dresses and things. It has been the custom to pick about ten children to perform, but actually the whole Sunday School belongs to The Band of Hope and it is a large stage at the Winter Gardens, so I would like to see as many boys and girls used as possible."

The three girls went into consultation.

"Ten shillings sounds a lot," said Isobel, "but it isn't so much if we use lots of children, so it's no good thinking of anything that wants much dressing up."

It was Louise who had the bright idea.

"Why not nursery rhymes? I could join some together to make one piece of music."

They were in Isobel's little painting room. Victoria, as she always did when she was seized with an idea, began pacing up and down.

"They could dance in two and two and then sing

255

while some acted the parts. I think the great thing will be to do it all very fast."

Isobel had her sketch book.

"I tell you what. I expect each of the girls has a white frock; why couldn't they have a pleated skirt with their frocks tied back over them, like fishwives have?"

"And couldn't we dye their stockings?" Louise suggested. "That would look fun."

Victoria hung over Isobel's shoulder.

"What about the boys?"

"There is some frightfully cheap stuff of a sort of cotton."

Isobel made a few rough sketches.

"Look, if the boys wore jerseys, they could have lengths of that stuff, with holes cut for their heads, and fasten them at the waist with any belt they have."

"What about their legs?" Victoria asked.

Isobel sketched out a few more ideas.

"I know. They can cross-garter with tape – like Morris dancers."

The idea was being born, the girls set to work. Victoria visited the church school and explained what she wanted and asked for volunteers. After last Christmas's successful play she had no difficulty in getting offers though, as the performers had to be free to rehearse on Saturday mornings, all who would have liked to take part could not. Finally, she selected twenty boys and twenty girls.

At the first rehearsal Isobel stepped in. Using one

girl and one boy as a model, she showed them what it was planned they should wear. Then she sent them all home with, in the case of the girls, a roll of bright blue crinkly paper, and the boys with lengths of green cotton.

"We're going to dye you girls' stockings ourselves, so they all come out the same colour," she explained, "so please will you bring a pair of white cotton stockings marked with your name to next Saturday's rehearsal."

Louise, with her usual competence, had strung a selection of nursery rhymes together which she could rattle off on the piano with immense verve. Victoria ruled the rehearsals and, since the boys and girls performing were proud to have been chosen, she got a well-drilled performance out of them.

The result exceeded anything the sisters had dreamed of. The standard of the entertainment, until the parish church children's performance, had been universally low: six girls dressed in kimonos had enacted a dreary routine with fans; a group of boys had given a tedious exhibition of Indian clubs, and a temperance song had been sung of which the refrain had been: "Drinking like a fish. Drinking like a fish" – and while they had sung it the children on the stage had shaken admonitory fingers at the children in the audience.

After an hour of this sort of thing the audience was comatose. Then suddenly, singing "Boys and girls come out to play", on danced the parish church team. They had good coloured overhead lights and these blazed down on what was really a pretty sight, for the girls looked charming with their white frocks pinned back over their blue paper skirts, and the boys most effective in their Robin Hood green. And as one nursery rhyme succeeded another the enthusiasm of the audience rose until, when the children danced off the stage, they were followed not only by clapping but by cheers and stamping of feet.

There were queries afterwards by the suspicious as to how such a performance was put on for ten shillings, but Isobel had her accounts to show. And any such pin-pricks were far outweighed for the girls by the pleasure they had given their father.

"This will be the talk of the town," he said, "and just what my parish wanted. They need to feel proud of themselves."

At the end of the term poor Victoria came home in floods of tears over her examination results.

"What's the good of working?" she sobbed. "My marks are hardly any better than last year. Miss French, whenever I see her, says I must learn not to be discouraged, but I am discouraged, and I don't care who knows it."

It was not possible for either her father or her mother to offer Victoria much comfort, as they both knew she was paying for having frittered away her time.

"Mummy and I know you have worked this term, and that is a beginning," her father said. "But you can't expect to catch up in one term. It will be in a year's time that we should see real improvement."

But there was improvement in Victoria's report; it was the only fairly good one she had been given since she was seven. There was no praise, but the words "Much improved" appeared several times.

"Well done, Vicky," said her father. "Those words 'Much improved' have been harder for you to earn than the 'Excellent' that I see on both Isobel and Louise's reports."

Then it was the Christmas holidays, and Victoria and Spot were at the station to meet John. Isobel had asthma, Louise had a cold and Dick had stayed at home to keep her company. The children's parents were at a prize-giving, and Miss Herbert had accompanied Victoria, but had left her to do some shopping. So Victoria was alone as the train was signalled. Suddenly her heart began to beat so fast it felt as if it was in her throat. John was coming home. She had not seen him since Christmas. How strange to be so happy it hurt. Suddenly the train turned the corner and puffed into the station – and John stepped down out of it. A year older, but even though he was now just sixteen, looking the same John.

"Hullo," he said. 'My word, it's good to see your comic face!"

Victoria grinned.

"Good to see yours. Miss Herbert's outside somewhere. Let's send her home with your luggage, and we'll walk."

18 Influenza

Nineteen-hundred-and-twelve began badly, for all the family had influenza. The boys had it first. Dick must have come home from school with the germs in him, and he shared them first with John. It was supposedly disappointing for the boys to miss the Christmas parties and dances (neither cared), but they were mild cases, so as soon as they were over the worst they managed to enjoy themselves playing ludicrous games, such as Snakes and Ladders and the then popular "Who Knows?", and working at elaborate booby traps to catch the unfortunates who brought in their trays. And for Dick there was the special treat of having Spot on his bed at any time when someone was not taking him for a walk.

Victoria was really the next to catch the disease, but no one knew this, as on the day John went back to school she disguised the fact that she was feeling most peculiar, in order not to be forbidden to go to the station. For this was a special occasion because, now that she was fourteen, she had been told she might go alone, provided she hurried straight home the moment the train had gone.

As it turned out, the journey to the station was not a success; John was cross, because he was only convalescent, and Victoria, who was feeling worse every minute, was monosyllabic. After a few abortive attempts at station conversation John lost his temper.

"You are a bore today, Vicky. I don't know why you bothered to come, if you've nothing to say. I wouldn't wait to see me off."

The easy tears of someone who is ill trickled down Victoria's cheeks.

"Don't be so mean. We've hardly talked all the holidays, because of your influenza and Dick being there. I don't know any of the things that happened to you last year."

John was disgusted by her tears.

"I'll tell you at Easter. There's no need to blub."

"I can't help it," Victoria sniffled, reduced at last to truthfulness. "I feel simply awful."

John, who until that moment – like most male invalids – had thought of nobody but himself, gave Victoria first a quick look and then a concerned one. He felt her forehead.

"You silly juggins! You should be in bed. You're awfully hot, I bet you're getting influenza, for that's just how I was when I started. Look . . ." he took some silver from his pocket, "go and find the station taxi and when you get back go straight to bed, and let Aunt Sylvia send for the doctor."

Victoria felt too ill to argue, and was thankful to fall into the taxi and be driven home, with her eyes shut. When she reached the vicarage, how she arrived – or in what condition – passed unnoticed, for Louise had collapsed with influenza in a far more

261

dramatic way; she had what was then called "fainted dead away". Though she did not know it, the children's mother was also catching influenza, and so was not entirely herself, or, even though she was worried about Louise, she would have noticed that Victoria was ill. Instead, Victoria, slowly pulling herself upstairs to bed, was greeted by:

"Don't crawl about like that, Vicky. Louise is ill. Run to the kitchen and ask Annie to put on a kettle for a hot water bottle." Then, hanging over the banisters, she called: "Hester, haven't you found that brandy?"

Annie saw at once that Victoria was ill.

"You sit down by the stove, ducks. I'll take up the bottle, then I'll fill one and put it in your bed. Could you fancy something hot to drink?"

Victoria had reached the stage where she wanted nothing but to lie down.

"No, thank you, Annie."

Annie filled the bottles and took them up.

"And this other one is for Miss Vicky," she said, passing Louise's bottle to the children's mother. "Very queer she looks; proper go of the flu, I'd say – worse than that one." She nodded at Louise.

Louise, looking unbelievably frail, was receiving her mother's whole attention. Except that she was not feeling well herself, the children's mother was in her element – with Louise wholly dependent on her. She did not want to believe that Victoria was also ill; in some way it detracted from the excitement surrounding Louise's fainting attack.

"What a nuisance! I'll have a look at her presently, but I don't suppose it's anything. She's never ill. She's as strong as a horse."

Annie gave the children's mother a look which, as she told Hester afterwards, "should have cut like a knife", and with a sniff she swept out of Louise's room, saying:

"If you don't want to trouble, madam, you needn't. I'll look after Miss Vicky."

And Annie did. She helped Victoria upstairs, undressed her, and tucked her into bed.

The children's mother did, later on, look in on her second invalid but, inexplicably even to herself, could only say grudgingly:

"Oh, that's right, you are in bed. The doctor's coming to see Louise, so he may as well have a look at you at the same time – but I expect it's nothing."

Victoria turned her face to the wall and tears trickled down her nose. Why did Louise have to be ill at the same time? It would have been nice, for a change, to be the one Mummy fussed over.

When the doctor came he confirmed that both girls had influenza.

"But it's Vicky who has the sharp attack," he said. "Her temperature is 103°. Let me know if it goes higher."

True to form, though Victoria had bad influenza while it lasted, she recovered quickly, while Louise, who had not had nearly so high a temperature, was still too weak to get up. Then Isobel caught the complaint. She awoke shivering in the middle of the night and Victoria had to run for her mother, who was then in the crawling-about stage.

Isobel was very ill indeed, and was left with a chest weakness – something which terrified her parents, haunted by the knowledge of Mother's mother who had died of the so-called galloping consumption. Then to cap everything, while they were still awaiting news of the results of the tests the doctor had made on Isobel, the children's father, Miss Herbert and Annie all succumbed on the same day.

The children's mother, still convalescent herself, was distracted. She was good in a sick room, but a wretched cook and no good at all at arranging attractive trays. Hester could barely cook, and had no idea about trays other than slapping on to them food which had been prepared by others.

Victoria realised these things, and was worried that her father might be neglected, so she slipped into the kitchen when no one was about and started to prepare what she thought would please him: tea, toast cut in fingers, and a boiled egg set on a tray covered with the best tray cloth, on which she pinned a spray of winter jasmine. She was hurrying out of the kitchen with this offering, trying to get it upstairs before her mother came down, when she ran straight into her. The egg fell off the tray and smashed on the kitchen floor and the tea splashed over the best tray cloth. Any woman run off her feet might have been annoyed, but the children's mother, barely convalescent, saw this accident as a last straw.

"Really, Vicky! I would have thought a great girl

like you would try to help, not to hinder. And why is this flower pinned on to my nice cloth?"

Victoria's mouth set in an ugly line.

"It's for Daddy. *I* care if he's looked after, even if nobody else does."

Her mother could have slapped her.

"He's asleep and he's only to have liquids. I wish you would ask me before you do things. There's plenty for you to do if you want to help."

Victoria, also barely convalescent, looked more mulish than ever.

"All right. I'm asking now."

Somehow her mother kept her temper.

"Then take that tea to Miss Herbert."

But the next day when the doctor called she asked: "Do you think Vicky could go back to school? She's no help to me, and there is no point in her hanging about the house."

The doctor was very sorry for the children's mother, who always looked delicate but at that moment as if she might dissolve at a rough word. Kindly he patted her shoulder.

"What you need is a good holiday; this is a nasty influenza and leaves the patient run down. I'll have a look at Vicky on my way out."

After the doctor had gone the children's mother said almost triumphantly to Victoria, who was listlessly lolling in a chair by the fire:

"You are going back to school tomorrow. The doctor says you are quite fit now."

Victoria was convinced she was not fit to go back

to school, and the injustice bit into her soul. There was Louise, just as much recovered as she was, lying in bed, while she was turned out into the cold.

"It's mean. It's mean," she muttered. "Annie says Louise's looks pity her. I wish mine did. I should think I would get pneumonia from going out too soon, and then if I die Mummy will be sorry."

At least Victoria had expected to have a triumphal entry into Laughton House. As she travelled on the bus to school (a concession to her weakened state), she could almost hear the cries of "Hullo, Vicky!" "Are you better, Vicky?"

But her arrival caused no stir, for half the school were late in returning after influenza or colds. Someone in her form did say commiseratingly: "Your face is yellow like a Chinese."

Because of her promise to her father and to Miss French, Victoria, according to her lights, worked hard; but because she felt ill-used, she had a chip on her shoulder which made her crave for notice – even, if necessary, for notoriety. It was this which impelled her to spend part of the money she had been given for Christmas on green hair ribbons.

It was the fashion that year for teenage girls to hold their front hair back with combs, and fasten their plaits back by a huge bow of wired ribbon – usually black – at the nape of the neck. Victoria's school dress that term was a top and skirt of coarse grey material with a green stripe running through it.

It was this green stripe which gave her the idea of matching it with a green hair ribbon. She had noticed

266

this ribbon in a shop in the town before she had influenza.

Victoria was not, of course, allowed in the town alone, but that did not worry her. If everybody else was going to loll about at home while she went to school, then she had a right to do what she wanted to – as a way of making up. So on Saturday morning when she was supposed to be taking Spot for a quiet walk round the parish, she caught instead a motor bus into the town. The green ribbon, six inches wide and stiffly wired was still, looking glorious, in the window. Victoria bought enough for two large bows.

Miss French seldom had cause to speak to her girls about their clothes. She was so perfectly turned out herself that she set a standard which the school struggled to live up to. Now and again after a birthday a gold bangle would appear, but usually "Very pretty but I should keep it for the holidays" was enough and the bangle was never seen again. To wear coloured hair ribbons was unheard of.

Victoria had not dared to put the ribbons on at home, for not only would she be ordered to take them off but there would be awkward questions as to where she had bought them. So, though she had tried them on and admired them in her bedroom, they travelled to school in her coat pocket.

Louise was returning to school for the first time that day and Victoria had feared she might be a nuisance hanging about the day girls' cloakroom, but Louise was no trouble for she wanted to see her friends, so for a few minutes Victoria had the looking glass to herself and she thought the effect superb.

"Almost," she thought amazed, "I look pretty."

Her appearance in her form was greeted by gasps.

"Vicky!" – "Your hair!" – "Wait until Miss Brown sees you."

But one girl said what Victoria hoped to hear.

"You won't be allowed to wear them, but I must say they suit you. Quite divino."

Adding Os to words was fashionable amongst the young at that date.

To the form's surprise, Miss Brown, though she gave Victoria a startled look, said nothing. The truth was, she was not in a position to say anything. The staff knew there were unwritten laws about dress and jewellery, but they had no instructions to enforce them; that must come from Miss French. So Victoria wore her startling green hair ribbons until French literature, a class taken by Miss French which A and B shared. Then quietly, but so that the whole room heard, she said:

"We don't want to see those green ribbons tomorrow, Vicky. Black, please."

It was too much to hope that Louise would keep that story to herself. The moment she got home she was recounting it to her mother, her father – who had not yet been allowed outside the house – and to Isobel.

"You should have seen the way the girls looked at Vicky – sort of half laughing. I would have sunk right through the floor with shame. But *she* didn't.

She just looked as though Miss French hadn't said anything."

"But where did you get green hair ribbons, Vicky?" her mother asked. "I bought you black."

"I bought them when I was shopping at Christmas."

"That's a lie," Louise declared, "because you had to borrow sixpence from me for Mummy's present. I bet you bought them out of your Christmas money – and now it's wasted."

The young in those days had very little pocket money. The Strangeways had threepence a week until they were twelve, when it was raised to sixpence. But even then the money was not entirely their own: a penny had to go on the plate on Sundays, and since they had received sixpence a week Isobel and Victoria had to buy their own postage stamps. As a result the exact state of everyone's finance was common knowledge.

Trapped, Victoria completely lost her temper. She would punish smug, tale-telling Louise! In a second she had seized Louise, thrown her to the ground, and was banging the back of her head on the floor.

"You beast! You beast! If I say I bought them at Christmas, I bought them at Christmas."

Their father separated them.

"Really, Vicky, what behaviour! You might be a savage. But, Louise, you too are to blame. You shouldn't tell tales."

"Well, make her show her Christmas money,"

said Louise. "If she's still got it I'll say I'm sorry –
but she hasn't."

All the family had received two and sixpence,
from one of the uncles, and Grand-Nanny had sent
each a shilling. There had been no other money at
Christmas except the sixpence in the plum pudding
and Dick had found that. Victoria should also have
had two weeks' pocket money; she had spent the
rest on paper books and transfers when she had been
ill.

Louise was still looking pale from influenza and
she had black shadows under her eyes. It had horrified her mother to see her frail baby's head being
banged on the floor. Coldly she said:

"Yes. Go upstairs, Victoria, and fetch the money.
But don't come down until you feel you can control
yourself. How could a great girl like you treat poor
little Louise like that?"

Every word was calculated to inflame. There was
nothing Victoria hated more than to be called "a
great girl" – and the "poor little Louise" was the
last straw. She strode to the door, out of which she
intended to stalk, slamming it after her, but Isobel
came to the rescue. Her words tumbled out on top
of each other for she was, since her chest infection,
even shorter of breath than usual.

"When you come down would you bring me
another handkerchief, Vicky? I've been coughing."

Victoria and Isobel had few secrets from each
other, so at once Victoria knew what Isobel meant:

under her handkerchiefs was a sachet in which she kept her money.

So the door was not slammed and in a few minutes Victoria was back. Her mouth set in a hard line, for she loathed lying to her father; but in her hand was half-a-crown, a shilling and tenpence in coppers. She held the money out for Louise to see.

"Half-a-crown, one shilling and two weeks' pocket money, less twopence for collection on two Sundays. Now apologise!"

Louise could always find a way out of her troubles.

"You are a silly! I never thought you hadn't got it. But if you want me to I don't mind saying I'm sorry."

The children's father said gently:

"Now the subject is closed. I think Vicky, like the rest of us, is still feeling the effects of being ill." He gave Victoria a smile which made her feel so ashamed it hurt. "Now Mummy and I have some nice news for you: next week we are all going for five days to Granny and Grandfather to blow away the last of the influenza."

The five days at Granny and Grandfather's certainly put the family on their feet again, for Grand-Nanny had great ideas about "feeding up" – something they all needed. But Victoria, for once in that house, was not happy. It still rankled that she had been sent back to school while Louise stayed comfortably in bed. She still carried a chip on her shoulder for she had convinced herself she had been sent back to school because she was not wanted. She kept turning over in her head ways of making herself noticed and admired. And her conscience continued to give her a sharp prick when she remembered how she had lied about her money.

Of course Granny and Grandfather saw that something was wrong and both tried to find out what, Grandfather during morning prayers, Granny by one of her little talks.

"Holy Father," Grandfather prayed at morning prayers, "please help my granddaughter Vicky. That she may grow in gentleness. Thou knowest how hard it is for her to accept correction meekly. But with Thy help all things are possible . . ."

Granny, eager to help, on the family's second morning in the house sent Aunt Sophie for Victoria.

"As I have told you before, Vicky, I have a very special corner in my heart for you, but I am not very happy about you on this visit. Granny's old eyes are sharp and what she sees worries her. She does not like that droop at the corners of your mouth."

Had any other adult talked like that, even her father, Victoria would have resented it; but Granny was special. She did her best to explain.

"Although I really am working hard I hardly ever get more than Bs and that makes me feel terribly inferior – which I do anyway, for day girls are despised at Laughton House.

Granny stopped her.

"Yet dear Isobel and little Louise seem happy enough."

"It's different for them. They're good at things. But I'm good at nothing . . . And then they're both prettier than me."

Granny could not deny this last, but she could find something to praise.

"I seem to have heard wonderful accounts of parish entertainments arranged by you. I should scarcely call that being good at nothing."

Victoria dismissed this for she sincerely longed to get to the heart of her discontent.

"I know the doctor said I could go back to school after influenza. But Louise, who started when I did, didn't have to. But it wasn't just that once – it's always that I never seem to matter as much as the others."

Granny was shocked.

"That is nonsense, ain't it? But you probably are having growing pains and they may make you think you feel things you do not." Gently she took one of Victoria's hands and patted it. "I do not want to preach, for that is not what grannies are for – but suppose you try showing a little more love instead of always asking for it? I think you will be surprised how it will help you, and how soon that mouth will turn up again at the corners."

Granny and Grandfather were really worried, and after a discussion behind closed doors decided they must talk to the children's father.

"Though I think the difficulty is really dear Sylvia," Granny said. "This is sad, for I notice that when they are doing something which both are enjoying, Vicky and Sylvia are happy together."

Grandfather knew what she meant.

"I agree. But I think it will be better if we talk to Jim alone; after all, he is our son. Sylvia might think we were interfering."

So that evening Aunt Sophie was instructed to take the children's mother to the kitchen to choose home-made jam to take back to the vicarage, so that Granny and Grandfather should have the children's father to themselves.

Granny opened the conversation. "We wanted to speak to you about Vicky, Jim dear. She looks so unhappy."

Horrified, the children's father stared at his mother.

"Unhappy! But how can she be? Ours, as you know, is such a happy home."

"To you and to Sylvia and the other children, no doubt," Grandfather agreed. "But your mother is right. That child is not happy, Jim."

Granny patted his knee.

"Something must be done, dear. Do you think that school is right for her?"

The children's father was surprised at the question.

"Laughton House! It's a splendid school. And Miss French is not only delightful but a most sincere Christian."

Grandfather spoke dryly.

"A sincere Christian may not necessarily understand Vicky. Would you perhaps try keeping her at home next term, and allow her to learn with that admirable Miss Herbert?"

That, distressed though he was, made the children's father smile.

"Miss Herbert is indeed admirable, but I'm afraid Vicky does not find her so; I should fear bloodshed if I tried that experiment."

"Then what?" asked Granny. "Something should be done, dear."

The children's father was most disturbed; it was appalling that his parents should have to say a child of his was unhappy. Then an answer came to him. He spoke slowly, as one repeating what he had been told.

"Vicky has a difficult nature, far more difficult than have the other children. She therefore needs more help. I had planned that she should be confirmed next year, but now I know it should be this year. She is to start her classes immediately."

Convinced that God had spoken, it never crossed the minds of her father and grandparents to wonder if Victoria should also be consulted. And indeed, at that date young people seldom were consulted when plans were made for them.

"We must make Vicky's confirmation a great day for her," Grandfather said. "I shall of course attend and so will Sophie." Then he looked at Granny. "I think for so important a day even your dear mother will be at the service."

"And so will as many other members of the family

as can get away," Granny promised. "Dear Vicky; she shall be surrounded with our prayers and with our love."

19 Confirmation Day

The children's father did not tell Victoria she was to be confirmed until they got home. Then he called her into his study.

"Vicky, I am going to prepare you for confirmation."

Victoria had no idea why she had been sent for; certainly being confirmed had not entered her thoughts. She answered like a flash.

"No, thank you, Daddy. I don't feel suitable for that yet."

Her father, who was sitting at his desk, held out a hand and when, unwillingly, Victoria came to him he pulled her on to the arm of his chair and put his arm round her, laying his face against hers in the way that made one of his eyebrows tickle her cheek.

"Granny and Grandfather talked to me about you. They said you don't look happy, Vicky." He paused for a moment.

In that pause Victoria felt for a second almost a friend instead of a daughter. Daddy knew she was not happy. Now, since he had said that, she could explain everything. Perhaps, as he was so wise, he would understand why she felt inferior, and tell her how you stopped feeling it. She took a quick breath and opened her mouth, but before she could speak her father went on.

"I told them that was nonsense. With a happy home such as ours how could any child not be happy, and that I was sure you liked Laughton House, for it is a splendid school and Miss French a wonderful woman." His lips twitched. "Granny wondered if perhaps you would be happier doing lessons with Miss Herbert."

The enormity of this suggestion swept every other thought out of Victoria's head, so the moment when absolute truth might have been spoken passed, and was never in that form to be revived.

It was probably a good thing, Victoria decided later, for would her father have accepted that he had a daughter who would be happier living away from her family? With his feeling about his home and the way he was brought up, could he have faced the truth that one of his children did not find the vicarage perfect?

Victoria was stunned.

"Lessons with Miss Herbert! Daddy!"

Her father chuckled.

"I knew that was how you would feel. Mind you, Miss Herbert is a wonderful woman and a great help, not only to Mummy but to me; but I don't think she would like teaching you any more than you would like doing lessons with her. Now, about these confirmation classes . . ."

Victoria's chin shot up.

"I told you, Daddy, I don't feel suitable for them."

Her father held her closer to him.

"I am not going to allow you to decide, Vicky darling. You have a more difficult nature than your sisters or Dick, so you need special help. That I know will come to you when you are able to attend Holy Communion. Your confirmation will be a big occasion, for many people will want to be present to pray that you may be especially helped and blessed."

Victoria tried to wriggle out of her father's arm so that she could face him. But she could not for he held her tightly.

"Please no, Daddy. I know you think it will be lovely for me, everybody praying and all, but . . ." she was going to say "I'll hate it," but she had the sense to bite that back. Instead she said: "I won't like it, I mean, I can see it's good of everybody, but oh, Daddy *please* no."

If he had never had that, to him, shocking talk with his parents and had not been convinced God had suggested the answer, the children's father might have yielded to Victoria's pleas and postponed her confirmation for a year; but the talk had taken place and now he was dedicated to giving this much-loved but wayward child the spiritual help he was convinced would change her life. He took his arm from around her and got up and led the way to his prie-dieu.

"We will ask God together for a very special blessing on me when I prepare you; and on you, not only on your confirmation day but for all your life."

Although her sisters did not understand why Victoria was making such a fuss about being confirmed they were sorry for her.

"I don't see why Vicky's got to be confirmed, if she doesn't want to be," Louise said to Isobel. "Lots of girls aren't confirmed until they are fifteen, so she could have waited until next year."

Isobel was puzzled.

"I don't understand why she is so worried about it. I liked my confirmation day."

John wrote sensibly from school.

"What a state to get in about it! You knew it would happen some time. As you know, I was done last year and it was all right. All the same, I can't understand why Uncle Jim is making you be done if you don't want to be. Still, I daresay you would not have felt any more like it next year."

Not to anyone could Victoria explain the horror with which she faced her confirmation day, for she did not understand it herself. She did talk about the subject to Isobel.

"Being me, I ought to look forward to it. Everybody staring at me and praying for me. Half the parish there and heaps of relations all on their knees saying: 'Let this be a turning point in Vicky's life.' But instead, I feel sick when I think about it – and I don't know why."

"It's different being looked at for ordinary things," Isobel said sagely, "than being prayed

280

about. But when you are being confirmed you'll find you don't think about the congregation."

"You didn't, because you're different. You never do anything bad. Nobody was praying you'd behave better, but just that you'd have less asthma and things like that. And it's not only the confirmation day, it's those awful preparation classes."

Isobel could not follow that.

"They're all right. Like lessons. You will be told by Daddy what to do, and how to prepare for Holy Communion, and about the Holy Ghost. Why do you mind that?"

Victoria shuddered.

"It's bad enough having talks and praying with Daddy when I'm alone. But in front of other girls – some of them like Olive Gay who are my friends – I'll be embarrassed all the time. I don't think anyone could like their father to talk about God and all that in front of their friends. God should be kept private."

"It won't be as bad as you think," Isobel consoled.

"It won't," Vicky agreed, "but only because at my confirmation classes I'll be a deaf adder that stoppeth its ears."

This was what happened. Victoria had to attend her classes, but she was an experienced non-listener, so all the wise helpful things her father said, which were absorbed by the rest of his class, passed her by.

It was not only over her classes that Victoria was obstructive, it was over everything to do with confirmation. Had she not been so wrapped up in herself she would have realised that she had a sympathiser in her mother who, on principle, disapproved of a fuss being made about a religious ceremony. Since her marriage she had conformed to her husband's wishes and, except for a cup of tea which she insisted helped to keep her tickling cough at bay, went to Holy Communion fasting. But that did not say she approved either for herself or for delicate Isobel. How much more sensible, she thought, was the way she had been brought up – to attend once a month after morning service, with a good breakfast inside her. She therefore admired Victoria's fight, as it was one she wished she had the strength of mind to take part in herself. As a gesture to show understanding she cut down her list of necessities for the garden, so that one day she was able to say:

"Vicky, you never have a new frock so, instead of squeezing you into Isobel's confirmation dress, you can choose your own. If you will find a pattern you like, and choose the material, the dressmaker can make it."

Alas, Victoria was determined to like nothing to do with her confirmation. Without a thought as to where the money had come from she stuck her chin in the air.

"Thank you, Mummy, but Isobel's cast-off will do nicely."

It was that sort of remark that usually made the children's mother's temper rise. But on that occasion she refused to be upset.

"Choose something not too warm and I'll have it dyed for the summer, for I don't think a girl of your age looks her best in white."

Stubborn to the end Victoria would not ask Isobel's advice about design – still less Miss Herbert's, who was knowledgeable about materials. Instead, with heaven knows what garment in mind, she had a real monstrosity made – acknowledged as such even in the badly dressed vicarage. The dress proper was made of a coarse, shiny, dotted cotton. But on the shoulders was a flapping trimming of what looked like broderie anglaise. The neckband and the wrists were finished off with the same kind of trimming.

When Louise saw the dress she said to her family: "That looks like her drawers, not a frock." And no one disagreed with her.

The confirmation was towards the end of March. For days beforehand every post brought small packets addressed to Victoria. In those days little limp-back books were sold for special occasions and also white books with gold on them. Isobel, seeing the pile of little books growing in Victoria's bedroom, said:

"I should think you've been given the lot."

Victoria scowled at her presents.

"I can't see a girl is likely to be better because she has thirteen copies of *The Imitation of Christ* and seven of *Thoughts before Holy Communion.*"

It was Grandfather who really drove Victoria almost to frenzy. He had taken rooms for himself,

Granny and Aunt Sophie on the seafront and, true to his belief in laying your troubles publicly before God, he suggested that a little prayer meeting should be held in church before luncheon (the confirmation was at three), which should be attended by Victoria, her godparents and all relations.

"Oh no!" said the children's mother when she heard what was planned. "Say no. Vicky will hate it."

The children's father could not believe his father could have a bad idea.

"I don't quite think I can say no since my dear father has suggested it."

"Then for goodness' sake keep it as quiet as possible. Vicky is very strung up as it is. If your father must say prayers let him say them in the study."

Although to Victoria the study was better than the church nothing was bearable on that embarrassing day. From the time she woke she thought she heard a special voice being used. It was not entirely true; Isobel and Louise spoke normally and so did the servants, but to Victoria everybody was offending.

"Don't talk to me in that tip-toe way," she shouted at Miss Herbert in the middle of breakfast.

Miss Herbert refused to be cross; instead she put on a brave bright smile.

"I did not mean to, dear, but this is a very, very special day, isn't it?"

It had been planned that Victoria should go to morning school with her sisters and that they should all come home to lunch, but Grandfather's prayer meeting made that impossible for her. Instead it was decided that she should do a few lessons with Miss Herbert in Isobel's painting room.

"Nothing to worry you, darling," her father said, "just something to keep you occupied, for Mummy, Annie and Hester will be busy over luncheon, as the Bishop is coming."

Miss Herbert had chosen Victoria's lessons with care. She would read some poems to her suitable for the day, and she had found an edifying little book on the last days of Lady Jane Grey, which she thought was just right. If they had more time she would tell the story of her favourite saint – Dorothea. Victoria, grinding her teeth, bore with the poems and with Lady Jane Grey, but St Dorothea, told in Miss Herbert's special confirmation day voice, was more than she could take.

"St Dorothea was exceptional even amongst saints . . ."

Miss Herbert got no further for Victoria picked up the ink pot and threw it at her. The pot hit her on the forehead but fortunately not hard enough to do real damage, except that ink cascaded down her face and on to her high-necked blouse. At that exact moment the door opened and in came Grandfather followed by Aunt Sophie.

"Forgive me disturbing you, Miss Herbert," said Grandfather. "I wanted to give my grand-daughter . . ." He had been going to say "a confirmation kiss". But by then he had seen Miss Herbert.

It was extraordinary what grown-ups could do about pretending something had not happened when their minds were set on it. Not a word was said. Miss Herbert was led away by Aunt Sophie and when next seen was quite clean if rather red in the face from scrubbing, and Grandfather quietly disappeared.

"I thought," Victoria confided afterwards to Isobel, "that I'd have the most terrible punishment I ever had and, of course, that the Bishop wouldn't confirm me. But he can't have been told, for all he said when he saw me was: 'Hullo, Vicky. I hope I confirm you nicely.'"

Somehow – the girls never knew how – the incident was smoothed over and unbelievably reduced to mischief, and the ink-throwing was never mentioned again.

Granny, who with the aid of her chair and Aunt Sophie's arm, had been able to attend Victoria's confirmation, with the same aids came afterwards to the vicarage to tea, and from the sofa on which she was lying turned her attention to Isobel.

"You will be sixteen this summer, won't you? When are you bringing her out, Sylvia?"

Granny never asked that sort of question without a reason. Isobel was a pretty girl and, though of course too young yet, must not be allowed to spend her life in a studio – something Granny was certain could only too easily happen.

The children's mother hated Granny's question. Eastbourne, in its own way, was quite a fashionable place. Most of the girls were taken to London to be presented at court. Afterwards they made their début in local society, either at a dance given for them or at the Hunt Ball, for which a party would first be entertained to dinner. But whatever form the entertainment took, on the first and future occasions the girl's mother was always present to chaperone her daughter, and had to remain to the bitter end to drive home with her.

The thought of sitting up half the night wearing evening dress filled the children's mother with loathing. She was not a good sleeper and needed eight hours in bed to have the strength for the daily round. How was she to endure next year and all the future years as the girls grew up if she was expected to be out of bed until two or three in the morning, knowing she would be called as usual at seven? Other mothers could lie in bed half the morning to get over late nights, but they did not live in a vicarage where, whether you were up late or not, you were expected to be down to morning prayers at 7.45.

"We haven't made any plans yet. We've still a year to make them."

Granny had expected that kind of answer and was determined to put up a fight. She was not worldly-minded, but a girl should marry and Isobel would have no chance of doing that sitting alone at her easel.

"I imagine there will be young people's dances next Christmas to which John can escort you, Isobel. Do you still take dancing lessons?"

That was another awkward question. In the last parish they had attended a weekly dancing class in a private house. There they had learnt national dances, Greek dancing and those who had what was called accordion pleated frocks had learnt skirt dancing. They were also taught ballroom dancing. But at Eastbourne there had been no dancing classes for the school dancing class was on Saturday afternoons and was for the boarders only, and the children's mother, thankful to save the money, had decided that the girls knew how to dance and need learn no more. Isobel, conscious that there was purpose behind Granny's question, spoke even more quickly than usual.

"Not now – I mean, we did but we know all the usual dances."

"I think a few polishing classes this autumn would be a good idea, Sylvia. I will pay for them and I will also pay for a dress, something nearly grown-up. Next year I shall give you a real ball dress, Isobel."

Isobel and her mother replied gratefully but they also exchanged a look. It was hard to say who dreaded next year the most.

20 The Punt Summer

That summer the holiday was a landmark, for it was a family occasion. It was at Christchurch in Hampshire and there Granny and Grandfather had rented a house, and so had all their children who lived in England or were home on leave. Each family lived its own life but there were many joint family occasions: giant bathing parties; giant picnics; giant expeditions to church; giant funerals on Sunday afternoons, and giant hymn-singing on Sunday evenings. Family groups were photographed at the house Granny and Grandfather had rented. The sort of family group that was popular in those days taken round a tea table.

But for the children what made that holiday at Christchurch was not meeting all the cousins and the uncles and aunts, though that was fun, it was the punt. They had all been able to swim since they were babies, otherwise their father would not have allowed them near the river, but never before had they had anything to do with a boat. On a holiday when he was a boy the children's father and his brothers had been lent a rowing boat, and he had never forgotten the joy of owning a boat, which must have been why, for that perfect August holiday, he had written in advance and hired a punt.

It was an ark of a boat which must at one time have been used as a ferry. It was large enough to take all the children, and a passenger or two, it was propelled by a punt pole in shallow water, but if it drifted downriver where the water was deep there were paddles. It was so immensely heavy and solidly built that, had the children lost control of it and allowed it to drift out to sea, and had there been a gale it would not have turned over.

Though the children's father had no idea of it when he rented the punt, it proved to have another value outside the pleasure it gave. At a time when the family might have split into two halves, with Victoria floating between them, the punt, enjoyed by them all, kept the family together. That August Isobel was sixteen, and John would be seventeen in November so they were included in certain of the grown-up doings. Because Isobel and John were counted as partly grown up, Louise and Dick, though Louise had just had her thirteenth birthday and Dick would be eleven in October, were classed with younger cousins as "the little ones". This meant Victoria belonged nowhere. Because of the punt, this widening gap in the family circle was not often noticed.

What glorious days were spent on the river Avon! Picnic lunches were taken and after the daily bathe the family were afloat often for hours, Isobel sketching, John master of the punt pole. Victoria, when it was not her turn to punt, felt a dreaming peacefulness which she had never before known – the ecstasy of being away where no one could get at you, of being with John and of moving with the river.

What did Louise and Dick feel that summer? Dick, with his arm round Spot who for the pleasure of being with the family endured rather than enjoyed boating, and showed his feelings by barking at every passing craft. Louise chatting away and calling out remarks to other boaters. Did they give up their rambles alone together to assert their right to places in the punt, or did they truly enjoy themselves?

Sometimes, when the little ones had been hauled off to join their cousins and Isobel was sketching on land, John and Victoria would go out alone in the punt. It was on such an occasion that John said:

"I know you don't think so but I think being confirmed has done you good."

Victoria had been dreaming so the remark caught her by surprise.

"Do you? Why?"

"I haven't heard you say 'it's mean' once these holidays."

Victoria was shy of talking of her personal life, even to John.

"I simply hated it on the day but I suppose it does help and all that. But actually there hasn't been much that has been mean since we came here. I mean it's been fairly perfect."

John looked at her thoughtfully.

"Well, whatever's happened has done you good. You're looking pretty."

Victoria grinned at him.

"Me! As if I ever could!"

"You are. It spoils you when your mouth turns down, it suits you to smile."

"But it doesn't make me pretty like Isobel and Louise are."

John studied her more carefully.

"I wouldn't be so sure. Not as pretty as Louise but then she takes after Aunt Sylvia's family while you are all Strangeway, but you could turn out just as pretty as Isobel – if not prettier."

Victoria thought he must be joking.

"But everybody knows I'm the plain one."

"Did – but, as I say, you're changing. Of course you still look a mess but you wouldn't if you washed more often and really gave your hair that hundred strokes every night you're supposed to give it."

"If I brushed it two hundred times it would still be greenish coloured."

John leant down from the punt pole and took hold of one of her plaits.

"I don't see any green. Actually, when it's just been washed, it's goldish. I noticed last week after the Herbert had washed you."

"Glory! Me with golden hair!" Then, after a pause: "If I'm not too sleepy, I'll start the hundred strokes tonight. I should think the Herbert will drop dead with surprise."

On another expedition Victoria heard of the rift that was growing between John and his father.

"I thought I did all right when he was home. I fished for hours. I learnt to play golf. I talked OTC and shooting eight until I was blue in the face and, as he thinks it soft, I hardly opened a book when he was about, but I can't have pleased him, for ever since he got back he's been on at me."

"What about? He must be pleased you do so well at school and are going to get a scholarship to Oxford."

"He's not worried about the scholarship because I'm going up whether I get it or not. But what is on his mind is the months between my leaving school and Oxford."

Victoria knew that John had plans but not exactly what they were.

"What is it you want to do?"

John leant on the pole, holding the punt stationary, his face alight with his inward vision.

"I'll leave at the end of next summer term. That'll give me a year. Imagine it, Vicky, a whole year to 'stand and stare'. A whole year to find out about me, something you don't get time to do at school. A year to think."

"But what will you do?"

"What I want to do is to travel, and I hope, write poetry."

"Not act?"

"Not then, I'll wait until I come down for good for that."

"Then what does Uncle Mark want you to do?"

Impatiently John moved and jerked the punt forward.

"He wants me to go to India. In fact he says I am going to India."

Victoria's knowledge of India was the teak, brass and ivory objects in Grandfather's house, the curious bracelets covered in little flowers the uncles brought home and the pictures she had seen of elephants. She thought a year in India would be superb.

"It would be fun to see it, wouldn't it?" she suggested cautiously.

John shook his head as if to shake something off it.

"No, it wouldn't, juggins. And I have seen it."

"You left when you were six. You can't remember much."

John's mouth was sullen.

"Oh yes, I can. I remember watching the gardener kill a snake. Ugh! And I remember when I was out with my ayah seeing a dead dog crawling with maggots. I was sick for days. My ayah died of cholera. I wasn't supposed to know, but I saw her before they took her away. Do you know, Vicky, it was so disgusting I dream about it still."

"Perhaps you'd like India if you saw it now; after all, you were only a little boy."

"I wouldn't, I'd loathe every minute. I'd be looking over my shoulder the whole time expecting to see something terrible. I know it's not supposed to be manly to be sensitive, but it's the way I'm made. Do you know, Vicky, if I knew I had to be a doctor with all the horrors they look at, I'd throw myself in the river."

Victoria thought he was being melodramatic though she knew his horror of anything unsightly was true enough.

"How are you going to get out of going to India?"

"I haven't an idea. I just know that somehow I will. I must have that year, Vicky. I need it."

"What will you do if Uncle Mark says if you won't go to India he won't give you any money?"

John smiled.

"I'll become a hermit and live in a shack on a mountain. 'And I shall have some peace there, for peace comes dropping slow, Dropping from the veils of the morning to where the cricket sings'."

Vicky chimed in softly:

"'There midnight's all a glimmer, and noon a purple glow, And evening full of the linnet's wings.'"

John smiled at her.

"You're coming on. If we can find a chaperone you shall come and visit me in my shack."

Either because of the beautiful holiday or because at last she was learning to concentrate, Victoria really did do better that autumn term, nothing startling but enough to give her a moderate report, which pleased her father. Her mother, however, was not so satisfied.

"I do hope they won't crush any talent Vicky has," she said. "She's quite clever at writing plays, but look what it says here about composition: 'Victoria uses too much imagination'."

"Well," said the children's father, "though it's

admirable in its place, imagination needs keeping in check."

"I suppose so," the children's mother agreed. "But if Vicky should turn out to be an author she'll need all she's got."

The children's father laughed, seeing in his mind's eye his harum-scarum daughter with her flying plaits.

"The only writing Vicky is likely to do is plays for my parish, and I don't think her gift for that shows any sign of being crushed."

The dress Granny had promised was made for Isobel. It had an almost long skirt and was a pretty soft blue.

"Isn't it gorgeous!" said Vicky when she saw it. "You'll look wonderful, Isobel."

But Isobel's artist's eye saw the dress as it was.

"I should say it was very suitable for the vicar's daughter. And I bet that's what John will think when he has to come to dances with me."

So that Christmas Isobel, when she was well, attended dances which did not finish until midnight, and Louise and Dick went to children's parties.

"You know what I'm like, Isobel?" Victoria said. "I'm a shuttlecock – sometimes I'm hit into the children's parties and sometimes I'm hit into your flapper dances."

Isobel was in bed that day with asthma. She gave a wheezy laugh.

"You don't care, so don't pretend you do. Anyway, next Christmas you'll have the flapper parties all to yourself while I'll have to go to proper grown-up ones, and I dread them."

Victoria lolled against the end of Isobel's bed.

"Do you suppose other girls are as bad at growing up as we are? Or is it the sort of life we lead in a vicarage which makes us slow?"

Isobel thought that over.

"I don't look my age outside, but I think I am growing up inside. I shall like being grown up, if only I could paint all the time; it's the thought of going to dances I hate, for I don't like dancing much and I don't know anyone to dance with. But you're different. You're changing every day and I think you will look quite grown up by the time you are."

"But I'm not growing up inside," Victoria confessed. "And I think looking grown up outside and feeling a child inside will make a muddle of me."

21 Isobel Comes Out

Louise, with an arm round Spot, sat on the floor of Isobel's bedroom. Victoria sat in the doorway between the two rooms. Isobel sat at her dressing table staring at herself in the looking-glass. The hairdresser had just gone, leaving behind her a head that looked strangely unlike Isobel's. Her back hair was piled up over a frame, and at the sides, with the aid of tongs, little curls had been set to brush her cheeks. Fixed on to her hair was a spray of tiny white roses.

"Don't you look lovely," sighed Louise. "I wish I was old and a hairdresser came to do my hair and Daddy gave me roses to wear in it."

"I can see it looks nice," Isobel agreed, "but it doesn't make me look like me. I think people shouldn't be so prinked up, they aren't themselves any more. I mean, think what a shock for the officers I dance with, if they see me tomorrow in my painting overall and my hair done by me."

"They won't see you. They have to go back to their ships," said Victoria.

A part of the fleet was visiting Eastbourne that summer on their way to manoeuvres and a ball was being given for the officers. On hearing the news, the children's mother, with more worldly sense than

298

anyone knew she had, decided that Isobel should make her debut at it.

"The tickets are rather expensive," she told the children's father, "but it will be money well spent, because all the officers will be unattached, so there will be plenty of young men for Isobel to dance with."

"But we shan't know them to introduce them to her," the children's father had protested.

But the children's mother had been making enquiries.

"No, but several of our friends will know them because they are giving dinner parties for them beforehand, and I have been promised introductions for Isobel."

Granny was written to, and in due course a box arrived from a London shop. Inside it was Isobel's first ball dress.

The ball dress was now lying on her bed with, beside it, white kid gloves and an evening cloak – this last provided by her godmother, Aunt Penelope.

"I wish the Herbert would come," said Louise. "I do want to see you with your dress on."

Victoria swung to and fro, holding the door handles.

"I expect she's having to sew Mummy into hers. She said it split the last time she and Daddy went out to dinner."

"You won't forget anything, will you, Isobel?" Louise pleaded. "What the most beautiful frocks were like and what you had to eat for supper."

Isobel got out of her chair and took off her dressing gown. In spite of her grandly-done hair she looked absurdly young in her ribbon-threaded camisole and slim petticoat.

"I hope skirts aren't so tight when I come out," said Victoria. "I like being able to kick if I want to."

Miss Herbert came in.

"Ready, Isobel? Your hair looks very nice, dear." She glanced at Louise and Victoria. "You two had better go downstairs, there isn't room for you here."

Victoria was going to answer but Isobel spoke first.

"Please don't send them away, Miss Herbert, the first ball is a family thing."

"Oh, very well." Miss Herbert carefully picked up the dress and draping it on her arms lifted it over Isobel's head.

It was made of white satin – a sheathlike garment with a draped bodice. Room to move was made possible in the hobble skirt by a triangle of pleated lace let in at the foot. There was lace, too, on the shoulders and edging the bodice. Across the bodice there was a spray of white roses. It was not a grand dress by the standards of the time, but it was pretty. Victoria and Louise were bursting with admiration.

"You look like Cinderella," said Victoria. "You ought to be riding in a coach drawn by white ponies."

Louise got up.

"I shall go and fetch Annie and Hester. I promised them I'd tell them directly you were dressed."

By the time Annie and Hester came into the bedroom, Isobel had on her long white kid gloves. They walked round her, examining her from all sides as if she were a horse.

"You couldn't look sweeter, Miss Isobel, could she, Miss Herbert?" said Hester. 'Not if she was Princess Mary herself."

Annie could always be trusted to keep the family's feet on the ground. She wagged a finger at Isobel.

" 'The rich and the poor, Their nakedness display. The poor because they must. The rich because they may.' "

After the taxi with their father, mother and Isobel had driven away – for because it was Isobel's very first ball her father had actually found time to attend – Victoria and Louise wandered aimlessly into the drawing room. It felt dull to be at home in everyday clothes while Isobel in satin would be waltzing in the arms of a sailor.

"What shall we do?" Louise asked. "Do you feel like Spillikins?"

Victoria shook her head.

"It's no good playing against you because you always win."

The door opened a crack and Annie's head poked around it.

"Is 'she' in her room?"

"She," said Louise, "is the cat's mother. Did you mean Miss Herbert?"

Annie was having none of that.

"I'll cat's mother you." She looked at Victoria.

"I've got a bit of treacle and that saved up. How would it be if we made some toffee?"

To her surprise Victoria had to turn her head away, for her eyes filled with tears. She knew that underneath she was minding this first breakaway into the grown-up world, but it had taken Annie's unexpected gesture of kindness to bring it to the front of her mind. In bed that night she puzzled over this. Until that evening it had been unfairness or meanness that she had known she would never forget, but here was something new.

"I suppose," she decided before she fell asleep, "just extra niceness can sort of hurt too. I must remember that."

Isobel, much to her surprise, enjoyed her first ball. Although she crept into her bedroom when she came home both Victoria and Louise heard her, and as soon as their parents' bedroom door was safely shut came into her room and sat on her bed.

"What was it like?" Louise whispered. "Did you dance every dance?"

Proudly Isobel picked up her programme with its small pencil attached.

"Look."

Victoria and Louise looked. The names were not readable but there was one for every dance, even the extras.

"Goodness!" said Victoria. "Aren't you tired dancing all those?"

"It was a lovely band," Isobel explained, "it made

302

me feel like dancing, but I didn't stay for the extras for Daddy looked so tired and I saw Mummy yawn."

Louise put the dance card back on the dressing table.

"I should think the Herbert will have to be trained up to be a chaperone. Mummy will never do; imagine when there are three of us."

Isobel was fumbling in the little satin bag which had come with her dress.

"I nearly forgot." She held out two cherries coated in glazed sugar. "I saved these at supper for you."

"Aren't they pretty!" said Louise. "Almost too pretty to eat."

Victoria bit hers.

"Did you dance all the time or did you sit any out with your partner?"

Isobel flushed.

"I did with the one I had supper with. His name was Charles Corn. He's asked Mummy to bring me to tea on his ship. We sat out because I told him about me, and that really I'd rather draw than come to balls, and he said why shouldn't I do both. And he found a piece of paper and I drew everybody he asked me to. He put my drawings in his pocket."

"I hope you aren't falling in love," said Louise. "I mean to marry first."

Isobel laughed.

"Idiot! There was nothing like that, he was just nice. And actually everybody was being invited on board the ships by someone. But you must go to

303

bed or you'll never wake up to go to school in the morning."

Unwillingly the girls went back to their rooms. Then, just as she was falling asleep, Victoria remembered something she had not asked Isobel. She got out of bed and put her head round the connecting door.

"Does it make you feel different all over to be treated as a grown-up lady?"

Isobel was just getting into bed; she paused with one foot on the ground thinking over Victoria's question.

"I think it does to other people but not to me. I mean, being called Miss Strangeway and dressed up in a ball dress hasn't changed the ordinary me, who will be told tomorrow by Miss Herbert to put on a jersey, or by Mummy to clear away my painting things. I know I'm grown up but at home I'm treated just the same as if I wasn't. I don't truly think being grown up has happened to me yet. I wonder when it will."

John won his scholarship to Balliol. The girls knew nothing about universities, but they could hear from the way their father talked about John that it was something very grand he had won. But John, in his letters to Victoria, did not write about his scholarship, except in a casual way, for he had still not won his free year.

"I think my father is weakening," he wrote. "At least he does see I don't want to go to India, but he won't agree I can have the year to do what I like with. He says I must work at something sensible."

But when he came home for the summer holidays he was jubilant. He shouted his news to Victoria before the train stopped.

"It's all fixed, Vicky. It's all fixed."

On the way to the vicarage he told her the details.

"You know my friend Henry? Well, he's going up to Balliol next year too, and until then he's to stay at home learning estate management for they've got a big place. I'm going to stay there most of the time. We must travel round a bit. The only stipulation is, I have to join the territorials."

"Goodness! The army! You'll hate being a soldier."

"Juggins! Territorials aren't real soldiers. They don't fight. You have to go to drills and things and there'll be manoeuvres in the summer. Henry's father is a colonel. Henry says it seems mostly dressing up."

Victoria looked up at John; he towered above her for he was now over six feet tall.

"You won't be coming to us, I suppose? Not even for Christmas?"

He grinned down at her.

"Don't worry. I'll keep an eye on you. As a matter of fact next year I'll get Aunt Sylvia to bring you and Isobel to the territorial dance. Henry says it's a big affair."

"I don't know when I'm coming out. Nothing's

305

been said. You see, I won't be seventeen till Christmas next year."

John looked at her, his eyes twinkling.

"The local girls had better look out. Nineteen-fourteen will be the year to remember. The year when you grow up."

Victoria made a face.

"I'm not growing up very fast. No one's actually angry with me now for I think they know I try, but I still am never at the top of my form."

"I wouldn't worry about that. It's how you look that matters to a girl, and I must say you are coming along splendidly in that direction. You might almost turn out a beauty."

Victoria's looking-glass had told her she was getting better looking, but not a beauty. She made a face at John.

"I'll never be that but I can still run. I bet I reach the vicarage gate before you do."

Regardless of her lengthening skirts Victoria raced up the hill with John pounding along beside her.

"Look at Victoria Strangeway!" John panted. "Oh the poor vicar! How dreadful for him having such a tomboy for a daughter."

22 Vicky Grows Up

The spring term started with an excitement. It had been decided that the school should give a performance of the songs from *Alice in Wonderland*. For this the singing mistress, who came twice a week, auditioned everybody to find who could take the solos. When she had finished auditioning Victoria she swung round on her music stool.

"How long have you been in the school?"

Victoria calculated.

"I came when I was twelve and now I'm just sixteen."

"That long! What do you do during my singing classes?"

What Victoria had done was to stand at the back surrounded by her giggling friends while she exercised her gift for talking to music. Long experience in church, making Isobel laugh by using her own words during the chants, had made a running commentary on school affairs to the tune of *Sweet and Low* or *Blow, Blow, Thou Winter Wind* child's play.

"I'm always at them."

"I know you are, but you have succeeded in disguising from me that you not only have a very nice voice, but almost perfect pitch."

As a result of the audition, when the list on the

board of who was to sing what part, Victoria found she was the Mock Turtle. This caused quite a sensation for, to make rehearsing easy, the solos were being sung by boarders. And also it was the first time Victoria had been distinguished in any way other than as a character who was frequently in trouble. Miss French sent for her.

"Had you some purpose in hiding from Miss Simpson that you had a nice voice?"

Victoria thought a lot of fuss was being made about nothing.

"She never asked if I could sing."

Miss French glanced at the clock.

"It's nearly tea time. Sit down, Vicky, you shall have your tea with me today."

Victoria sat down nervously. What on earth was coming? Some of the sixth-form girls had tea with Miss French. But never fifth-formers like herself.

"Thank you," she said gruffly.

Miss French was looking particular elegant that day in a rust-coloured dress.

"I was going to have a talk with you anyway, Vicky. You will be leaving school next year. Have you any idea what you want from life?"

Victoria was puzzled.

"Want from life? It's no good wanting things, is it? I mean, things happen."

The maid brought the tea. Miss French sent her away for another cup.

"Of course things happen which we none of us count on. But that does not mean we should not plan. When I was your age I had just begun to dream of having a school of my own. At that time it was only a dream, for my father, who was an artist, was alive, and we lived abroad. But he died when I was seventeen, and I came to England to teach languages. It was then my dream began to take shape in my mind. Not that at that time I saw any prospect of making it come true, but it's always good to have a plan to which you work."

The cup was brought and the tea poured out, and Victoria helped herself to a sandwich.

"I'm afraid I haven't any plan. Mummy said once we should all have to earn our livings. Isobel is going to teach art, but I haven't anything I do well, have I?"

Miss French sipped her tea.

"At the end of last term your form wrote essays about Christmas. You wrote about the Christmas tree and all the lonely who come to share it with you. It was shown to me, and I have kept it. Although naturally you will have to earn your living in some other way, for only the exceptionally gifted can earn it as an author, writing could supplement whatever you are able to earn."

Victoria's eyes shone. It was a truly glorious idea. It fitted in with what her mother had said: "Nothing ordinary." "I think you will be the one to surprise us all." But this talk of earning was worrying.

"I would love writing books, and almost I can see me doing it, but I can't see me being paid by somebody, can you?"

"I agree it is difficult to see the exact niche for you. Perhaps you could learn typewriting; I am sure a position could be found as a secretary."

Victoria looked reproachfully at Miss French.

"Haven't you forgotten how terrible my spelling is? Anyway I would hate to be a secretary. Imagine sitting all day long. Being a secretary is what Mummy thought Louise might be, just until she marries. She is marrying young and having lots of children."

Miss French was amused.

"Is she indeed! It would not surprise me. But to return to your future. I expect we could improve your spelling if we concentrate on it. But you are only just sixteen, we have time to think of work you would like to do. At the moment what I want you to think about is your writing. There is definitely a gift there – slight perhaps, but worth encouraging. Tell me, is John a cousin?"

Victoria put down her tea cup and took a cake Miss French was offering her.

"Yes. He lives with us, at least he always has because his parents are in India, but now he's living with somebody called Henry until they go to Balliol this autumn. He wanted to do nothing for a year, what he calls 'having time to stand and stare', but his father, Uncle Mark, said he must be a territorial."

"I noticed John in your essay. Singing *Good King Wenceslaus* with you and being so nice to the lonely people."

"John is nice. I miss him awfully but I expect he'll come back to live with us when he's at Oxford."

"You must tell him what I have said about your writing."

"But of course I will. I tell him everything. I always have."

But the first person Victoria told was Isobel.

"I don't want to tell anybody else yet," she confided. "I mean, it seems idiotic to talk about writing books, when you've only written a few essays at school."

"I won't tell," Isobel promised. "But I should think Miss French might be right. You've always liked writing plays."

"Wouldn't it be fun if we could do a book together some day? You'd draw the pictures and I'd write the story."

"I'd like that but I don't know that I'm going to try and illustrate. What I would like to do most is teach."

"I know that's what you think. But teach! Oh, Isobel, how awful! Why do you want to?"

"I don't know. I just feel I could. I'll have a chance to see this summer for Daddy is seeing about my having a proper studio. It's done by something called a mortgage."

"My goodness, aren't we changing? Imagine you with a studio of your own and me even thinking of writing a book."

But in spite of not meaning to, Victoria did tell her father what Miss French had said. It was a spring evening and she had walked down the road with him to deliver a note. Halfway to their destination her father paused.

"Vicky, I want you to tell me something. Suppose you knew you had something the matter with you that would eventually kill you, would you tell Mummy?"

Victoria did not accept right away the full meaning of her father's question. But she knew the answer.

"No, she would only fuss."

Her father put an arm through Victoria's.

"Thank you, darling. That's what I think. You can be a very sensible girl, Vicky."

Although she had not taken in the possibilities behind her father's question, Victoria had a feeling that her reply, though he was glad she had made it, made him feel lonely. She hugged his arm to her side.

"Imagine what Miss French said the other day."

Her father was amused rather than impressed. He never read modern books and could not imagine a child of his writing one. But it was good of Miss French to encourage Vicky.

"A great many things need saying, Vicky. It would indeed be wonderful if you were given the gift to say them."

"I don't think it's wise things Miss French meant. You see, it was Christmas evening I was writing about, so it was sort of remembering and putting it down so it was like a picture."

Her father left her to deliver his note. Victoria,

looking after him, knew for certain that this talk with him was one of those things she would remember for ever. And indeed, years later when she was in Australia and was told her father had died of angina, she could hear him say: "Suppose you had something the matter with you that would eventually kill you . . ." He had led a very full life and had become a bishop. So that he was ill had indeed been a well-kept secret, shared only with herself and his doctor.

John took the news of what Miss French had said quite seriously.

"I think that headmistress of yours might be right. Though at the moment I can't picture the sort of writing you might do. It can't be anything that needs brains. Wouldn't it be a joke if you wrote a play and I acted in it?"

There was to be no acting for John. That summer on 4th August war was declared against Germany. And John, already a partly-trained territorial, after a few months of more intensive training, was sent to France.

The ordinary English man and woman knew nothing about war. That it would all be over soon was the first reaction. It was not in any case expected to affect the lives of the ordinary citizen. Wars were fought by soldiers and sailors, who came on leave and were made a fuss of.

But soon it became apparent this war was not like that. People became nervous. "I don't like the vicar to be away even for a night," a woman said. "For what would we do if those Germans landed?"

That first winter fuel was either scarce or expensive – the girls did not know which, but before school Victoria and Louise had to saw logs.

"I haven't done this," said Victoria, "since I had to do it as a punishment for that awful report."

Food grew scarce. They kept hens in the field where it had been planned Isobel should have a studio. Isobel put an ostrich egg they had been given as a curio in the hen house and painted a Union Jack over it, writing under it: "A German hen laid this, now see what you can do."

Then came the casualties. House after house opened as a hospital. Isobel, when she was well enough, worked in one as a ward maid. But somehow for the girls the war still remained remote. Life went on more or less the same, except that there were no dances for Isobel, indeed, no parties for any of them.

Then John came on leave. The moment the news got round that he was coming presents of food arrived, among them a large rabbit.

"Would you lend me that for a day, Mrs Strangeway, ma'am?" the butcher said when he was asked to clean it. "I'll hang it in my window. It encourages people just to see food about."

Victoria was at school when John came home. It was June and lovely weather.

"He's in the garden," her mother said to her when she came in. "I think he looks peaky."

John was in that part of the garden the children had christened The Wood. He was in uniform with the star of a second lieutenant on his shoulder. He looked more than peaky: he looked thin, and his face was green. But he sounded in a way the old John.

"Hullo, Vicky! How's things?"

Victoria felt as if a cold hand had squeezed her heart.

"You look pretty awful."

John managed a smile.

"I've just been sick under the bushes there. It's nothing."

"Why were you sick? Have you eaten something bad?"

"Don't talk about it to the family, but I'm sick rather a lot."

She stared up at him. Then, why she did not know, she put a hand on his arm.

"Tell me."

It was then the dreadful thing happened. John, the self-contained, the poised, broke down. Tears rolled down his cheeks.

"Oh, Vicky. You'll never know how awful it is."

Suddenly she felt old.

"Tell me. Tell me every single thing."

So he told her. Of the squelching mud. The unburied bodies. The dying, screaming on barbed wire. The filth. The lice. The smells. Then, retching as he remembered, he whispered:

"And oh, Vicky, I have to go back."

Somehow between them she and John managed to keep to themselves that there was anything wrong with him other than fatigue. Victoria sent a pink note to Miss French:

"Please," she said, "I must miss school while John's on leave. We've always done things together. You do see, don't you?"

Miss French must have seen, for all she said was:

"Get your things on, dear. I will send a note to your parents."

So with Spot, John and Victoria went for long walks over the Downs; and though distant thuds sounded from the guns across the Channel, the air was fresh and clear, and after the exercise even John was able to enjoy a meal at a cottage table.

They never again spoke of conditions at the front. Instead, they lived entirely in the past. It was always: "Do you remember?"

The day his leave finished John refused to be seen off at the station. He had to catch an early train to link up with the troop train at Victoria.

"I don't want to be seen off. Just all come to the door. I'd like that."

So, as his taxi drove away, they were all there. The family, Annie, Hester and Spot. Perhaps he carried that picture to France.

Five weeks later the telegram came. Victoria knew something was wrong when she came in from sawing logs and saw Annie, her apron over her head, sobbing behind the kitchen door.

Her father called her into his study. "I don't know how to tell you, Vicky darling. You are so young to face sorrow."

Victoria gently stroked her father's hand.

"It's John. He's been killed."

"Yes, Vicky."

She stared unseeingly out of the window towards the front gate.

"I'll be all right, Daddy. I think I knew it was going to happen. Grand-Nanny once said growing up came suddenly. I grew up all in one minute, the day John came on leave."

WHITE BOOTS
by Noel Streatfeild

Even when the last of the medicine bottles were cleared away and she was supposed to have "had" convalescence, Harriet did not get well. Her walks along the towpath by the river did not put colour into her pale cheeks, her legs still felt cotton-woolish, and she looked terribly thin. Harriet's doctor, who had ordered the walks by the river, now suggested ice-skating; and though her mother couldn't believe that her poor spindly Harriet would even be able to stand up on the ice, at least it would be something for her to do if she couldn't be at school.

In her wildest dreams Harriet would never have thought that her being ill would have had so many repercussions. If she hadn't been ill, she wouldn't have gone to the rink. If she hadn't gone to the rink, she wouldn't have met little Lalla Moore, the future champion skater. And if she hadn't met Lalla – well, after she met Lalla, her whole life was changed for ever…

Collins
An imprint of HarperCollins*Publishers*
www.fireandwater.com

GEMMA
by Noel Streatfeild

Gemma is a film star – a beautiful, sophisticated girl with clothes to match. So when she's sent to live with her cousins, she's horrified. How *dull* to have to live with an *ordinary* family in an *ordinary* house!

And there's another problem: Gemma is terrified of school. She's never been to one before – and won't everyone sneer at a film star who's not a star any more? Well, she may be in the lowest class in the whole school, but *somehow* she's going to make herself stand out!

Also available:
Gemma & Sisters
Gemma the Star
Gemma in Love

Collins
An imprint of HarperCollins*Publishers*
www.fireandwater.com

Order Form

To order direct from the publishers, just make a list of the titles you want and fill in the form below:

Name

....

Address

....

....

....

Send to: Dept 6, HarperCollins Publishers Ltd, Westerhill Road, Bishopbriggs, Glasgow G64 2QT.

Please enclose a cheque or postal order to the value of the cover price, plus:

UK & BFPO: Add £1.00 for the first book, and 25p per copy for each additional book ordered.

Overseas and Eire: Add £2.95 service charge. Books will be sent by surface mail but quotes for airmail despatch will be given on request.

A 24-hour telephone ordering service is available to holders of Visa, MasterCard, Amex or Switch cards on 0141- 772 2281.

Collins
An *Imprint of* HarperCollins*Publishers*

The Grapes of Wrath

Born in Salinas, California, in 1902, John Steinbeck
grew up in a fertile agricultural valley about
twenty-five miles from the Pacific Coast – and both
valley and coast would serve as settings for some of
his best fiction. In 1919 he went to Stanford
University, where he intermittently enrolled in
literature and writing courses until he left in 1925
without taking a degree. During the next five years
he supported himself as a labourer and journalist in
New York City, all the time working on his first novel,
Cup of Gold (1929). After marriage and a move to
Pacific Grove, he published two Californian fictions,
The Pastures of Heaven (1932) and *To a God Unknown*
(1933), and worked on short stories later collected in
The Long Valley (1938). Popular success and financial
security came only with *Tortilla Flat* (1935), stories
about Monterey's paisanos. A ceaseless
experimenter throughout his career, Steinbeck
changed courses regularly. Three powerful novels of
the late 1930s focused on the Californian labouring
class: *In Dubious Battle* (1936), *Of Mice and Men* (1937),
and the book considered by many his finest, *The
Grapes of Wrath* (1939). Early in the 1940s, Steinbeck
became a filmmaker with *The Forgotten Village* (1941)
and a serious student of marine biology with *Sea of
Cortez* (1941). He devoted his services to the war,
writing *Bombs Away* (1942) and the controversial
play-novelette *The Moon is Down* (1942). *Cannery Row*
(1945), *The Wayward Bus* (1947), *The Pearl* (1947), *A
Russian Journal* (1948), another experimental drama,
Burning Bright (1950), and *The Log from the Sea of
Cortez* (1951) preceded publication of the

monumental *East of Eden* (1952), an ambitious saga of the Salinas Valley and his own family's history. The last decades of his life were spent in New York City and Sag Harbor with his third wife, with whom he travelled widely. Later books include *Sweet Thursday* (1954), *The Short Reign of Pippin IV: A Fabrication* (1957), *Once There was a War* (1958), *The Winter of Our Discontent* (1961), *Travels with Charley in Search of America* (1962), *America and Americans* (1966), and the posthumously published *Journal of a Novel: The* East of Eden *Letters* (1969), *Viva Zapata!* (1975), *The Acts of King Arthur and His Noble Knights* (1976) and *Working Days: The Journals of* The Grapes of Wrath (1989). He died in 1968, having won a Nobel Prize in 1962.